THE BROKEN CAGE

CROW INVESTIGATIONS BOOK SEVEN

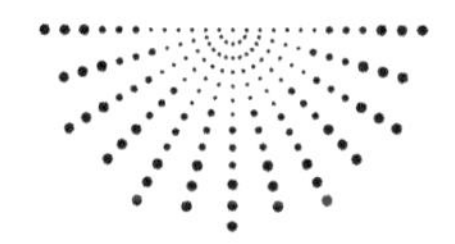

SARAH PAINTER

This is a work of fiction. Names, characters, organisations, places, events, and incidents are either products of the author's imagination or are used fictitiously. Any resemblance to actual persons, living or dead, or actual events, is purely coincidental.

Published by Siskin Press Limited

Cover Design by Stuart Bache

ALSO BY SARAH PAINTER

The Language of Spells

The Secrets of Ghosts

The Garden of Magic

In The Light of What We See

Beneath The Water

The Lost Girls

The Crow Investigations Series

The Night Raven

The Silver Mark

The Fox's Curse

The Pearl King

The Copper Heart

The Shadow Wing

This book is dedicated to the NHS with my deepest gratitude

CHAPTER ONE

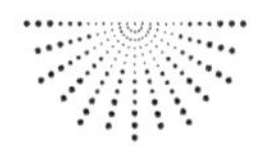

The cast had come off Lydia's left forearm two weeks previously and she was diligently doing her physical therapy exercises. Her broken nose had healed remarkably quickly and she no longer frightened small children with her bruised face. It was a drizzly Thursday and she was standing out on the terrace cradling a hot coffee in her favourite mug and watching the steam rise in the grey London dawn.

Fleet had slept at his own flat and would already be on his way to work. Jason was sitting on the sofa in the living room-slash-office of the flat, glued to his beloved laptop. A street-sweeping vehicle was making its noisy way down the lane which ran behind her building, its beeping joining the constant hum of traffic. A breeding pair of jackdaws were perched on the railing, preening each other with their beaks. Jackdaws were smaller than crows, the smallest corvids in the family, but Lydia had always had a soft spot for them. She raised her mug in greeting and two sets of black eyes swivelled to gaze directly into hers. Lydia stopped herself before she enquired after their wellbeing. There were limits.

Since throwing herself off a roof, killing her cousin Maddie in the process, Lydia had taken time off from Crow Investigations. Not so much because she wanted to, but because the rest of the world insisted. And, while she would never have admitted as much, she had been in a fair amount of pain ever since the morphine drops from the hospital had run out. She pushed back the sleeve on her hoodie and inspected the pale skin of her arm. There was still the faint blue tinge of old bruising. Although, Lydia would be the first to admit, that might just be the extremely pale colour of her normal skin. So white it was blue. Whatever, her skin tone hadn't benefitted from four weeks in a cast, but there were no visible signs of her broken ulna and radius. A compound fracture that the ortho guy had called 'unpleasant'.

It was fine that she had taken time to heal. She hadn't had a holiday in years and must have been owed the break. A couple of months of enforced inactivity had probably done her good. Okay, so she had felt like a caged bird and had spent every single night dreaming of flying, but whatever. She was fine.

The jackdaws were still sitting together, watching as Lydia drained the dregs of her coffee. As she turned away to go back inside, the larger of the two birds hopped along the railing. Its head ducked in a quick, jerky movement and then both birds took flight, wheeling over Lydia's head and up to the main roofline. Lydia stooped to pick up the small item dropped by the bird. Jackdaws were like magpies – they liked shiny things – so it wasn't entirely a surprise that the bird had been carrying something. What was unsettling was the deliberate way it had been left behind. Like an offering. Or a message.

Jason hadn't moved from his position on the sofa and he didn't look up when Lydia walked into the office holding the gift the jackdaw had left her. Flinging herself into her chair, she put her Docs onto the desk, one leg crossed over the other, and leaned back. The ceiling needed painting. She blinked away the image of falling soil, earth filling her mouth and nose until she couldn't breathe. Jumping off the roof had been almost easy after being buried alive in the Pearl court beneath Highgate Wood. She opened her hand. The pendant was gold. Or maybe brass, Lydia was no expert. An old-fashioned thing with diamond chips set around the edge and a fat pearl in the centre.

Lydia felt the blast of cold air a second before Jason spoke. 'What's that?'

He had moved to her side of the room, leaving the laptop open on the sofa. 'Jewellery.'

'Well I got that much.' Jason leaned closer and squinted at the pendant. He didn't need to squint, Lydia assumed, same as he didn't need to breathe or fidget or fold himself into a sitting position to use the sofa, but they were good signs. She only worried about Jason when he forgot his old habits and started floating above the ground like a proper ghost.

'Where's it from?'

Lydia gestured in the direction of the terrace. 'Jackdaw dropped it.'

'A bird?'

'Yep.'

'That seems ominous.'

Lydia was about to reassure him when an appalling sound split the air. It took Lydia a beat to understand that it was the fire alarm and another beat for her to think 'it's good the alarm works' before she realised that Jason was gripping her arm, sending freezing chills up to her shoulder. He was mouthing something. Saying something. Lydia's head was splitting with the sound and all she could think about was getting away from it. The cold brought her back to herself. She was halfway out to the roof terrace and she realised in that moment that she had been planning to jump. Not to jump, to take flight. Stupid, she berated herself, swivelling around and heading for the front door to the flat instead. Down the stairs, Jason keeping pace with her, and into the cafe.

It was just as loud down there, but Lydia couldn't feel heat or see smoke so she was beginning to relax and believe it was a false alarm. It was also mercifully early and the place was deserted. Not even open to the breakfast crowd, yet. The door to the kitchen opened and Angel appeared holding a fire extinguisher. Her dreads were caught up in a hairnet and her white apron was stained wet. Hopefully with water and not boiling oil. She hit a code into a wall mounted panel by the door and silenced the alarm. In the merciful silence which followed, Lydia waited for an explanation.

Angel wasn't stopping, though, and she was back

through the swing door, smoke billowing with the movement of the door.

'Don't,' Jason said, as Lydia made to follow Angel. 'You should get out.'

'It's fine,' she threw over her shoulder. If Angel was happy to go back into the kitchen, Lydia wasn't worried.

The kitchen, however, looked anything but 'fine' and Angel was coughing through a wet tea towel she had tied around her face. The smoke didn't seem that bad, but within seconds Lydia was fighting the urge to cough, too. 'What happened?'

Angel didn't answer straight away. She was occupied with moving a blackened pan from the stove with oven gloves and putting it into the sink.

'I think that's past it,' Lydia said.

Angel shot her an unreadable look. She looked wild. The whites of her eyes showing all the way round and Lydia realised that she had never seen Angel look properly panicked before. 'It's okay,' she said. 'Nobody got hurt. This is just... Stuff. Don't worry.'

Angel nodded tightly and turned back to the stove. A large soot mark stretched up the steel wall plate at the back of the hob and Angel reached for it, touching the surface lightly with one finger.

Her silence was getting eerie, so Lydia produced her coin and squeezed it in her palm, pushing a little Crow behind her next question. 'What happened?'

Angel's head snapped around and she looked directly into Lydia's eyes. For a moment, she was reminded of the jackdaws.

'I was distracted. I was making hash browns, just

shallow frying them in the pan...' she trailed off. 'Damn it.'

'What?'

'I liked that pan.'

Lydia wasn't sure how to phrase her next question without it sounding like a criticism, but she had to ask. 'What's wrong? This isn't like you.'

Angel's shoulders slumped even lower. It was disturbing. She was usually a force of nature. Terrifyingly capable and self-contained and so acerbic it was a wonder all her cooking didn't taste of lemon. 'We'll need to replace that,' Angel waved her hand at the fire extinguisher.

'Tell me,' Lydia said, refusing to be distracted.

The cook turned to face Lydia, lifting her chin. 'It's Nat. She's gone.'

A beat. 'When you say "gone"?'

'Left.'

Thank Feathers. It was hard for Lydia not to assume that 'gone' meant 'dead'. Still, it wouldn't be the appropriate response to hearing that Angel's wife had left. 'I'm sorry.'

Angel turned away and resumed the clean-up operation.

Lydia opened her mouth to ask if there was anything she could do. But she wasn't Angel's friend. She was her boss, the head of the Crow Family. And a PI who really needed to get back to work. 'Order a new extinguisher, pan and whatever else got damaged on the cafe account.' She hesitated for a second and then added: 'Feel free to close up today. Or the rest of the week. You can take some time off if you...'

'No,' Angel said quietly. 'Not necessary.'

JASON WAS STILL HANGING OUT IN THE MAIN PART of the cafe, concern etched across his face. He had one arm wrapped around his body and was fiddling with the sleeve of his suit jacket. 'It's fine,' Lydia said quietly. 'Small pan fire. Angel put it out.'

'That could have been bad.' His eyes were still worried.

'Could have been. Wasn't.'

'How are you so calm?'

Lydia wanted to say that being stalked by a contract killer who also happened to be her cousin or being in an underground cave-in of the Pearl court or being the head of the infamous Crow Family while simultaneously trying to dismantle the criminal side to the business had given her a high tolerance for stress, but she wasn't sure if it was true. It sounded good, but the truth was something less impressive and altogether more frightening. She wasn't sure she was capable of feeling anything anymore. As her bones had healed, sealing over the damage, she had felt another kind of covering stealing across her whole being. Her world felt muted. Everything experienced as if from behind smoked glass. Fleet had stopped asking her to see a PTSD counsellor, but she still caught him watching her with a creased brow when he thought she wasn't looking.

Her mobile vibrated in her pocket. It was Fleet, and

she walked away from Jason as she answered. He had been insisting that he hadn't been having any premonitions or 'weird feelings' but he always seemed to call when there was a chink in her habitual armour. Maybe it was just the finely honed instincts of a concerned boyfriend, or maybe it was the extra gleam that suffused Fleet and gave him an instinctual edge over mere mortals. She rolled her shoulders and forced herself to smile as she spoke, hoping to sound perkier than she felt. 'Hey.'

'I'm sorry to call so early.'

'No worries, I was up. You all right?'

'Me, yes. My detained suspect, not so much.'

Fleet had been working long hours on a missing person case. There was the suggestion of foul play and they had real fears about the missing man's wellbeing. Plus, it was a high-profile victim and there was pressure from top brass to get a result, but Lydia knew he had been hiding most of his stress. This didn't sound like the breakthrough he had been hoping for.

'He was alone for an hour,' Fleet was saying, his voice strangely flat. 'Tops. Now he's dead.'

'Feathers, I'm sorry.' People killed themselves in custody. It wasn't common but it happened too often to be called 'rare'. Given how Lydia had felt when banged up in Camberwell nick, she could understand the impulse. Escape by any means.

'I need to ask you something. I don't want to, I know you're not back at work.'

'I am back,' Lydia broke in. 'I keep telling you I'm fine. What do you need?'

'Do you know Mikhail Laurent?'

Lydia paused. She didn't recognise the name but took a moment to double-check her first response. Nope. Nothing. 'I don't. Is that your suspect?'

'He sometimes went by Mik the Drummer. And I had an informant who called him The Jekyll.'

'Not familiar. Sorry. Why?'

'Because he's asking for you.'

CHAPTER TWO

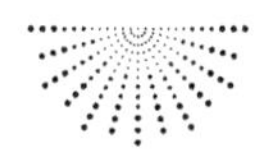

Fleet was heading up the Murder Team for the borough of Southwark, which included Peckham, Dulwich, Bermondsey and Camberwell. It wasn't exactly a promotion, but it was definitely the work he wanted. The Fleet that met Lydia on the front steps of Camberwell nick was suited, booted and had the air of command. He reminded her of the copper she had first met at The Fork after a hitman had attempted to throw her from her own roof terrace: pulsing with purpose and energy. He touched her shoulder. 'Thank you for coming.'

She opened her mouth to say 'no problem' but that would be a lie, so she settled for 'of course'.

She didn't want to go into the station. She knew she didn't want to be within ten metres of the place, but the feelings of animosity were as muted as all the rest. There were advantages to being numb.

Fleet swept Lydia past the security desk and into the non-public area of the station. A uniformed officer with a short ponytail and square fringe stepped in front as if hoping to waylay Fleet. Lydia didn't see the look he gave her, but it was enough to make her step smartly back.

The detention suite was swathed in police caution tape. Which seemed ironic. Fleet pulled on plastic booties over his shoes and handed a pair to Lydia. Then they double-gloved with thin latex and elbow-length gauntlets. 'Crime scene officers have started, but I've asked them to clear out for five minutes.'

A stone-faced man with very pink skin and slightly bulging blue eyes emerged from the crime scene, his white coverall rustling. He didn't so much as glance at Lydia and made a beeline for Fleet. 'This isn't-'

Fleet didn't let him get any further. 'I take full responsibility.'

Lydia could see Fleet didn't like the man, which was curious. He was usually excellent at hiding his feelings. Either she had got really good at reading Fleet, or he wasn't bothering to hide his antipathy for some reason. Maybe it was a perk of being the boss. Or perhaps it was the case getting under his skin.

Of course, everybody would be tense. A death in the station wasn't ideal. They knew fingers would be pointed, and the police had been getting plenty of negative press in recent times. Questions were being asked. Policies examined. Individual officers being held to account. It was a good thing as far as Lydia was concerned and she knew that Fleet agreed. We should be accountable, he said. We should be held to a higher standard, not a lower one. But whatever his moral standpoint, it still put pressure on his department and stress levels had already been high before a suspect died while in their care.

The SOC officer looked at Lydia, finally. 'She should be booked.'

Lydia's hands curled into fists and she felt the press of her coin. She tilted her chin, looking directly into the man's eyes until he looked away.

'Anyway,' he muttered, moving off. 'Don't touch anything.'

'Obviously,' Fleet said blandly.

As they approached the door, Lydia felt a prickling sensation across the back of her neck. She looked back, expecting to see Grumpy McGrumperson scowling at her, but the corridor was deserted.

The cell wasn't the same one that Lydia had been held in, but it was identical. Same obscured glass window with wide bars, same depressing tiled walls and stainless steel toilet, same thin blue wipe-clean mattress on a narrow platform. What was startling about this tableau, however, was the dead body.

'He's still here,' Lydia said, swallowing hard. She wasn't exactly taking deep breaths, but there wasn't a detectable odour. This was an extremely fresh crime scene. 'When did you find him?'

'Duty sergeant was doing a routine check at seven and found him like this. I called you straight away. Wanted you to take a peek.' Fleet was looking around the room with an expression that could be mistaken for anger, but that Lydia knew was just the way he looked when he was hyper-focused. 'You getting anything?'

He meant 'any sense of the magical Families'.

Lydia's special party trick. 'Nope,' she said, truthfully. 'Nothing at all.' Which was less truthful. She could, as always, sense Fleet's particular gleam. It was a sunshine warmth. A glowing hum of something out of the ordinary, something which told her that somewhere in his heritage was power. The sort of power that, despite it making her feel like an idiot, she had to call 'magic'.

Putting Fleet's mysterious signature to one side, Lydia focused on the corpse. It was a large man. He was sitting on the bed, elbows on spread knees and shaved head bowed. There was no visible injury and if it wasn't for the unmistakable stillness of death, Lydia could have believed that he was about to look up and ask them what the fuck they were doing poking around his cell. The shaved head segued into a wide neck, meaty shoulders and thickly muscled arms. He was wearing a black vest and sports trousers in navy with white stripes down the sides. Lydia was surprised to see that his skin was clear. His general aesthetic was the kind she associated with tattoos, but there weren't any visible.

As always, her curiosity had overtaken her initial revulsion. He was freshly dead, which meant that rigor mortis wouldn't have stiffened his body yet. Plus, he should have slumped down when he died. Pitched forward or backwards onto the bed. This seated posture was plain weird. She had clicked into the mode which allowed her to assess without emotion or revulsion and now she was ready to look at the dead man's face. She crouched down carefully, mindful of the importance of keeping her balance and not toppling onto the floor.

Fleet was out on a limb and she had no intention of ballsing up his crime scene.

The man's eyes were closed, which made a pleasant change from the other dead people she had met, and his expression was peaceful. Lydia blinked and looked again to make sure. That was the only word for it. If she hadn't thought it seemed fanciful, she would have sworn that he had the trace of a smile on his lips. Who died looking like that? Like they were welcoming an old friend?

She looked at his hands, which were hanging loosely, and revised her first impression of 'no injury'. One had bloodied knuckles, the skin split across the back of his hand, and the other had traces of blood on one fingertip.

Lydia straightened up, her knees clicking loudly in the quiet room. 'What about the CCTV?'

'He wasn't on suicide watch,' Fleet said, a touch defensively.

'I know, I just meant has the footage been reviewed yet?'

'I took a quick look. Got a PC reviewing it with the custody sergeant.'

'And?'

Fleet shook his head. 'Fuzzy. You know we pixelate the toilet area?'

Lydia grimaced and nodded.

'May as well have pixelated the whole lot. He went to that area, presumably to use the facilities, but then the whole feed goes fuzzy for approximately three minutes. When it clears, he's sitting there completely still. Dead or well on the way to being so.'

'Fuzzy like...' Lydia was thinking of the way Crows

sometimes showed up on CCTV or, more accurately, didn't show up.

'Yeah,' Fleet said, reading her mind.

'Well, that's disturbing. I see why you thought of me.'

Fleet gave her the briefest of smiles. 'Well, yes. That. And the obvious.'

Lydia had been avoiding looking at the obvious, wanting to take in all the other aspects of the scene before she got flooded with thoughts and feelings. Now she let her gaze rest on the writing. It was smeared on the industrial-grade rubber flooring just in front of the seated man in what looked like blood. The penmanship wasn't perfect, but the words were perfectly legible. Get The Crow.

CHAPTER THREE

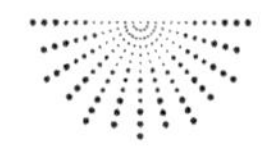

'We've got a problem, Boss,' Aiden said when Lydia answered his call. She had just stepped out of the front entrance to Camberwell nick and her heart was still racing, adrenalin flooding her system and telling her it was time to get far, far away. She breathed in slowly through her nose and took a moment before she replied. 'Can it wait?'

'Not this time.'

Aiden never contradicted Lydia. He was all 'no worries' and 'yes, boss'. This was not a good sign. 'Where are you?'

'At the house. Family meeting.'

He meant Charlie's house in Denmark Hill. Lydia frowned. 'I didn't call a meeting.'

'Can you get here soon?'

Fleet appeared and, thank feathers, he was on his own. Walking out of the station, she had heard a whispered threat from one of the uniforms and the sound of someone hawking up a globule of phlegm. It might have been coincidence, but it had felt like an insult. Safe to say, her standing amongst the police community of Camberwell hadn't been improved by the dead man's last words. Which was hardly fair.

Fleet ran a hand over his face, rubbing the day-old stubble. He must have been called into work early, before he'd had a chance to shave. 'You can look through the footage if you want. The PC I put on it hasn't got very far, yet. Like I say, I don't think there's anything there, but you never know... What's wrong?'

'Family stuff,' Lydia said. She went on tiptoe to kiss Fleet. 'I'm sorry to bail. Keep me posted?'

'Of course. You, too.' He was frowning, but that might have been his dead suspect. He took a step like he wanted to come with her, then shoved his hands into his trouser pockets. 'Go careful.'

'It's just Aiden,' Lydia said, keeping her voice light. 'Probably wants a raise.'

THE OUTSIDE OF CHARLIE'S HOUSE WAS LOOKING increasingly unkempt. Lydia had never had to worry about things like gardeners before, but now she made a mental note to get Aiden to check whether they were still being paid and, if so, to stick a rocket up them vis-à-vis their performance. A magpie was sitting on the roof ridge in front of the TV satellite dish and the path was lined with jackdaws. A single crow was on the front gate, acting as sentry. Lydia greeted the birds and unlocked the front door.

Raised voices from the kitchen. Lydia hesitated, caught between wanting to listen in and not wanting to be caught doing so. If they had heard the door open, they would guess what she was doing loitering in the hallway and that was not behaviour becoming of her position. She straightened her shoulders and gave herself a brief talking to. This was Aiden and the assorted cousins. She was the head of the Family. She didn't need to listen in or worry about what they thought of her. They needed to worry about her. Still. Aiden had sounded rattled.

Game face on, Lydia walked into Charlie's kitchen and made straight for the coffee machine. Six young men and one woman were sitting around Charlie's dining table. They looked like they had just come from a bar fight. Aiden had a black eye and there were other assorted injuries on display. Lydia recognised Jon, the youngest, and Daniel, who had been tight with Aiden when they were little. She didn't know the others well, not even their names, although she thought perhaps the woman was Anya. Or Annie. Something like that. She really ought to pay more attention.

The group went silent as she made an espresso. She purposely took her time finding the cup and matching saucer, and then turned to face the table.

'We've got a problem,' Aiden said. 'You know the betting shops?'

There was a spare seat around the table, but Lydia leaned against the central island and took a sip of her coffee. Charlie had stayed away from drugs, but he hadn't minded gambling. Lydia knew that one of their income streams came from a string of betting shops in

Camberwell. Back in the old days, there had been plenty of off-the-books stuff and illegal gambling, but she had thought it was all above board, now. A government-sanctioned way to part the gullible and the desperate from their cash.

'This crew... They've been running their own books. One of our shops heard about it when their income took a nosedive. A few of the regulars stopped turning up, and they poked around until they found they were getting their fixes elsewhere.'

'It's a free country,' Lydia said mildly.

'Not really, boss,' Aiden said.

Lydia looked at him in surprise.

He swallowed hard but continued speaking. 'We run those shops. We staff them and watch the books. Charlie stopped the council from approving any others if anyone tried to move in on the legit side and nobody dared do anything else. But now... The Brixton Mob have just started their own thing. Like we don't exist. Like the Crows don't run the gambling in Camberwell. It's not right. The Family aren't happy about it.'

The assembled Crows looked variously at the table, their hands, the ceiling and the floor. Anywhere, in short, that wasn't in Lydia's direction. She took another measured sip of coffee. 'Is that a fact?'

The group continued to studiously avoid looking at Lydia. None of them spoke.

Lydia sighed. 'Just tell me what happened.'

Aiden cleared his throat. 'Just a bit of gang trouble. Nothing we couldn't handle.'

'Good, then,' Lydia pushed away from the counter and made to leave. 'Next time you want to tell me everything's fine, maybe just do it on the phone, eh?'

'We killed one of them.' Aiden spoke in a rush. Part scared, part proud.

Lydia stopped moving. 'Accidentally?'

'Yeah,' Aiden said. 'Mostly.'

Hell Hawk. 'Start at the beginning. Don't leave anything out.'

ONCE THEY HAD FINISHED THEIR REPORT, TOLD haltingly and with lots of looking at each other and stopping until Lydia had lost her patience and produced her coin in order to focus their minds and get them through the damn story, she dismissed them all. Except Aiden.

She pocketed her coin and gave him a long stare. To his credit, he didn't look away.

'So,' she said finally. 'Where exactly was I unclear?'

Aiden didn't flinch. 'You said to wind down anything that wasn't legit.'

'Good. That's how I remember the conversation, too.'

'But some of those people.' He gave a half-shrug, his chin jutting out in defiance. 'Some of those things. They don't go easy. There's a struggle. We can't run our legit gambling if they're running the off-the-books stuff in the same street. It cuts our profits. And it makes us look weak. Three of our shops have been getting hassle for months now. Gangs trying it on, causing bother. A couple have been knocked over. Known Crow establishments, getting robbed. We can't allow it.'

Lydia closed her eyes. She wanted to ask him why he hadn't told her things were so bad, but she knew the answer. She hadn't wanted to know and Aiden was a good solider and he hadn't wanted to bother the brass.

When she opened her eyes, the situation was still just as messy. 'Does the deceased have family?'

'One sister. I've paid her off.'

'Good,' Lydia nodded. 'Is it going to catch attention? I assume you cleaned the scene?'

Aiden shook his head. 'Shouldn't think so. He's a known villain. Roadman geezer, only recently left Her Majesty's bed-and-breakfast. Body wasn't cleaned away, there wasn't time, but there aren't any witnesses. No loose ends.'

Well that would remain to be seen. Just because Aiden didn't think there were any loose ends, didn't mean there weren't any. 'Weapon?'

Aiden smiled, and Lydia didn't like the look of it. 'His own blade. He must have got all turned around in the scuffle.'

There was a meanness to Aiden these days. A hardness that hadn't been there before. I did that, she thought dully. I can't blame Charlie anymore. This is on me. 'So was it a hit? Retaliation?'

Aiden's smile disappeared. 'I told you. They've been stepping up to our establishments, ripping them off. We had to show a bit of strength. It's not my fault they went for blades, made it messy.'

He seemed to anticipate Lydia's next suggestion.

'You can't pay them off. Sister's different, she's not in the life. But the gang, you give them money, say we're going legal and above board and we don't want no bother, next thing you know, there's a queue of them outside this door with one hand out, wanting a bit more and a bit more.'

If Lydia hadn't been so numb, she would have been angry. 'I know that,' she said mildly.

'It doesn't end,' Aiden persisted. 'We had to stop that little rebellion with the language they understand. We've been looking weak for too long. Rep will only hold so long without being backed up. And he came for us. I didn't have a choice.'

'I understand,' Lydia said. 'Do you think that will be an end to it?'

'For now,' Aiden said. 'Should do for now.'

Lydia wanted to put her head in her hands, to block out the conversation and the cold look in Aiden's eyes. Instead, she told him to leave. 'I'm heading upstairs. Let yourself out.'

'Training?' Aiden asked, picking up his phone from the table and shoving it into his back pocket.

'Yes,' Lydia lied. She wasn't going to tell Aiden that she intended to lie down in one of Charlie's spare rooms and have a sleep. Shut out the Crows and the world for a few precious hours.

. . .

Back at The Fork, Angel was presiding over a thankfully not-on-fire kitchen. 'Coffee,' Lydia said, by way of greeting.

'Help yourself,' Angel said and Lydia was relieved she seemed back to herself.

'And food. What's good today?'

'Everything,' Angel said in a monotone. 'Everything's good. Everything's always good.'

Okay, not completely back. There was an absence in Angel's gaze, like she was watching something entirely different play out in her mind's eye.

'Lasagne,' Lydia said, resisting the urge to snap her fingers in front of Angel's face. 'And chips.'

Angel blinked slowly. She put down the spatula she was holding on top of the display cabinet which was in an unprecedented state during cafe opening hours. Empty. Eventually, as if dragging the word from some long-forgotten room in her mind palace, she asked, 'Salad?'

Lydia shook her head. 'Bread, though. If there is any.'

Angel didn't answer, disappearing through the swing door.

Lydia took her seat at her usual table and leaned her head back. She didn't want to think about Aiden plunging a knife into another human, even if they were a gangster. She had to harden her heart, she knew. They had been coming for the Crows, for her Family. Back in the day that was a known suicide mission. So, things hadn't really changed. She was only one person, what could she do?

The words 'get the Crow', written in blood on the floor of a cell, flashed into her mind and she gratefully turned her thoughts to Fleet's dead detainee. Mikhail. She had been telling Fleet the truth when she said she didn't know the name and she hadn't recognised the man, either.

Fleet's missing person case had been going on for weeks and he had been excited about this suspect. A breakthrough, he had called it.

She scrolled through the news sites to check that nothing had leaked about the body in the station. The missing person case involved an actor called Rafferty Hill, and had dominated the headlines for a couple of weeks after it broke. It still merited page one treatment for even the smallest update. That's what happened when the victim was moderately famous. And young and good looking. It wasn't fair, but what was?

Rafferty Hill had been to a minor public school and UCL before turning away from his chemistry course to study theatre. Unlike ninety-nine-point-nine per cent of his compatriots, he grabbed an agent and a moderate role in a BBC drama and dropped out of his course. Lydia paused on a picture of Rafferty in costume for the Dorian Gray adaptation that had been his big break. He had the requisite cheekbones and striking eyes, full lips and luxuriant black hair for his chosen profession. He had gathered positive reviews, all of which used words like 'promising' and 'new talent'. At twenty-three, he wasn't especially young for making his acting debut, but the media love a story. The fact that his parents weren't in the theatre business, meant they were painting him as a working class breakthrough into the profession. A genuine raw talent. Never mind that his mum and dad ran a successful chain of estate agencies and he had never worked a minimum-wage job in his life.

There was nothing in his past or recent history to suggest trouble. His star was on the rise and he had been invited to some notable parties, at which he had done a little coke, but who hadn't? Stable middle class family with a house in Cricklewood. Lived with his best friend from university in a flat share in a converted Victorian school on the Old Kent Road. Fleet said the interviews indicated that the arrangement was due to change, now that Rafferty had some money coming in, but that he hadn't been in a rush. He wasn't at home all that much with shooting on location and touring with a stage production of Dracula. The best friend/flatmate, who was called Amber Robertson, indicated that this was perfectly fine and expected. No animosity there, apparently.

Lydia had asked Fleet whether there was a romantic entanglement with the best friend. She was thinking of jealousy or unrequited love as a motive. Women didn't often commit murder, but it wasn't unheard of. Lydia ought to know.

'Best friends from childhood, apparently. Completely platonic. Amber talked about a time when they were teens and they 'gave it a go' but it had been 'gross, like kissing her brother'. It all rang true, but I followed up with friends and family. Everyone agreed that they had always just been good friends.'

'What about relationships? I don't see a significant other listed.'

'That's because there was nobody significant to note. Last relationship lasted four months and ended two months earlier. Amber said he hadn't been too bothered and that it had been an amicable split. We followed up her details, but she was excluded very quickly on account of her being on a film shoot in America at the time of Rafferty's disappearance. A hundred people and a time-stamped camera make a great alibi.'

'Two months with nothing at all? With that face?'

'Amber mentioned a one-night stand the week before he went missing, but we haven't tracked down the girl.'

'Woman,' Lydia corrected absently.

'Barely,' Fleet said. 'According to Amber, anyway.' He paused. 'She wasn't very complimentary about Rafferty's choice of partner on that occasion.'

'Which was why you were so thorough on their relationship. You're sure Amber isn't jealous? Harbouring a secret passion?'

'Pretty sure,' Fleet said. 'But you don't have to be romantically or sexually interested in a person to be overly possessive and controlling.'

There was still the possibility of Amber's life changing for the worse as Rafferty's star was on the rise. Real estate was no joke in London and it was conceivable that Amber was seriously concerned about her living arrangements. What if Rafferty was dumping his old pal for fancier digs?

'So where was Amber on the night in question?'

'At her parents' house in Cricklewood.' He pulled an unhappy face. 'Family, I know. Not the best alibi in the world. But we've got CCTV of her on the tube and in the local Tesco store which confirm she was in the right area for a parental visit.'

So many dead ends. Nothing close to a promising person of interest. Nothing resembling a motive. No wonder Fleet had been overjoyed to have a suspect. And now that suspect was dead.

WHEN LYDIA WORKED A JOB SHE DID WHATEVER hours it took. This was both the beauty and curse of being her own boss. And it came with the freelance territory. She didn't get paid until the job was done, so there was an extra incentive. Fleet, however, was on a salary. However much he cared about his job, and he cared a great deal, he tried to keep it within his contracted hours. Of course, these often included overtime. He wasn't entirely successful, but he was certainly better at compartmentalising than Lydia had ever managed. He called at half six. 'We still on for eight or shall I push the reservation back?'

'Dinner?' Lydia asked in surprise. They had planned to go to the new Thai restaurant that had opened near to Fleet's flat, but she didn't think he would be able to leave the office, much less be in the mood for a date.

'If you're not caught up in family stuff. Was Aiden all right?'

'I can make it,' Lydia said, side-stepping the question.

. . .

Over spring rolls and lemongrass-infused crab cakes with sweet chilli dipping sauce, Fleet tried very hard not to talk about his case. He asked her about her day (fine) and her arm (fine) and made a truly heroic effort to flirt a little.

Lydia, who had never been any good at a work-life balance, and didn't really see the point, responded with an observation. 'It had to have been quick and painless. You saw his face.'

Fleet put his chopsticks down and took a swig of his Singha beer.

'You've seen more dead people than me,' she persisted. 'You ever see one look like that?'

'Sure. Old folks who popped off in their sleep.' He raised his eyebrows. 'What? When I was a constable I saw plenty. Mail piling up inside the door. No family or friends visiting. Finally, we get called when the smell hits the hallway.'

'You should put that on the recruitment poster.'

A small smile. 'We don't have a cause of death, yet. Heart failure, obviously, but not what caused it.'

'Could be an underlying condition.' A Fox had died in the disused tunnels of the underground, once. He'd had a weak heart and had been frightened into a catastrophic cardiac event. 'What about his brain? Would an aneurism look peaceful? They're fast, aren't they?'

'We'll have to wait for the pathologist's report. It's a priority case so hopefully we'll get it tomorrow. They're short staffed, though, so...' He shrugged. 'I'm keeping my fingers crossed.'

'And you're a bigwig, now. I bet they'll rush it through.'

'I'm not a bigwig,' Fleet said. His eyes crinkled. 'And who says 'bigwig' these days?'

'You must be if you're risking bringing me into a crime scene. In your station. In full view of everyone.'

'It didn't matter who saw. You had to be entered on the log, anyway. It wasn't going to be a secret.'

That was another thing that differed about Fleet's world and hers. His had a lot of rules. A lot.

He reached across the table and took her hand. 'This is supposed to be a romantic evening, you know.'

'What's more romantic than solving your case?'

He squeezed her hand. 'I'm serious.'

'So am I. This is on your mind. You don't have to pretend it isn't. There have got to be some perks of being with me and this is one of them. You don't have to be normal.'

Fleet smiled properly at that.

'It was a risk, though,' she took her hand back and attacked her food. 'Everyone with the last name 'Crow' is now a person of interest. It wasn't a subtle message.'

'It's a lead,' Fleet conceded. 'But I'm not worried about getting flack. As long as I get a result on this missing person case, all will be forgiven.'

'What makes you so sure?'

'I'm not,' Fleet dropped his gaze. 'Just being optimistic.'

'You have protection? Friends in low places?'

Lydia was goading him, she knew. He had refused to go into the details of his deal with Sinclair at the secret service and it was a pebble in her shoe. Well, more like a boulder. She forced herself to move onto more neutral ground. 'I do have one question. Why was Mikhail known as the Jekyll?'

'As in 'fake'. He had a side-line in selling counterfeit at one time. I guess it stuck.'

Lydia was familiar with rhyming slang, but this one made no sense. 'Jekyll and Hyde doesn't rhyme with 'fake'.'

'Jekyll and Hyde, snide. Snide means being fake to people. Second generation rhyming slang.'

'Got it.' Something else was bothering Lydia. 'How did he get the bloody knuckles? Was he violent when he was brought in?'

'Not at all. Booking officers said he was surprisingly polite. And he was uninjured when he was put in the cell. He must have got worked up after and punched the wall. If the CCTV hadn't gone weird, we would have it recorded.'

'Which means you don't have evidence that he did the injury himself, unprovoked. That's not ideal.'

Fleet had a spring roll in one hand and he gestured with it. 'That's it, no more shop talk. We're out on a romantic evening and we're going to be romantic, damn it. Now, tell me my eyes are dreamy.'

She laughed at that, feeling a wild happiness break through the wall for a moment. She stood up and leaned across the table to kiss Fleet.

When they came up for air, Fleet had one hand

tangled in her hair and was breathing hard. His pupils were dilated and Lydia knew from the tingling that was running through her body that hers would be the same. She spoke quietly, not breaking eye contact. 'Shall we go home?'

'Yes.'

CHAPTER FOUR

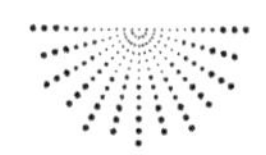

Lying on her back in Fleet's high-thread-count sheets, with one arm behind her head and one hand entwined with Fleet's, Lydia waited for her breathing to return to normal. It seemed impossible that she still felt as urgently attracted to Fleet as she had when they had first got together, but it was true. And seemed entirely mutual. It was a kind of small miracle and she thanked feathers for it as she moved and felt the muscles of her body pleasantly stretch. *This was something that Maddie would never do again.* The thought came swift and sharp and cut through her afterglow.

'What are you thinking?' Fleet had turned onto his side and was gazing into her eyes.

Lydia shook her head, forcing a smile. 'Nothing coherent. Not after that.'

He smiled slow and happy. 'Good.'

Her mind flicked away from Maddie and to the man sitting in his police cell. Strangely, calmly dead. She could understand why Fleet had wanted her to see the scene. Not just because of the message, but there had been something odd about the whole thing. How had he died in that eerily calm position? She knew that people sometimes went quickly and peacefully. An octogenarian settled in their favourite armchair, thinking about a boiled egg for lunch and then... They were found with their knitting on their lap and an air of being just about to say something. It happened. Just not to muscle-bound men in their thirties who were sitting upright in a police holding cell.

It hadn't really been a surprise that the staff of Camberwell nick hadn't been thrilled to see her. Not only was she part of the infamous Crow Family which, in turn, was tarnishing the reputation of one of their finest, but she had recently come off a building. That little incident connected her to the highly suspicious death of a young woman, and it had caused significant danger to the public. An officer had spent some considerable time explaining to Lydia exactly the damage she could have done to an innocent pedestrian had she landed on them. As if, in fact, she planned to make a habit of flinging herself from tall buildings.

Maddie's death had been cleared away. In all senses. Fleet had told her that Maddie's body had been moved extremely quickly after only the most cursory of forensics. The police had been involved purely for show. Uniforms guarding the scene until it was cleared and that was it. No police inquiry. No investigation. A Met spokesperson had been ready to brief the press, but it hadn't been necessary. There were no questions. No press coverage. No mobile phone videos or pictures leaked by the general public to social media. 'Quite impressive, really,' Fleet had said. 'I didn't know things could still be hushed up so effectively these days. Especially in central London. It wasn't exactly a deserted spot.'

'Okay, you're definitely thinking now,' present-day Fleet broke into her thoughts. His face was relaxed and his eyes were soft, but Lydia could sense that a frown was hovering and ready to land.

She touched his warm cheek and leaned in to kiss his concerns away. And his questions.

Fleet was lying still and almost asleep when Lydia knew she had to get up and leave. Her sleep had never been particularly reliable, but it had become elusive in the extreme. She was an expert in predicting when she was about to lie for hours next to Fleet, trying not to wake him up with her movements. She sat up and kissed the side of his face. 'I have to go to work.'

He opened his eyes and began to sit up but she pushed him gently down. 'Go to sleep. I'm meeting Aiden.' So that last bit was a lie, but it was the first thing that popped into her head.

'Family stuff?' Fleet murmured, already slipping back to sleep.

She was almost dressed and just about to creep out of the door when Fleet spoke again, his voice clearer. 'Watch out for the blue van.'

Lydia paused, waiting to see if he was going to say anything else. She was caught between waiting to ask him what he meant and not wanting to wake him up. A fully awake Fleet might decide he needed to be a gentleman and walk her to her imaginary meeting.

Rain had fallen while she was at Fleet's, but it was nothing more than a light mist, now. She walked fast along the wet pavements, breaking into a run to try to clear her thoughts. If she exhausted herself, physically, perhaps she would be able to sleep when she got home. She focused on the rhythm of her feet striking the slabs, the splash of the puddles and the pull of her breath.

Hitting a parade of shops and takeaways close to home, the foot traffic increased. There was a woman stumbling along with an open polystyrene box, shovelling kebab meat into her mouth, and Lydia dodged into the deserted cycle lane to avoid getting too close. She looked the kind of drunk that could easily fall over if surprised. At that moment, lights veered from the line of traffic as some idiot decided they were in a hurry and needed to use the cycle lane to attempt an illegal manoeuvre.

Lydia jumped back onto the pavement just as the van course corrected back to its lane. She stood for a moment, breath heaving and looked at the skid marks on the road. The blue van pulled away with the line of traffic, as if it hadn't just come close to killing her.

Back at the flat, Lydia felt too wired to sleep. She sat at her desk and splashed a little whisky into one of the mugs which littered the surface. It had dried dregs from her last coffee in the bottom, but that was okay. There was nobody around to judge. She leaned back and sipped the alcohol, willing her mind to stop whirling. The gold pendant from the jackdaw was in the middle of the desk where she had left it. It was an ugly piece with a fat yellowish pearl decorating the middle. It had given her a small jolt of 'Pearl Family' the moment she had picked it up, but Lydia had wondered if that had been pure suggestion because of the actual pearl. Or paranoia on account of her own fears. She picked it up to check. There it was, again. The faintest touch of Pearl. A yearning sensation.

That was it. A faint longing and the impression that the necklace had, suddenly, become a shade more attractive. Both things she associated with Pearl magic, but in their diluted, trace form. With her eyes closed and a bit of concentration, Lydia could feel an echo of something else. A whisper. A woman's voice, but so quiet that she couldn't make out any words. Well, that was new. Which begged the question – why had the jackdaw brought it to her?

Another question was why was she now able to get a 'read' from an inanimate object that seemed to go beyond the usual 'Family vibe'? It was an element she didn't really want to examine, a sense of her growing power and ability that she had been shoving away, locking in a dark room and hoping she wouldn't have to confront. The numbness wasn't post-traumatic stress. Or, more accurately, it wasn't *just* post-traumatic stress. It was a side effect of the sheer amount of denial Lydia was using not to confront one essential fact. She had killed her cousin. And, in accordance with what her father had told her about Crow Family power, it seemed as if she had gained a bit of whammy in return. More specifically, Maddie's power. The reason she had this neatly locked away and was considering setting fire to the box, was that if she openly acknowledged this power transfer, she would have to wonder what else had come along with it.

Enough.

Lydia swallowed the whisky in one fiery gulp and waited for the effect. There wasn't one, which meant that her inhuman tolerance for alcohol seemed to have increased alongside her Crow power. She pushed the mug away in disgust and leaned back in her chair, closing her eyes.

When she woke up, a crow was cawing outside the window and her neck and back were sending urgent pain signals, a not-so polite request that she stop bloody sleeping in her office chair.

The necklace was in the middle of her desk and she picked it up absently. If she was the superstitious sort, she would count it as a message. Which was followed, quickly, by one scrawled in blood on a cell floor. If this was a fairy tale, there would be a third.

Her mobile rang making her jump.

'Just checking in,' Fleet said, sounding disgustingly awake. 'Everything okay?'

Lydia rubbed a hand over her face. 'Yeah. Yes. All good.'

'Take it easy today, won't you? You're not back to full-'

'I'm fine,' Lydia said, trying to make it sound genuine. She appreciated his concern, of course she did, but she was sick of being treated like a delicate invalid.

'I'm nearby, can I pop in?'

She tilted her head to one side, stretching her sore muscles. 'Of course.'

Lydia swept the necklace into the top drawer of her desk and went to brush her teeth.

RAFFERTY HILL HAD GONE MISSING FROM HIS HOME and, despite police investigation and public appeals for information, there had been no new leads on his whereabouts. The case hadn't been acted on immediately, or even classified as a MISSPER. Rafferty was an adult and not considered especially at risk. It was assumed that he had needed some time to himself or had gone partying or on holiday without telling his flatmate and family. But then a witness had come forward to say they had heard raised voices in the flat on the day before he disappeared. The building had been canvased a second time and, on this round, another neighbour mentioned that they had heard shouting and banging, had assumed that Rafferty was having a heated debate with his flatmate. Added to the statements from Rafferty's friends that he had been on a health kick for an upcoming film shoot, and hadn't touched drugs or alcohol in weeks, it cast sufficient doubt on the party theory. When Rafferty failed to turn up to a pre-filming meeting for his upcoming role and his agent began phoning the police daily, voicing concern about his whereabouts, suddenly Fleet had a missing person case with a high-profile victim. Problem was, the new evidence didn't point to anything concrete. Just left unanswered questions.

Fleet had talked to Lydia about Rafferty when it had first landed on his desk, but it had been five weeks ago and she had been distracted by the pain and the after-shocks of dealing with Maddie. Thinking about it made Lydia realise how far she had come since that point. Those first couple of weeks had been blurry with pain medication and relief. A relief which had quickly morphed into guilt and exhaustion and finally a numbness that she still couldn't shake.

Lydia rinsed the toothpaste from the sink and washed her face with cold water. She avoided looking at herself in the mirror.

Fleet arrived fifteen minutes later. He was wearing a work suit and, as usual, it made Lydia want to take it off. Unfortunately, Fleet was in work-mode in all respects. He peered at her face like he was a medical professional, and checked the bottles of pain killers and muscle relaxants in the kitchen. 'These are still full.'

'I told you, I don't need them anymore.'

He leaned against the door jamb, regarding her with a serious expression. 'It's not just the physical side of things. It's a lot to process. You don't have to pretend to be okay.'

Luckily, Lydia knew exactly how to distract Fleet

from this tiresome line of questioning. 'Anything more on your dead suspect?'

'No.' Fleet's eyebrows were drawn together and his mouth was tight.

Mikhail had been Fleet's big hope. A man with a well documented record for burglary had seemingly targeted Rafferty. Someone matching his description had been captured on CCTV on Rafferty's street on three occasions and on one of these, could be seen entering the paved communal front garden and looking up at the building as if casing the place. There was also evidence that he was moving into extortion and bribery as the footage caught him pushing a white envelope through the letterbox, which was later recovered from the recycling bin. It was addressed to Rafferty by name, but with no flat number, and the handwriting matched that on the piece of lined paper – clearly torn from a cheap notebook – which was found crumpled with the envelope. The note warned Rafferty that his secret would not stay hidden if he didn't agree to the deal. The envelope had been torn open and the note was no longer inside, so it had definitely been seen and then discarded. It gave a deadline of midnight that Friday. Rafferty went missing on the Saturday, with his last known conversation being with his flatmate Amber.

Lydia fixed Fleet with a long stare. 'What did Mikhail say about the note?'

'Nothing.'

'Did he deny writing it? Or...'

'He said nothing. Not a single word. Not during booking. Not during questioning. That was why he had been left for a while. It was anticipated that a little bit of stew time would make him reconsider his pact of silence. And I was hoping I would find a new angle or a bit of leverage.'

'He's a thief, right? And occasional purveyor of dodgy goods. What made him move into blackmail?'

'That's the question, isn't it? My guess... The opportunity presented itself. Something too juicy to pass up. Rich young actor on the rise in the public eye. Must have seemed like an easy mark.'

That still didn't make sense to Lydia. A mark for burglary, sure. But to jump to blackmail? When he had never done anything like that in the past? That was plain weird. 'So you trace Mikhail's movements over the last couple of months. See where that opportunity came from.'

Fleet shook his head. 'Already done.' He turned his palms face up. 'I've got nothing. He hasn't been arrested in over five years, the address we've got on record is old, and his last parole officer is off long-term sick. He doesn't use social media or credit cards. The man doesn't even have a Netflix subscription.'

Lydia paused. She was still annoyed that Fleet had suggested she was holding out on him, but she also knew he was desperate. 'You want me to ask him?'

To Fleet's credit, he didn't point out that Mikhail was dead. 'You think he'll speak to you?'

Lydia shrugged. 'He did ask for me.'

She moved closer, putting a hand to his chest.

He put his hand over hers, but still looked troubled.

'I had hoped you knew him. That would have made things easier.'

Was she imagining it or was there an accusatory note in his voice? 'He's not a Crow, I told you.'

'But he clearly has had dealings with your Family. I was hoping something might have come back to you.'

'So this isn't a social call.'

He straightened. 'I wanted to check on you. But, yes. I did want to talk about Mikhail, again. He left you a message. Could he have...' Fleet trailed off. 'Never mind.'

'Could he what?'

'Nothing.'

'You want me to look through Charlie's things? See if there's a picture of them together with a heart drawn around their faces and a handy note on the back with the guy's address?'

'Of course not.'

'But you think I'm holding out on you? Even after everything. You think I would do that?'

Fleet met her gaze, unblinking. 'If it was to protect your Family, sure. You've said it before. This is just my job, it's not my life.'

Lydia allowed her gaze to drop. 'Your job matters to you so it matters to me. Besides, I'm not so far gone that I don't care about finding a man before he turns up dead. Or about a man dying in a police cell. I'm not so far gone that I don't care.'

Fleet looked shocked at that. 'I wasn't saying you were... Gone. You're a good person, Lyds.'

She snorted. 'Don't spread it about. I'm barely hanging onto my rep as it is.'

He went still. 'Family trouble?'

'Nothing I can't handle. And nothing I can tell you about without compromising your professional ethics, so best we drop it, eh?'

'Oh shit,' Fleet said.

'Indeed.'

CHAPTER FIVE

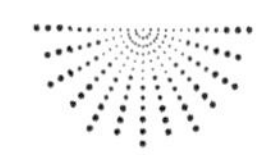

The next morning, Fleet took a phone call while Lydia was in the shower. She was towel-drying her hair when he walked into the bedroom, looking unhappy. His superior had vetoed the possibility of Lydia walking back into the cell to take 'another look'. Since Fleet wasn't about to explain why Lydia needed to see the place again, and she wasn't even sure Mikhail's ghost would be available and able to speak, he said it was better if he dropped the matter.

'Are you in trouble?' Lydia asked him.

'No more than usual.' Fleet slipped his hands under her t-shirt. 'Nothing I can't handle.'

She twisted in his arms and dropped the towel. They were just getting to an interesting part of the proceedings when Fleet's mobile rang.

He broke away. 'Damn it. Sorry.'

'Don't worry about it.' Lydia combed her damp hair and adjusted her clothes while Fleet paced the room. It didn't sound like good news.

'I've got to get to the office,' he said when the call finished. 'The post-mortem report is in. Nothing useful. Cause of death is unclear.'

'I'm sorry,' Lydia said. She could see the stress etched on Fleet's face. A nice clear-cut pre-existing condition leading to perfectly natural causes would have really helped him at this point.

'Not your fault,' Fleet said, planting a quick kiss on her cheek. 'I just want to read it for myself.'

'Go,' Lydia made a shooing gesture.

'Right. I'll see you later.'

'Pub?'

'Pub. Not The Hare, though.'

'Why not?'

Fleet paused. 'I have no idea.'

They settled on The Crown instead and Lydia didn't push Fleet on his sudden aversion to their favourite Camberwell establishment.

Once Fleet had left for the office, Lydia found Jason to tell him they weren't taking a field trip to look for Mikhail's ghost, after all. He trailed her to the kitchen and flipped the switch on the kettle. Lydia didn't bother to say that she didn't want a hot drink. She had learned that it was easier to just say thank you and not drink it than try to stop Jason from making something when he was in the mood.

He paused, one hand in the box of teabags. 'Where do you think he went?'

Lydia was pretty sure who he meant, but she asked to play for time. 'Who?'

'The dead guy. Mikhail. You said you didn't see a spirit when you saw the body and I would think you would. A fresh murder like that and your power's so strong these days.'

'We don't know that it's a murder,' Lydia said. 'Unexplained death at the moment. And he was alone. That means-'

'Not a lot in our world,' Jason said. 'But you didn't see his spirit or sense it?'

'Nope. Nothing.'

'So where did it go?' Jason seemed agitated, but Lydia was at sea with existential conversations and she didn't know how to comfort him. She didn't like to think too much about souls and where they went, but it seemed more pertinent now that she had hastened a few people on that journey. The guilt flared and she rubbed her arms, suddenly cold.

'Sorry,' Jason said, stepping further away.

'It's not you,' Lydia said, forcing her expression into something less bleak. 'I just don't have an answer. And I don't like thinking about it.'

The kettle hadn't boiled, yet, but he picked up the kettle and poured water onto the teabag. 'Because of Maddie?'

'I suppose. But I always used to be sure. I knew that we were just self-aware animals that had made up some stories to explain our existence before science came along. We're just atoms and electrical impulses in the brain. When we died we just died. End of. Now I know that's not always the case. So who else is out there? And what does that mean?'

Jason moved to the fridge. 'You're right. It's a stupid question.'

'I didn't say "stupid",' Lydia objected.

'I'll make you some toast.'

He took butter from the fridge and put it onto the counter, not looking in Lydia's direction.

'It's fair enough to think about,' she tried. 'I mean you don't know what's going to happen when you do pass on, pass over, whatever...'

He turned back. 'Yeah, but neither do you. And neither of us know what's going to happen next year. Or tomorrow. Or whether this will break or bounce if I drop it,' he picked up a mug from the side. 'It was a stupid question because the point is that we don't know. That's what being alive is. Uncertainty. And I like being alive. I mean, I like it being like I'm alive.'

'That's good,' Lydia said gently. She smiled, hoping to lift him from his philosophical mood. 'And, for the record, I'm pretty sure that mug will smash if you drop it in here.'

Lydia had set up a Google alert on the pub, The Hare, and wasn't entirely surprised when something popped up mid-afternoon. A stabbing incident in the bar involving a twenty-three year old and a seventeen year old. The place would be closed and taped off as a crime scene and most definitely not available for a quiet drink.

Fleet was due to finish at six, but Lydia had arranged to meet him at half-seven. The man wasn't known for his ability to leave work on time and it was usually best to build in buffer zones. He would say the exact same thing about her, which meant everything was nice and equal. In fact, Lydia had built in so much of a buffer that she had got caught up doing research on Rafferty Hill and had lost track of time. Fleet was sitting in the corner with a pint of ale and a glass of red on the table.

'You saw the news about The Hare?'

'Yeah,' Fleet took a sip of his pint, avoiding her gaze.

'So that's why you didn't want to go there. You knew.'

He shook his head violently. 'I did not know anything.'

'Not true,' Lydia picked up her glass. It was cold and she knew the wine was going to taste harsh. She knocked it back anyway. 'You knew something. You had a gut feeling.'

'Maybe,' Fleet conceded. 'Lots of people have gut feelings, though. It's nothing to get excited about.'

So Fleet was still in denial about his growing ability. Lydia filed that fact away and turned the conversation to more neutral matters. His day. Her day. Dead people, murder suspects, gang problems and crime figures.

Once they were onto their second drinks and had a couple of bags of crisps split open, the conversation wound its way to the Rafferty Hill case. And Mikhail the Jekyll.

'There was one thing,' he said. 'There was some paper in the stomach contents. A mass consistent with a small piece. Just a slip, pathologist thinks, but it's hard to be certain. It depends on the weight of the paper.'

'He ate some paper?'

'Properly chewed it, too. That and the stomach acid means we can't tell what was written on it, if anything. It could also have been a habit.'

'Like chewing gum?'

'More like a compulsion. It's a thing, apparently. Well, a disorder. Xylophagia. I looked it up.'

'Or it was something he didn't want anyone to read. A phone number or an address. I assume it wasn't found when he was booked in? You've spoken to whoever took him to the cell?'

'We only take items which could pose a danger.' Fleet sounded defensive.

'I know,' Lydia said quickly. 'I was just thinking out loud. Wondering if one of your staff might have seen it. Might remember it.'

'I'll ask them again, but nobody mentioned anything in their reports. They log everything. It wouldn't have been left out.'

He was still sounding defensive, so Lydia moved the conversation on with another question. 'Where are you with Rafferty?'

Fleet glanced around, confirming that nobody was in earshot. 'The blackmail is still our best lead and it doesn't give us anywhere to look. Only gives a possible motive for him disappearing.'

'Parents?'

'Nothing.'

'Friends?'

'Dead end.'

She licked her finger and pressed it into the crisp crumbs left in the packet. The salt burst on her tongue. 'And I assume you spoke to his manager?'

'His agent. Of course. Nothing to suggest he was going to do a flit.'

'What about the blackmail? What's he supposed to have done?'

'Doesn't say.'

'Not even a hint?'

'Totally generic threats. No details. Could be literally anybody taking a punt on a payday or a terrible practical joke.'

'Except you have linked it to Mikhail, because he was caught on CCTV hanging around Rafferty's building?'

'And the CCTV which showed him delivering a white envelope. It could be argued that it's not conclusively the same white envelope which was retrieved from the recycling bin, but it was a good start. But now that's a dead end, too.'

The words hung in the air between them for a moment. Then Fleet sighed. 'Only thing I do know is that if he doesn't turn up for the first day of shooting, he'll be in breach of contract. But before that, they will recast it on the quiet. They have to wait until he breaks contract before they can formally replace him, but have no doubt they will be making contingency plans. He's an ambitious young actor and this is a lead role.'

'It really doesn't look like he's gone missing of his own accord, does it?'

Fleet shook his head. 'But it doesn't fit the profile for a kidnapping situation, either. Where are the demands?'

'Could his family be keeping quiet about that?'

'They're under light surveillance and we've got phone taps. If they were dealing with kidnappers, we would have picked up on something by now.'

Lydia thought about that for a while. Could a couple of frightened civilians successfully hide their activities from the police? If they were sufficiently motivated, it wasn't entirely impossible. But, she had to admit, not likely.

'One thought,' Fleet said, looking unhappy. 'If it was an unsuccessful extortion situation. Kidnapping gone wrong.'

'That would leave Rafferty in a shallow grave somewhere.'

'Yeah. That would explain why they didn't follow through with demands.'

'Hell Hawk. That's not a cheery possibility.'

'On a brighter note, maybe he has just had some kind of breakdown. Maybe he's taking a rest cure somewhere quiet?'

'On his own?'

'Or he's in a fugue state. Can't remember who he is, but he'll just show up when he gets his memories back.'

'Or maybe it's a publicity stunt. A way to drum up interest in his latest project?'

Fleet smiled properly. 'That would be even better. Just some silly arse wasting police time. Then he can turn up alive and well. And make a substantial donation to charity to salve his conscience for all the trouble he's caused.'

'And while we're at it, pigs can fly, politicians will tell the truth, and I will start drinking kale juice.'

LYDIA LURCHED AWAKE, HEART THUDDING. FLEET was sitting up in the bed next to her, breathing heavily. She reached out and touched sweaty-damp skin. 'What's wrong?'

'Nightmare,' Fleet said. 'Just a nightmare.'

Lydia clicked on the bedside lamp, blinking in the light. Fleet looked awful. Like he was about to throw up. 'Are you going to be sick?'

He swallowed hard a couple of times. 'I don't think so.'

Lydia hauled out of bed and padded through to Fleet's kitchen. She grabbed the basin from out of the sink, grateful that they were at his place where dirty dishes went into the dishwasher and didn't just sit in the basin for days at a time, and carried it through to the bedroom.

'I'm okay.' Fleet was leaning back against pillows, now, and he had wiped his face so it was no longer glistening. There was still an ashy tone to his skin, though, and his eyes were glassy and afraid.

'Bad one?'

He nodded, accepting the basin and putting it on the floor on his side of the bed.

Lydia waited. He would tell her in his own time. Fleet had a lot of bad dreams. And a lot of waking visions. His gift seemed to give him foresight into future events, but it appeared that the atheists were right and there was no grand plan. Fleet often saw several versions of an event. Or saw things a split second before they happened. Largely useless premonitions, in other words. And a relatively high price of rarely getting a decent night's sleep.

She climbed onto his lap and held his face with both hands, looking into his wild eyes. 'It was just a dream. It's okay. You're okay.'

Gradually his eyes lost their glassiness and he focused properly on Lydia. His hands flexed on her hips, pulling her against his waking-up body.

'Well, since you're awake, too...' His lips quirked into a devilish smile. It was a shadow of his usual full-watt expression, but was still appealing. They kissed, breathing quickening for a more pleasant reason.

Later, once they were tired again and curled up together, ready to attempt sleep, Fleet murmured something into her hair.

'What did you say?'

'It was Rafferty Hill.'

Lydia squeezed his hand. 'You're doing everything you can. You have nothing to feel guilty about.'

'It wasn't a guilt dream. It was more like a message, like there is something huge I'm missing.'

Lydia twisted in his arms, turning to face him. 'That could be good. What was the message?'

It was too dark to see his expression, but Lydia could sense him frowning as he hesitated. 'You can tell me.'

'I might have it wrong, but it seemed to be saying that Rafferty Hill is still alive.'

CHAPTER SIX

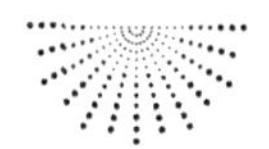

Uncle John had never been Lydia's biggest fan, but that frosty relationship had become positively glacial in recent weeks. It was understandable. The official line was that Lydia and Maddie had fallen from the hospital roof accidentally, distracted by a heated debate. Death by misadventure. Lydia hadn't challenged the story given by the police, but Uncle John and Aunt Daisy were pretty damn certain that their little girl wouldn't have done anything so clumsy.

The Crow Family meeting at The Fork was the first time Lydia had been in the same room since it had happened. They had held a small memorial service at their house for Maddie, but Lydia hadn't been invited. The story went that they couldn't do anything official, and had to keep it very low key. That was partly true. They had a death certificate but no body. Maddie's remains had vanished, courtesy of the secret service, and according to Aiden, a visit from a couple of suits had resulted in a cash compensation and an extracted vow to keep very, very quiet.

John was sitting at one of the tables against the back wall. Lydia had to pass him as she entered the cafe from the internal door. She paused at the table to greet him. She had intended to say 'I'm sorry for your loss', the standard platitude, but the words stuck in her throat the moment she saw his face, etched with cold hatred. 'Where's Daisy?' She asked, instead.

'Sick.' John was staring determinedly to Lydia's left, avoiding her eyes.

If she was Charlie, she would tell John to go home and fetch his wife, sick or not. This was a Family meeting. Capital 'F' and everybody in the inner circle had been called. If she was Charlie, she would have found a way to kill Maddie and cover her tracks at the same time so that John and Daisy would be lining up to shake her hand and to beg retribution for their daughter.

But she wasn't Charlie. And she couldn't pretend to be sorry that Maddie was dead, any more than she could pretend she hadn't killed her. Lydia put both hands on the table and leaned down in front of John so that he had no choice but to look at her face. 'Daisy gets a free pass in recognition of her loss. On this one occasion. Are we clear?'

John's nod was so tiny it was hardly there at all.

Lydia straightened and made her way to the middle of the room. The room fell silent as soon as she began to speak.

. . .

Aiden was standing with his hands clasped in front of his body, back straight. He looked more like a soldier every day. He gave a report of the recent trouble.

Lydia followed up with a brief description of the message left by Mikhail. 'I need to know if any of you had recent dealings with Mik. Or have any insights about why he might have turned to blackmail from burglary, or why he might have left that message. It certainly looks like it's calling for our help, but it's also given us a bit of unwanted police attention.'

'The attack is the serious issue,' Uncle John said. 'That shows we are perceived as weak.'

'I dealt with it,' Aiden said. 'That sends a message that we're not weak. Come for a Crow and you'll go home in a box.' He seemed disgruntled at having his experience side-lined, which Lydia could understand. He had taken a life in defence of himself and the Family.

Lydia soothed his ruffled feathers by focusing on the gang attack. 'Aiden has protected our reputation. He gave a quick and clear response and, hopefully, that will calm things down. But everyone must be on their guard.'

'We need to show we're strong.' Uncle John again, stating the bloody obvious.

'Showing we're strong is all well and good,' Lydia said. 'But we are strong. Let's not forget that.'

Uncle John opened his mouth again, but Lydia rolled right over him. 'Aiden, Daniel, and Annie. How do you feel about some training?'

'Like martial arts? Gym work?'

'Like this,' Lydia produced her coin and then created a thousand duplicates. She let them hang above the

Crows' heads, motionless in the air, and then sent them flying around the cafe in formation. Breaking and swarming and moving together like a murmuration of starlings at dusk.

'I can't...' Annie began.

'Not yet. But you're a Crow. I might be Henry Crow's daughter, but we share the same bloodline. And it can't be the only thing. Look how strong Maddie was. She wasn't my sister.'

John flinched.

Lydia ignored him and carried on. 'I am stronger than I used to be and that is because I have been training. Practising.' She decided not to mention the possibility that she had accidentally stolen Maddie's power. That wasn't a helpful detail. 'You can train, too.'

There was some murmuring and a lot of uncertain faces. One or two avid ones, though. Aiden stepped forward. 'It's a good idea, boss. Worth a try, anyway.'

After the last Crow had filed out of The Fork and Lydia was alone, Jason pushed through the door from the kitchen. In the past he would have simply appeared, quick as blinking, but he seemed to have really caught the corporeal habit.

'Were you listening?'

'Yeah. Well, I got distracted in the middle for a bit. John goes on a bit, doesn't he?'

Lydia sat down and rubbed a hand over her face. 'John and Daisy hate me, and that's fair enough, but I don't think it's bothered the rest. I think it'll be okay.'

'Why do you care that people are running illegal betting in Camberwell?' Jason asked. 'If the Crows are legit, why does it matter? Can't you just opt out of the gangland pissing contest?'

'That's what I hoped,' Lydia said. 'But illegal business takes away from the on-the-books shops which we run.'

'Does it? I would have thought they were separate clientele.'

'Some are, but the space where they overlap is huge. And it's not just that... It's about optics.'

'Optics?'

'How it looks. If the people of Camberwell running betting shops and paying their business rates and their taxes perceive that underground shops are taking their customers and running down their profits, they are going to be unhappy. I'm not just battling the business community of Camberwell who are used to the Crows stepping in and sorting out any little problem in return for a cut, I'm also trying to pacify my own blood relatives. Second and third cousins and in-laws, running our betting shops and blaming my new policies every time they have a week of low takings.'

Jason moved back toward the door to the kitchen. 'Would toast help?'

'Always,' Lydia said, forcing a smile. 'Let's go upstairs, though.' The darkness outside the large windows of the cafe was unnerving. With the lights on she felt suddenly vulnerable, as if there was somebody outside on the street, staring in.

'You all right?' Jason followed her gaze. 'What did you see?'

'Nothing,' Lydia said. But her feet carried her to the door she had locked behind the last Crow. She pulled the bolt back, turned the key, and stepped into the street. A car shushed past on the wet road. The lights of the surrounding buildings and the street lamps meant that it was only London-dark. Dark in name only. Lydia knew true dark. Under the ground with earth in her nose and ears and total blackness pressing onto her eyes.

A young couple walked by on the opposite side of the road, arms looped around each other. The woman was holding a closed umbrella loosely at her side and their heads were tilted toward each other. Oblivious to anything except each other. Lydia scanned up and down, looking for the source of her disquiet. Her skin was prickling and she could feel the urge to spread her arms. The stretching of wings ready for flight.

A single man appeared around the corner, just as the couple reached it. He loped past, large headphones clamped on his head.

There was nothing. Nobody peering in. Lydia forced a long slow breath. Maddie was gone. She wasn't watching, waiting. Charlie was incarcerated. Alejandro was banished. She had vanquished all threats. She was fine. And if some roadmen of Camberwell were stepping up to the Family and taking pot shots, it would be nothing she couldn't handle. She felt her coin in her hand and made a fist around it. She was stronger than ever. She was safe.

Still, she scanned the windows of the buildings

opposite and looked up and down the road. There was something. Somebody watching. She could feel it.

UPSTAIRS IN THE FLAT, LYDIA PUT HER FEET ONTO her desk and leaned back in her chair. The ceiling was as unhelpful as always so she closed her eyes and counted her breaths. Emma had been extolling the virtues of meditation on their last phone call. She had an app for it on her phone and said it was helping her to stay calm on the school run.

The sound of the plate landing on the desk and the cooling air interrupted her count. She was up to over fifty breaths and she still felt tense as hell. Jason was clearly worried as he had made four slices of toast instead of two. 'It's okay,' she said, digging into the carbs.

'What if you let the Crows go back to the off-the-books gambling? If they can reopen their illegal betting operations, they won't be missing out on that side of the revenue anymore and they won't have anything to complain about.'

'I said we had to go legit.' Lydia chewed a lump of toast and swallowed. 'I am dating a copper.'

Jason shrugged. 'Maybe it's being dead, but whether the gambling is legal or not doesn't feel like that big a deal. Morally speaking, I mean. And you have to give your family something.'

The dodgy side of the Crow business had always leaned on protection rackets. When Charlie had taken over, he had shut down the drug side as far as possible and used the Family reputation to keep the really bad stuff out of Camberwell. You still had addicts, of course, and people buying and selling weed or ecstasy or LSD or even a bit of snow was by-the-by, but heroin was harder to stumble across. You could stroll into Brixton or Peckham and any passing school kid could point at your nearest dealer, but in Camberwell, not so much. And if you did, it wouldn't be a Crow that sold it or had brought it in on a ship. That was Charlie's legacy and Lydia had no interest in destroying it. She had no problem with people taking drugs, if it was their own free will and they had the cash to do so, but the supply chain was rife with bad business. And she wasn't about to let the Crows join in the other streams of criminal income, either. Human trafficking. Guns and knives. It was a murky world and it only got darker the deeper you went. Maybe illegal betting was the lesser of the evils. Or maybe she had lost all perspective. Maybe, a very small voice said, this is Maddie talking. Her beautiful, morally broken cousin jumped into her mind's eye. *What else did she give you when she died?*

CHAPTER SEVEN

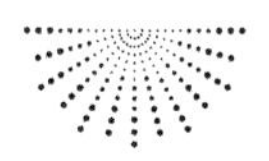

Six weeks earlier, the Pearl King had died along with the rest of the Pearl court. Lydia had worried that releasing them from their contract would leave the Pearls free to roam London, wreaking havoc, but instead they had shrivelled and died in front of her soil-clogged eyes. She didn't like to think about that time. The terror of the earth shaking, the rocks raining down as the underground cavern collapsed around her. Earth pushing down and in and around until she was cowering in her tiny space beneath the Pearl King's throne. Hoping to live and then, eventually, waiting to die.

Still, Lydia had been half-expecting a surge of Pearl magic above ground. It was such a seismic event that it seemed unlikely to not have some kind of knock-on effect.

As she ran the streets of Camberwell, she stretched her senses out, listening. It was past midnight and the pavements were quiet. She had started walking when she couldn't sleep, but now only running would do. It was the closest thing to flying and, bonus, it was bloody exhausting. She was convinced that if she could just run far enough, then she might be able to sleep properly. It hadn't happened, yet, but that was just a matter of distance.

She caught the usual mix of Family notes. Lots of Crow, of course, glimpses of Silver and the occasional Fox. The Pearl was the same as before. Just the weakest glimmer, diffuse and almost-toothless. Generations of Pearl power disseminated and spread throughout London. Walk into any independent shop, especially one that didn't seem like it ought to be making a living, and you'd get a whiff. Just be careful not to linger, or you'd find yourself walking out with a pastel-coloured dog coat for the pet you didn't even own, courtesy of an eleventh-generation Pearlie.

Lydia was nearly at the river. She usually looped Burgess Park and headed back to home, but tonight she had run straight through and kept on going. She passed The Shard, lit up like a beacon, and found herself at the Thames. She paused for a few breaths, looking at Tower Bridge and the black water flowing beneath and then downriver to Docklands. The lights of the city suddenly felt strange and, for a split second, Lydia imagined them all put out. The city as it had once been at night. Dark. Dangerous. A primeval mass of people, living intertwined like one organism. No. Not one organism. Many little creatures. Scurrying in the dark. Huddling in rooms. Too busy fighting and fucking among themselves to notice the predators swooping above.

'All right, darling?' A man in a suit with his tie loosened had broken from his group of mates, heading home from a club. 'Bit late for that, isn't it? Come and have a drink with us.'

Lydia didn't bother to answer. She took off running again. Heading home.

After a couple of hours of light sleep, Lydia spent an hour buried in the paperwork she had brought back from Charlie's home office months ago and then hadn't looked at. As she expected, it made for dry reading. It wasn't as if the really dodgy stuff had been written down clearly, but alongside information from Aiden, a fuzzy picture was emerging. And that picture was complicated and multi-layered, with so many connections that Lydia couldn't see a way to excise portions of the business without affecting the whole. Lydia knew that telling Aiden to shut everything down wasn't enough. He didn't have enough information to carry out the command, let alone the time and clout. Now that she was fully recovered from her injuries, she needed to get properly involved. And that meant making sense of Charlie's empire.

At nine, she drove over to Beckenham and parked outside Emma's house. It was high time she caught up with her closest friend and this was one of the best windows in her day. After the school run and, in Emma's own words, well before she 'passed out from exhaustion' at around eight pm.

At a nearby cafe, Emma pushed her sunglasses to the top of her head and put her bag on the spare chair at the table. 'I'm starving.'

'Me too,' Lydia said, realising it was true. When had she last eaten? Yesterday?

They had caught up on Emma's news on the walk over. Tom was fine. Maisie and Archie were fine. Archie didn't like his main class teacher, but he had a different one on a Friday who he loved and the teaching assistant who was in full-time was probably his favourite person in the whole wide world, so he had reversed his initial refusal to attend. Maisie had decided she was a dragon and Emma had to call her food 'dragon food' and address her as 'princess dragon'. Plus, if you displeased her, she breathed fire.

'That sounds hazardous,' Lydia said.

'You have no idea,' Emma replied. 'And what about you? Are you still taking it easy?'

'Mostly,' Lydia said.

Emma opened her mouth to speak, but Lydia rushed on. 'I had to get back to work. I was climbing the walls. And I'm fine.' She held up her hands. 'I promise. I'm completely healed.'

The waiter arrived, saving Lydia from whatever Emma had been about to say. They both ordered the huevos rancheros and coffee. 'And two orange juices, please,' Emma added. 'What?' She looked at Lydia. 'You need the vitamin C.'

'How do you know?'

'Just a hunch.'

Lydia thought about arguing, but then she recalled

her diet over the last week and realised that Emma was probably going to prevent her from developing scurvy.

Once they were alone, Lydia tried a more truthful answer to Emma's question. 'I've been having a bit of trouble with the Family business. It's been distracting me from my other work.'

'What sort of trouble?'

Lydia had sketched out some of the Crow Family business in the past, reassuring Emma that she was keeping the family away from the nasty stuff and the deeply illegal. Now, she explained that her plan to keep everything squeaky clean hadn't entirely worked. 'It's too entrenched and there are too many variables.'

'People?'

Lydia nodded. 'All doing their own little deals with their own mini networks. It's not as if Charlie kept a lovely big spreadsheet with everybody's business and details and financial records. I keep finding things out, usually too late to do anything, but I didn't think there was anything too bad.'

Emma went still. 'But there is something? Really bad?'

'Not really. I don't know. I can't tell.'

Emma raised an eyebrow and waited.

'We own a load of betting shops and have shares in many more. And Charlie did a lot of deals for the development of Camberwell. Regeneration projects with council funding.'

'Well that's all legal, by the sounds of it.'

'On the surface, yeah. But to keep hold of lucrative sites and to land deals, it all involves kickbacks and favours. And you don't want to know about some of the favours.'

Their drinks arrived and Lydia took a fortifying sip of her coffee.

'Okay. But it used to be worse stuff, right? And you're only one person. You can't change everything overnight, it's going to take time. You're not doing those deals, so in a few years, the fallout from your uncle will have settled.'

Lydia stared at Emma in surprise. 'I thought you would be more horrified.'

'Beckenham isn't Camberwell, but it's not another planet. I heard the rumours. And it sounds like you've done a brilliant job in cleaning things up. You should cut yourself some slack.'

'I don't know about that,' Lydia mumbled, embarrassed.

'Well I do. You think Charlie was worrying about people gambling when they didn't have the money? Or intimidating people?' She stopped. 'I just realised. That's probably not your only problem, is it?'

'Not really.'

The waiter brought the food and put it down.

Lydia picked up her fork, although her appetite had disappeared. She couldn't look Emma in the eye. She wanted, suddenly, to tell her that Aiden had stabbed a man. A bad man, no doubt, but still. But that would open Emma up to the true darkness of her Family.

Emma was grinding pepper over her eggs. Without warning, she put the grinder down and grabbed Lydia's hand across the table. 'I know you feel bad about Maddie.'

Lydia's eyes were suddenly stinging. She blinked back tears. She didn't deserve sympathy. She wasn't a victim or the bereaved. She was a killer.

Emma didn't let go of her hand and, eventually, Lydia managed to look at her face, dreading what she would find there. Her expression was just the same as it always was when she looked at Lydia. Fond exasperation, a touch of amusement and a world of love.

Lydia swiped her face with her free hand.

'I don't know if I thanked you properly,' Emma said, squeezing her hand a little. 'You did me and my family and most likely many more people a true service.'

'I didn't...' Lydia hadn't told Emma exactly what had happened on the roof. Just that Maddie had been intent on sending her over the edge and that they had both gone over in the ensuing struggle.

Emma shook her head gently. 'You did the right thing and I'm so proud of you.'

Lydia swallowed hard. 'I didn't think you were in favour of the death penalty.'

Emma released her hand, shrugging. 'Funny how you don't really know what you believe in until your kids are in danger.'

After brunch with Emma, Lydia took the tube to the hospital. She felt both comforted and raw from her conversation, like the top layer of her skin had been ripped away. It was good not to feel numb anymore, she reasoned. Although, when she got in sight of the hospital building and felt a swooping sickness, she wasn't entirely convinced it was an improvement.

She walked through the main entrance and then, navigating by memory, found the patch of tarmac beneath the roof where she and Maddie had landed. It was the edge of a carpark, a walkway for pedestrians hurrying from their cars to make appointments; nervous, sad, sick, or all three.

Lydia stood on the pavement and looked up at the hospital roof. It was a long way up. Ghosts often seemed to end up connected to where they died. Not that she was claiming to be an expert, but that had been her experience so far. A man speaking loudly into his mobile, a Pret bag in his other hand, almost walked into her. He took evasive action at the very last moment, but was close enough for Lydia to get a blast of his coffee breath and cologne.

Behind him, an elderly couple were making their way a little slower. Lydia waited for them to pass, stepping out of the way and watching the way the man fussed with his wife's coat collar, turning it the right way out and taking her hand firmly as they approached the corner, as if she might dart away.

Once they turned the corner out of sight, there was the sound of a car door slamming shut and she knew she wouldn't have long to be alone in this place. She closed her eyes and took a slow breath, reaching out her senses. She called to Maddie silently, and, once, speaking out loud. Lydia wasn't sure if she wanted to hear an answering voice, but she kept trying, pushing with everything she had and straining to hear. She gripped her coin in one hand and ignored the gathering crows, searching the empty air for a trace of Maddie. But there was nothing. Not a whisper. Not a faint outline. Not a shimmer in the air. It was over.

CHAPTER EIGHT

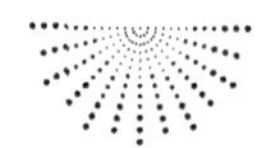

Lydia had her eyes shut and her face tilted up to the sky. The sun was warm on her skin and there were kids playing with a football nearby. She could hear them laughing, the thud of the ball against the path, and smell something sweet in the air. The scent was overtaken by one of warm earth and fur as she felt the Fox arrive. He hesitated before sitting on the bench to her left and she saw flashing red, disappearing into dark undergrowth. She followed the image in her mind's eye, willing her heart to slow to normal.

He didn't speak and Lydia opened her eyes, expecting to see the unsettling gaze of Paul Fox. Instead, it was one of his brothers. She didn't know his name.

'I've got a message for you,' the Fox said.

'From Paul?' Lydia hated that she was worried for Paul, but she was. She clamped her lips together to stop herself from asking after him.

'He said to tell you that he's busy.'

'Right...' Lydia raised an eyebrow, waiting for more.

'That's it. He's busy. Very fucking busy.'

Lydia tilted her head, considering. The Fox was smiling a little. Enjoying himself. Enjoying the delivery of the message. Which meant she was still deeply unpopular with the Fox clan. That was no surprise and no worry. What was new, was Paul washing his hands of her. Or appearing to. Sending a message that things had changed between them, that maybe she couldn't count him among her friends.

'I am the head of the Crow Family and I demand respect,' Lydia said, fixing the Fox with a long stare. 'I had something for him, but he can find out all on his own. You tell him that,' Lydia stood up. 'When you can walk again, that is.'

She opened her fist, revealing her coin lying in her palm. She turned her flat hand upside down and the coin remained stuck fast, ignoring the laws of gravity.

The Fox didn't look particularly impressed and certainly not alarmed. That would come in a few seconds when he tried to get up from the bench. Lydia walked away.

BACK IN CAMBERWELL, LYDIA CHECKED IN WITH each of the betting shops run by the Family. Aiden had said it would be good to smooth some feathers. Charlie had taught her that nothing was better than the personal touch. No matter how busy or important he got, he always made time to visit the smallest businesses, checking in and making sure he was seen doing so. Lydia had put it down to a personal power trip, but now she could see the sense of it. Besides, you picked up information in the most unlikely places, and information was everything.

The shops ranged from clean and bright, radiating a good-time vibe, rich with promise, to the dingy rooms she had imagined. Shabby, depressing rooms with nicotine-stained walls and hollow-eyed punters staring at screens. The air thick with desperation. Lydia wondered if you could trace a gambling addict's descent from one type of emporium to the other, a metaphorical journey illustrated in bricks and mortar. More likely, of course, all types of gamblers, both addicted and recreational, chose where they went purely on location and habit. If Lydia scratched the surface of the shiny-happy betting shop, she would find the same spectrum of despair.

She could feel a depressing weight pushing down when she contemplated it, so she locked the thoughts up and shook hands with the proprietors and tried to look interested at the repeated complaints about internet gambling, illegal bookies, and back-room poker games. She distracted herself by asking every Crow whether they knew Mikhail the Jekyll, but drew a blank. The members of the Crow Family who had chosen to run legal gambling establishments were the most law-abiding of her beloved flock, and genuinely not connected to the shadier side. Which said something about the Crow Family and its history, but not something Lydia particularly wanted to dwell upon.

. . .

Back at The Fork, Lydia checked in with Angel. 'Any news about Nat?'

The cook shook her head, turning away to pour Lydia a coffee without being asked.

She took it and wondered what she could say that would sound comforting, coming up with nothing. 'She'll be back' was only good if it was true and what right did Lydia have to make pronouncements on Angel's marriage?

Her phone rang and she walked outside the cafe, into the street to answer it. She had been expecting Paul Fox's voice and she wasn't disappointed.

'Jasper is very unhappy with you.'

'How long did it take him to get home?'

'He was paralysed for three and a half hours. He's not amused.'

'But you are.'

'No,' Paul said. 'Well, yes. Okay, a bit. But that wasn't very polite.'

'Neither was sending your little brother to meet me.'

There was a silence. One which Lydia let run. She was standing outside The Fork and could see Angel through the window. She was staring into space with a blank expression.

Eventually, Paul spoke. 'Things have been... Tricky recently. There are people, things, that I've been dealing with. I didn't meet you personally because I was busy. It was not meant to hurt your feelings.'

'You didn't hurt my feelings,' Lydia snapped. 'It's protocol. Respect.'

'I know that's important to you.'

Lydia smiled at his careful diplomacy. 'It's not, really. But it's the look of it. You know the game. You know the position I'm in these days.'

'I do,' Paul said. 'But you have to understand... It's not all about you. Not all about the Crows.'

'You have a problem?' Lydia turned away from the window and began pacing up and down the pavement. She wanted to say 'maybe I can help', but wasn't sure she could truly follow up on that kind of promise. Her plate was full and in danger of tipping over.

Paul side-stepped her question with one of his own. 'What were you going to tell me?'

'I got a message, thought I should let you know.' She took a fortifying breath before speaking the words out loud. 'In case it's connected to the Pearl court.'

'The ones you buried under Highgate Woods?'

'It's a pendant with a pearl in it. I'm getting a faint Pearl Family read from it, nothing strong, but it was brought to me by a jackdaw.'

A moment of silence, and then Paul's voice, sounding amused. 'Little Bird, that's not a very scary henchman for a crime boss.'

'I'm not a crime boss,' Lydia said. She stopped pacing. 'And I just wanted to let you know. In case it meant something.'

'I think you just wanted to see me,' Paul said, sounding altogether too happy. 'I think you were missing me and wanted an excuse.'

'That's not...'

'A necklace from a bird? Come on. Trouble in paradise? All not well with your shiny copper?'

Lydia started. She hadn't told Paul about Fleet's gleam. 'Shiny?'

'Good as gold,' Paul clarified. 'On the side of the angels. Or the law, anyway.' He paused for effect. 'Unlike us.'

'I was just telling you as a friend,' Lydia said. 'As allies. That's all.'

'Well, isn't that nice,' Paul said. 'Keep your friendship, Little Bird. Call me when you're ready for a real alliance. But don't wait too long.'

Upstairs, she found Fleet waiting. He was lounging on the sofa with his phone and Jason was sitting at Lydia's desk, scowling at him. She wondered whether Fleet could see Jason or sense his presence. He had caught glimpses in the past, but seemed to have settled on wilful blindness when it came to her ghostly flatmate.

'He's in my spot,' Jason said.

'And you're in mine,' Lydia said.

'What?' Fleet had put his phone down to greet her and was now frowning in confusion. 'Oh. Is he here?'

'Yes. He's waving at you.' That was the politest way to interpret the gesture that Jason was making.

She raised her eyebrows in a question and Jason shrugged. 'Just amusing myself. It's been a slow day.'

While Lydia had been taking it easy over the last few weeks she hadn't appreciated that Jason had had less to do, as well. And she hadn't realised how much he had come to rely on the distraction and sense of purpose that working for Crow Investigations provided. 'We'll have some cases that require your hacking skills soon,' Lydia spoke without thinking.

Fleet had straightened and was looking from Lydia to the empty air in front of the desk.

'And I use hacking in the non-illegal sense of the word,' she added. 'Not hacking. Typing. That's what I meant.'

'I didn't hear anything.' Fleet stood and crossed the room to kiss Lydia. 'Hello, you.'

After a minute or two of Fleet's finest work, she felt a draft of cold air pass over her back and shivered slightly. He increased his efforts, probably mistaking Jason walking behind her for uncontrolled passion.

Lydia opened her eyes and found Fleet's own gaze wandering.

She broke the clinch and looked around. 'He's gone.'

'Good.'

Fleet's smile was borderline smug and Lydia wondered if he could possibly be feeling jealous of a ghost. Surely not.

LATER, AS LYDIA WATCHED FLEET SEARCHING vainly for something to eat in the small kitchen that wasn't toast, she had an unusual thought. Maybe they should leave London together. Get away from her family, his job, everything. Just start over somewhere entirely new, where they could be normal people with a normal relationship and normal lives. As soon as the thought came, she felt the impossibility of it and the weight settled back over her shoulders. She had killed the night raven, the contender for the crown, and that meant she couldn't abandon the Family. She had taken the power, so now she was saddled with the responsibility.

Besides, as Fleet turned to hold up an extremely expired unopened packet of bacon and give her a look of mock-exasperation, she caught a blast of his signature gleam. It wasn't just a glimpse of sunshine coming out from behind a cloud, it was like standing close to a burning star and feeling heat that could melt an entire world. She realised that she had been damping down her own senses to make it bearable, instinctively turning them down like she was adjusting the volume control on her phone. She opened her mouth to ask Fleet if he had noticed the change, but he started speaking at the same time. 'You go first.'

'I've been wondering something,' Fleet began.

He looked uncertain and that set alarm bells off in Lydia's mind. 'What?'

'It's something that Sinclair said.'

'I don't want to talk about your new friend.'

'It's about your uncle.'

Lydia forced herself to keep looking at Fleet. 'What about him?'

'Is he still being detained? I mean, now that Smith is no longer running his department.'

'That's a question for your friend. How would I know?'

'You're not curious?'

Was she curious? Lydia dug her fingernails into her palm to stop herself from shouting. Hell Hawk.

'We've got to assume that someone else has picked up where Smith left off. Sinclair says not, but that doesn't mean anything. She might be out of the loop.'

'Or she might be lying to your face.' Lydia was trying not to think about Fleet and Sinclair having cosy little chats about her Family. She knew that Fleet was on her side, but she still felt a sting of betrayal. She had been raised not to speak about her Family to outsiders and Sinclair was most definitely in that category.

Fleet nodded 'Or that, yes,'

'I told you not to have anything to do with her. Learn from my mistakes.'

'I could ask her about Charlie. If you want?'

'I don't,' Lydia said.

'But why?'

'Because I assume he's dead,' Lydia said. 'And I like that assumption. I don't want to learn otherwise.'

'Wouldn't it be better to be warned? If he's alive and there's a chance he will get free. Or a chance that he's already free.'

'I would rather not know,' Lydia said, hoping the repetition would be an end of the conversation.

No such luck.

'That makes no sense. Why wouldn't you want warning? You love knowledge. You want to know everything about what everyone is doing. What they need, what they like, their strengths, their weaknesses, their family histories. Everything. Why don't you want to know about Charlie?'

Lydia allowed herself a sigh. 'Because it won't help.'

THE NEXT DAY WAS SUPPOSED TO BE A DAY OFF FOR Fleet. While Lydia had been recuperating, they had made all kinds of grand plans about regular time off, days out of Camberwell, and maybe even a holiday out of the country. Truth to tell, Lydia wasn't all that bothered, but it made Fleet happy to talk about being normal. Even if she knew that in his bones it wasn't for him. A Fleet on a sun lounger in Spain would be a very bored Fleet indeed.

Still, it didn't mean he was thrilled to be called in for an unscheduled meeting with the top brass. As he said on the phone when he called to let Lydia know he couldn't get to her place until the afternoon. 'Now I'm here, I've been sucked into some other things. And there's paperwork that needs looking at today. Apparently it can't wait until tomorrow.'

'No worries,' Lydia said. She was still in bed, doing half-hearted research on her laptop. 'Call me when you're free. See what we feel like then.'

'It's going to be much later, I think. I'm sorry.'

'Honestly, it's no problem,' Lydia reassured him again. He was being overly apologetic and it made her feel as if there was something he wasn't telling her. She shoved away the thought. 'Call me later.'

ONCE SHE KNEW THAT FLEET WASN'T ABOUT TO JOIN her, bed no longer seemed quite as attractive. Lydia got up and put on leggings, a vest top and her running shoes. After a lap of Burgess Park, her mind felt calmer and her muscles pleasantly warmed. She showered and got changed before settling down with Jason to watch the drama that had been Rafferty Hill's big break. It wasn't her usual kind of thing, but it was well done. And Rafferty was compelling. He definitely had that thing, star power or whatever it was called. The indefinable quality that made you want to watch him closely, made the scene come alive, and made you miss him when he wasn't there. Could be talent, good looks and charisma. Or it could be a drop or two of Pearl blood. Pearls could sell anything, including themselves.

She went to YouTube and found a clip of an interview Rafferty had done as part of the publicity effort for the drama. There were three actors being interviewed, but when Rafferty spoke Lydia felt a flash of Pearl energy. It sent a bolt of longing from her scalp to her toes, and she wasn't surprised to note that the interviewer directed all of her questions to Rafferty, all but ignoring his co-stars.

There were a lot of Londoners with a little Pearl magic. But only a trace. Just enough to make people like them, to ease their passage through the world. Some, like in the case of the grocers which had opened on Camberwell high street, had enough to make their produce irresistible. The place had a steady stream of customers, never mind the Tesco Metro a few doors down and the outrageous price mark-up.

That ability had been nothing when compared with the Pearl court. The original Family with a capital 'F'.

Underneath the ground, in an enchanted place which had defied the physics of time and matter. Lydia's skin broke out in bumps just thinking about it. The tang of magic in the air and those beautiful faces and lithe bodies. The music, the dancing, the party which never ended. And the Pearl King's perfect features, their casual cruelty. No, not even cruelty. Something beyond that. Something inhuman. Lydia didn't want to wander into this tangled thicket, this particular memory lane, but it was too late. The air was filled with choking earth and she was desperate, gasping, crawling underneath the fallen throne to shelter while the earth caved in. The absolute dark. The cold. The creeping knowledge that she was going to die there. Alone.

CHAPTER NINE

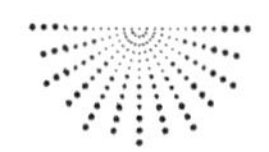

Lydia knew that she hadn't been focused on Mikhail and his cryptic message. Between the problems in the Family business and the ongoing fallout from Maddie's death, not to mention the growing feeling that something wasn't quite right with Fleet, she had been distracted. But Mik the Jekyll had left a cry for help and she was sure it was directed at her. First off, she needed to know what part he had played in Rafferty Hill's disappearance. Mikhail was dead and Rafferty hadn't spontaneously appeared. That meant he was either imprisoned somewhere with access to food and water, or dead. Or, that Mikhail hadn't anything to do with his disappearance and the blackmail was a separate crime.

Lydia thought about the flash of Pearl she had caught from Rafferty Hill's video clip. The interviewer had been leaning in slightly, gazing up at Rafferty like he was the answer to all her hopes and dreams, but when he had smiled back at her with that movie star grin, Lydia had felt something. Not just a bit of attraction, but a full blast of lust, hunger, and thirst. Like she had been fasting for one hundred days and Rafferty Hill was a steak dinner.

She called Fleet. 'I want to speak to Rafferty's flat-mate. Amber, was it?' Lydia said.

'We interviewed her thoroughly.'

'I'm not criticising your work. But there might be something else I can pick up.'

A pause. 'Is this because of Mikhail's message?'

'Partly.' Lydia didn't want to talk about the Pearls out loud. It felt like an invocation.

She could hear somebody speaking to Fleet, demanding his attention. He was distracted, pulled away from her by his myriad responsibilities. Lydia knew that the Rafferty case was nowhere near the only thing on his roster. After he broke away to answer his colleague, he came back onto the line. 'If you think it will help.'

Rafferty's flat wasn't far from the eastern edge of Burgess Park, right on the edge of Bermondsey where it was bounded by the Old Kent Road. Amber agreed to meet Lydia there after seven, when she would be home from her job at a talent agency in Soho.

Knowing that Amber had known Rafferty for a very long time, Lydia didn't bother to masquerade as an ex-girlfriend or old friend of Rafferty's. Instead, she went with dealer. Pissed-off dealer who was owed some cash. Fleet might have believed Amber's protestations of non-romantic interest but Lydia wanted to double-check. Fleet was an excellent copper with superhuman instincts, but there was no harm in being thorough.

To play her part, Lydia could wear her usual clothes. She added a couple of burner phones to her pockets. She could have gone with her true identity, of course, and leaned on her Crow power, but she felt like keeping it old school. Maybe because she still believed that people told you unexpected truths when you weren't leaning too hard. And maybe to prove to herself that she hadn't changed that much.

The flat was in a converted red brick Victorian school on a busy section of the main road. When Amber opened the door to Lydia, she wanted to tell the woman that she shouldn't have agreed to meet a dealer in her home. She should have insisted on a meeting in a public place with plenty of exit points. And she definitely shouldn't have turned away so quickly without properly assessing Lydia as a potential threat, or spoken to her with that offhand 'talking to the staff' tone. 'This is a waste of time.'

The flat was significantly nicer than Lydia had been picturing. Which, in London, meant there was some serious money floating around. Rafferty and Amber had been living at this address even before he landed his big break, which meant that the money preceded it. Family cash? Or Amber's job was more lucrative than expected.

'I told you on the phone, I don't know anything about Raff's debts. He's dead. You can't collect them now. When did he buy from you, anyway? What was he after?'

'Nice place,' Lydia said, ignoring Amber's questions and taking her time to walk around. The living area had huge windows, an exposed brick wall, and a mezzanine accessed by an iron staircase. The kitchen was stocked with high-end cabinets and what looked like granite counters. There was recessed mood lighting and large iron lanterns hanging down. Lydia didn't know much about interior design but her instincts were telling her that the uncomfortable-looking sofa cost more than her car and that at least some of the art on the walls was original. There was a sheen to expensive and this flat was covered in it.

Amber was hovering by the kitchen island. There was a single wine glass out and she seemed to be wondering whether to get a wine bottle and finish the ritual, or whether she would then have to offer Lydia a drink and prolong her visit.

Lydia saved her from having to worry about it any longer by opening the fridge and extracting an open bottle of white wine. She poured Amber a generous glass. 'Drink up.'

For the first time, some appropriate fear crossed Amber's face. 'Would you like...'

'The talent business must pay well,' Lydia said, leaning against the island and watching Amber. 'This place is beautiful. Really impressive.'

Amber's hand was on the stem of the glass, but she didn't lift it. 'Thank you.'

'So which is it?'

'Sorry?'

'It doesn't pay this well. Not at your level, anyway. I did my research. And I'm guessing from that wine choice that you don't come from money. It's nice enough, but shows you're not to the manor born.' This last bit was a complete guess on Lydia's part, but Amber's reaction confirmed she was on track. Her lips went into a thin line and a flash of fear passed across her face. 'Which leaves one option. One of you was making extra cash.'

Amber straightened. 'You're not Raff's dealer. I didn't think he was going to someone else, not off his own bat.'

'No,' Lydia said. Then she gave Amber her shark smile as the truth fell into place. 'That would be you.'

The wine in Amber's glass slopped dangerously close to spilling. She steadied herself with a visible effort. 'If you weren't selling to Raff, what are you doing here? Who are you?'

'An interested party,' Lydia said. 'Very interested to hear that you think he's dead. What makes you so certain?'

'Does he owe you money?' Amber had regained her poise. She took a sip of her wine. 'Gambling?'

Lydia held out a hand flat and tilted it up and down. If you didn't give people much, they tended to fill in the blanks for themselves. It could be illuminating. Rafferty clearly had an addictive personality. That could lead to risk-taking and other dangerous behaviour. It also widened the number of people who might consider kidnaping him for cash. 'All you need to know is that I want to find him.'

'And then what?'

'I don't want to hurt him,' Lydia said. 'I want him back at work and earning money.'

Amber nodded in understanding. 'Me, too. I only

said he was dead because it's easier. You're not the first to come looking.'

'So let's help each other out. Tell me what state he was in when you last saw him. Is there a chance he is wandering a park somewhere bollock-naked with no idea of his own name?'

'He was clean when he disappeared. He was only recreational, anyway. No danger.'

Well that wasn't strictly true. 'Spare me the caring sharing stuff. Who else has been looking for him? Where does he owe money?'

Amber's features smoothed out. 'You know I can't tell you that.'

Softly softly old school investigative work had its place, but Lydia was sick of Amber's company and her cowardly self-preservation. She produced her coin. 'I think you can. If you try.'

Amber's gaze was drawn to the coin and lines appeared between her brows. Lydia wasn't sure if she recognised its significance. They weren't far from Camberwell, but not all Londoners remembered the old stories.

'Why?' Amber said. 'What does it matter? You're not police.'

'Correct.'

'So why are you busting my balls? What's it to you?'

Lydia moved her coin over the back of her knuckles, not looking at Amber. 'Maybe I just want to find him. Alive and well.'

Amber picked up her wine and slugged some back. 'I don't know where he is. If I did, I'd have brought him home myself.' She turned to get another glass from the cupboard. 'You want a-?'

When she turned back, Lydia had flipped her coin and it was hanging in the air, spinning slowly. 'Dealing makes you vulnerable. It's something people could use against you, but you weren't the target. What do you know about the blackmail?'

'What blackmail?' Amber spoke far too quickly. Lydia almost felt sorry for her.

'There were a couple of notes hand-delivered here. Maybe more.'

'How do you know about those?' Amber's eyes were so narrow, they were little slits. 'That's not public information.'

'Did Rafferty talk to you about them?'

Amber didn't answer for a moment.

Lydia watched her coin spinning in the air, and watched Amber do the same. The muscles around her eyes relaxed and then her mouth fell open. If Lydia could have sold her coin trick in a bottle, she could make a fortune from the pharmaceutical industry.

'He didn't see them,' Amber said slowly. 'I hid them. He wouldn't have coped very well. He didn't need any added pressure, was already super stressed. I had to look after him.'

'What was he stressed about?'

Amber blinked, her trance-like state breaking for a moment. She gave Lydia a funny look, as if it was obvious. 'With being a rising star. The pressure to perform. He was terrified he was going to fuck up his big break.'

The words rang true, but they didn't fit with the

confident man she had seen in the interview. But the man was an actor. It was his job to appear in whichever way he chose. To hide his true nature in favour of a persona. With that thought, another clicked into place. Amber could also be an actress. 'That was nice of you,' Lydia said. 'Have you always been so protective?'

Amber shrugged. 'I suppose. We've been friends for a long time. I love him like a brother.'

Well that covered a multitude of sins. 'And you didn't think he could handle the notes?'

'No. He was already fragile enough. Leaning on my help a bit too much, if you know what I mean.'

'Pharmaceutically speaking?'

'Yes.' Amber sniffed delicately and went for a piece of kitchen roll to dab at her bone dry eyes. 'I think he must have overdone it that night. He wasn't in his right mind. He must have done a bit too much and then gone walkabout. He might have walked into the river for all we know.'

Lydia looked at Amber without blinking. She had swapped her 'clean and sober' story about Rafferty to 'emotionally unstable user' without missing a beat. Lydia was clearly supposed to buy this as the reluctant truth dragged from a loyal friend but every single instinct in her body was screaming that Amber was still lying. Which would have been impressive if it wasn't so irritating. 'Do you feel responsible?'

'Of course,' Amber sniffed again. 'A bit. I know it's not my fault, of course, but I keep going over that night. Wondering if there was something I could have done.'

'Where were you?'

A slight hesitation. 'At home. With my mum and dad in Cricklewood.'

Lydia nodded. 'When did you first realise he was missing?'

'Really quickly,' Amber said, her voice full of earnest concern. 'I came back late that night and his bedroom door was shut so I didn't disturb him. Next day I knew something was wrong, though. He had a meeting with his agent and they called me looking for him.'

'Had that happened before?'

'What do you mean?'

'How did they know to call you?'

'Oh. I just mean, they called the landline here and I answered.'

'Okay. So he wasn't in the habit of letting people down? Professionally.'

'He was doing really well, I told you. He was in a good place.'

'So what did you do?'

Amber settled back. 'I knocked on his door. He didn't answer but I went in. Thought he would be sleeping. But he wasn't there. Bed was made.'

'What did you think had happened?'

'Then? I assumed he had hooked up with someone.'

'His girlfriend?'

'He didn't have one. Just one-night stands.'

'When did you think something was wrong? When did you report him missing?'

Lydia knew the answer to the second question, but she wanted to give Amber a chance to lie to her again. She didn't disappoint.

'The next day when he wouldn't answer his mobile. And then he didn't come home that evening. That wasn't like him and I got worried.'

She nodded like she believed every word out of Amber's mouth, then scribbled the number for one of her burner phones onto the note block on the kitchen counter. 'Call me if you hear from him. If I can collect the money he owes me, there's a percentage in it for you.'

Back at The Fork, Lydia found Aiden sitting at a table by the window. His beanie was pulled low and his chin was on his chest. She expected to see his phone in his hand, but as she got closer she realised his eyes were shut.

She slid into the seat opposite and watched Aiden open his eyes and straighten himself with an obvious effort. He had purple shadows under red-rimmed eyes and his expression was one of utter exhaustion. Aiden was a main bloodline Crow and he had youth on his side, so he had to have been seriously sleep-deprived to look this rough. Lydia clamped down on the urge to ask him if he was all right. She wasn't his mum. 'What did you find?'

'There's a high stakes poker game being run every week at the Ruskin Hotel.'

'I don't care about that.'

'Fingers have been pointed at a few bookies. I'm still making enquiries. There's a lot of chat, a lot of complaining.'

'Is that all? What about debt collection? Did you find the main players?'

Aiden shrugged. 'It's in progress.'

'What about the other matter?'

Aiden straightened a little. 'I spoke to the older guys. They know his name. He did a few jobs for Charlie back in the day.'

'It can't be that long ago, Mikhail was only early thirties.'

'He started young. Phil said he remembers him doing a B and E when he was thirteen.'

'Hell Hawk.' Charlie Crow. Corrupting the youth of Camberwell. Or maybe that was unfair, maybe Mikhail had already been corrupt before he'd met a single Crow. Yeah, right. The kid had been... A kid. Her stomach turned over.

'Nothing recent, though,' Aiden said.

'You believe them?'

Aiden raised his eyebrows. 'Of course. They know who I am and that I was asking for you.'

'Why does that ensure honesty?'

'You don't trust family?' Aiden looked like she had just told him Santa didn't exist.

'I don't trust anyone,' Lydia said.

CHAPTER TEN

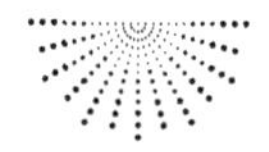

Lydia had just finished giving Fleet her report on Amber, when she realised that he was radiating tension. A really good girlfriend would have noticed earlier, but she figured Fleet would understand. Especially since she wasn't going to bill the Met for her investigative work. 'What's wrong?'

Fleet opened the fridge without answering. 'You're out of beer,' he said after a moment.

'Is it to do with your secret mission?' Two months ago Fleet had disappeared on a job which involved Sinclair and, apparently, his own father. He had maintained a dignified silence about the whole episode, which was infuriating. Lydia had taken a break from asking him about it, hoping that feigning disinterest would somehow spur him into sharing. Needless to say, it hadn't been successful.

He closed the fridge with more force than was strictly necessary. 'I told you. It's better if I don't talk about that.'

'Just because I don't trust Sinclair and I told you not to have anything to do with her and I don't trust the secret service doesn't mean we can't talk about it.' Lydia attempted a cheeky smile, in the hopes of being charming, rather than combative. It wasn't her strong suit.

Fleet's lips compressed and Lydia could see him mentally counting to ten. She wondered, unworthily, whether her new powers could be used to make Fleet confide in her. She pushed it away immediately, repulsed by herself. That was coercion. Abusive behaviour. Morally bankrupt. But it might be effective, a tiny voice pointed out.

'You want to go out to eat?' Fleet had already turned away. 'Or order pizza?'

'I want you to tell me what's wrong. Is it the Mikhail death?' Somebody dying in police custody was never good news. 'Is someone on your team getting blamed?'

He leaned against the counter and folded his arms. 'It really doesn't help that we don't have a clear cause of death. The Met standards committee is not a fan of unexplained events.'

Lydia felt a rush of relief. It was work. Fleet's day job wasn't her favourite thing but she understood it. Understood the stresses he was under. And it wasn't a secret, wasn't something that could drive a wedge between them.

'I'm sorry I haven't turned up anything useful.'

Fleet closed his eyes and shook his head gently. 'Don't apologise.' A moment later, his voice very soft, he added: 'I'm sorry. I'm in a terrible mood.'

'Pizza, then? And garlic bread.'

Fleet didn't smile. Or open his eyes.

Lydia felt her coin in her hand and she squeezed it for comfort before putting it into her jeans pocket. 'Have you spoken to Mikhail's family? Are they the problem?' She could imagine Mikhail's nearest and dearest demanding answers. Understandably.

'His ex-girlfriend has been informed. He doesn't have any other family that we know of but, to be honest, we're drawing a lot of blanks. We don't even have a permanent address for him. Everything that requires a postal address goes to his ex-girlfriend's place, but she swears he hasn't lived there for over two years. They're on good terms, apparently, and he stays regularly to spend time with his son. She seemed to think that he was sofa-surfing the rest of the time, but couldn't give us any names.'

'Sad for him.'

Fleet shrugged.

Lydia's patience snapped. 'Please just tell me what's wrong.'

'You know I said it wouldn't be a problem?'

'Me coming into the station to see the crime scene? Or the message Mikhail left?'

'Both. Turns out, I was a bit optimistic.'

'Your MI5 pal let you down?' Lydia couldn't help needling Fleet about his connection with the secret service contact, Sinclair. She was still wildly curious about Fleet's relationship with the service and what Fleet had done for them, promised them.

'Not exactly. It's more a question of optics.'

Lydia realised what he was getting at. 'You can't be seen to be with me?'

'It would help if we could be discreet. Just until this case is sorted. Top brass are particularly skittish at the moment.'

Lydia thought that it was business as usual for management, but she didn't say anything.

'It won't be for long. And it won't change anything. We weren't exactly high profile, anyway.'

'Don't worry about it. This isn't exactly new.' Fleet had been pressured several times to cut his ties with Lydia, and he had chosen to ignore it. Despite this knowledge, she did feel a small squeeze in her chest. This continual outside pressure couldn't be good for a relationship. She just had to hope they were strong enough to withstand it.

Fleet still looked unhappy and Lydia realised there was worse to come. 'What else? Just tell me.'

'Is Aiden in trouble?'

Well that wasn't what she had been expecting. Fleet was watching her carefully and she kept her face neutral. Or, that was the plan, at least.

He nodded as if he had read something in her eyes. 'I thought so.'

'Did you have a dream?'

'Yeah, but that's not why I'm asking.'

Lydia waited. Suddenly it felt like their early days, again. Being guarded about her family and wondering whether to trust the copper. Which was ridiculous. Fleet had proven his loyalty and his love time and time again.

'I didn't tell you because I didn't want to put you in an awkward position, professionally speaking.'

'I understand,' Fleet said. 'But Sinclair sent me a message this morning. She wants to meet with you. She said it concerned Aiden and that you would want to hear her out.'

'You spoke to her?'

He shook his head, still not moving his gaze. 'She sent a minion.'

Lydia knew when she was backed into a corner. 'Give me the details. I'll go.'

Fleet let out a breath. 'So it's true?'

'I'll handle it.'

WHEN LYDIA WOKE UP SHE REACHED FOR FLEET before remembering that he hadn't stayed the night. He had said that 'lying low' wouldn't change things but had made excuses about needing an early start the next day. The bed was cold on his side and she starfished her limbs in an attempt to reclaim the space. She had always enjoyed sleeping alone in the past, and there was no reason for that to change. 'No need to fall apart, woman,' she said out loud. Or to panic about her relationship. They had weathered worse.

Jason opened the door. 'Did you call me?'

'You opened the door.'

'Sorry. Yes. I didn't knock.'

'No, I mean you opened the door. You didn't just appear.'

'Right,' Jason looked at the door as if surprised to see

his hand resting on the edge. It sat on the surface, fully obeying the rules of physics.

'You are really here, now, aren't you? When did you last... You know?'

'Vanish?' Jason frowned. 'I don't remember. It's been a while.'

More signs of her increased power. The power she had taken from Maddie when she killed her cousin. It wasn't a good feeling, but the new strength was like a warm coat. It made her feel protected and prepared. Feelings she couldn't bring herself to hate.

'You want something to eat?'

Lydia focused on Jason. 'Why not?'

The sunlight was pouring through the windows into the main room of the flat. It lay a bar of bright white across Lydia's desk and another across the floor. Jason was already in the kitchen and the telltale sounds of brunch-making came from within.

'I've been thinking,' Jason said when she joined him.

He had a spatula in one hand and was pouring oil into the frying pan with the other, so she was expecting an egg-related comment or question.

'The man in the station. Mikhail the Jekyll?' Jason turned the heat on under the pan and turned back to face her. 'He might not have been asking for you.'

Lydia opened her mouth to argue. She was 'The Crow'. The main one. If you were going to refer to a 'the' it would be her. That wasn't ego, it was common sense.

'Just hear me out. If it was a complete sentence, it makes perfect sense that it was referring to the most senior Crow. The head of the Family.' He indicated

Lydia with a wave of his spatula. 'But if it wasn't finished... He could have been going to write something else. Like 'Get the crow with the big nose' or whatever.'

Lydia forced herself to consider his words. Jason was smart and she hadn't exactly been giving his matter her full attention. After a moment, she asked: 'Why wouldn't he just use their name? He was writing in blood as he breathed his last, doesn't make sense to add more words than needed.'

'Yeah, exactly,' Jason said, growing more animated. 'If he knew your name, he would have written Lydia, right? Or the letter 'L'. That's the quickest. So if he didn't know the name of the Crow, maybe he was halfway through describing them.'

'I mean, it's possible,' Lydia got a couple of plates from the cupboard and put them on the counter next to the hob.

'And you don't know him, right? So why would he be asking for you?'

'To investigate his death? It's my job.' Or to avenge it. Mikhail wasn't a Crow but he belonged to Camberwell. And after all the work he had done for the Family, he probably felt he was owed some Crow payback.

'Maybe,' Jason had opened a box of eggs and was now expertly cracking them into the hot oil. 'But what if it was more an instruction to the police? Pointing them at the killer, kind of thing.'

Lydia stiffened. She picked her words carefully. 'You think a Crow murdered him?'

Jason turned wide eyes to her. 'I'm sorry. I know they're your family, but it's possible, isn't it?'

There were advantages to being dead, Lydia thought. And advantages to having a dead friend. He was able and willing to suggest things that nobody else would dare to voice. And, much as Lydia didn't want to admit it, the ghost had a point. Luckily, she had the perfect excuse to cut the conversation short. 'I'll think about it,' she said, taking the spatula and manoeuvring a fried egg onto a plate. 'I've got to go and meet a different kind of spook.'

SINCLAIR WAS SITTING ON A BENCH ON THE embankment. She was wearing soft cashmere in earth tones, draped in complicated folds around her tall frame. Lydia had no doubt that the same item on her would make her look like a toddler in a blanket, but Sinclair had the air of a catwalk model. She had a paperback book open on her lap and Lydia was carrying a takeaway bag and a tall cardboard cup of coffee.

Anybody watching would see two strangers, happening to occupy the same bench for a matter of minutes. That was the idea, at least. Lydia could only hope that nobody was watching closely. She put her coffee onto the ground at her feet and concentrated on liberating her tuna melt panini from its wrapper.

Keeping her eyes dipped to her novel, Sinclair murmured a greeting, her lips barely moving. The woman was good.

'I'm leaving when I finish this,' Lydia said, not looking at Sinclair, 'and I'm a fast eater.'

'Very well,' Sinclair said quietly. 'You have a problem I can solve.'

'Why would you do that?'

'In return for a favour.'

Lydia took an experimental bite of her panini. It had cooled enough not to burn her mouth.

'A small favour,' Sinclair continued quietly. 'Neither illegal nor particularly dangerous.'

'I don't have a problem,' Lydia said, after she had swallowed her mouthful.

'Not yet, perhaps. But there was an unfortunate gang-related killing in Camberwell. It is low priority and there are no leads. That could change suddenly. As soon as today if this chat goes poorly.'

Lydia looked out to the river as if contemplating the view. She raised the sandwich to hide her lips. 'Blackmail is a terrible way to make people do your bidding.'

'Really? That's not been my experience.' Sinclair flipped her book closed and rose from the bench. She stowed her book into a brown leather tote and adjusted the cashmere folds. 'You start tomorrow morning. Churchill's War Rooms. I do hope you won't let me down.'

CHAPTER ELEVEN

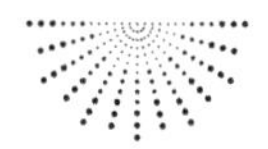

Churchill's bunker opened to the public at nine on the dot which was why Lydia found herself stepping out of the tube at Westminster at the unholy hour of six-thirty. She would have a good sixty minutes before even the earliest of early-bird staff members showed up at seven forty-five. Time to walk the facility in peace.

Sinclair hadn't given her any further details, but there had been a message from a Rebecca Collier on her landline answer machine when she had returned to the office, confirming that she would be her contact during her 'discreet' investigation at the Churchill bunker.

A woman was waiting at the public entrance of the bunker, which was tucked at the bottom of a vast flight of white stone steps and dwarfed by the imposing architecture of Her Majesty's Royal Treasury above. She was wearing a dark grey trouser suit and had a staff lanyard hanging around her neck with another in her hand. 'Wear this,' she said, thrusting it at Lydia.

She turned back and strode through the door, not waiting, and not introducing herself. Perhaps she thought her lanyard did the job. Or perhaps, like, Lydia, Rebecca Collier wasn't a morning person.

Inside, the ticket desk was empty and the rope barriers had an abandoned air. They made no sense until they were corralling hordes of historically minded tourists. 'Who is picking up the tab for this?' Lydia had been wondering whether this was a personal crusade of Sinclair's or part of some other reciprocal deal. It would also to be handy to know whether it was mandated by the museum trust who owned and ran the site. These days, knowing who was behind what seemed increasingly important. Not to mention, who believed in the Crows and their powers.

Her mouth twisted. 'Howard Shireton. Head of PR. He seems to believe there's something to the accounts.'

'So, what exactly is the problem here?'

Lydia was braced for a suspicious death and, knowing her current luck, something which pointed to the Crow Family.

'It's utter nonsense.' Rebecca Collier was moving at a brisk clip as she spoke, as if hoping to leave Lydia behind.

They had entered the bunker and, apart from the modern signage and information panels, Lydia felt as if she had walked into the nineteen-forties. A nineteen-forties during an apocalyptic event.

She turned down one corridor and then unlocked a door marked 'private'. Inside was a small neat office, kitted out for the twenty-first century. 'A number of staff members have reported seeing a white lady in Churchill's bedroom. Crying. It's one of our biggest draws and this kind of rumour is not helpful to our message of education and cultural significance.' Her eyes blazed momentarily. 'It's Churchill's bedroom!'

'When you say 'white lady'...'

'In a white dress, apparently,' Rebecca said. 'Well, not in a white dress. Because there is no such figure.'

'You don't believe your staff?'

Rebecca shrugged. 'People let their imaginations run away with them. Working late, end up alone after a day underground. It can be creepy if you're that way inclined. Plus there are the pipes.'

'The pipes?'

'Noises from the pipework. They run along the outside of the walls in lots of places.'

Lydia nodded as if this was reasonable. If witnesses had reported seeing a mysterious sobbing woman in a white dress, that didn't tally with noisy plumbing, but she wasn't about to argue with her guide. 'So you haven't experienced anything unusual down here?'

Her mouth twisted. 'Unusual, yes. Inexplicable, no.'

Right then. It was clear that Ms Collier was following orders and she wasn't delighted about it. 'Will I be able to speak to the others?'

'Who?'

'The people who have seen the ghost.'

Rebecca's lip curled. 'If you must.'

. . .

Lydia was given a place to work in the cafe. It was housed in the original switch room of the bunker and it was impossible to forget that they were deep underground. It wasn't as bad as walking the disused tunnels of the underground, but Lydia still wasn't a fan. The air was scented with coffee and the cleaner that the waiting staff had used on the tables, but Lydia was convinced she could smell soil and stone and the dry earth of a long-forgotten cavern. A young man with an athletic build and an open smile was stacking juice cartons in the display fridge and he offered her a coffee which she gratefully accepted.

The first up for interview was an older woman with a bowl haircut and heavy-rimmed glasses. Her fingers were swollen with arthritis and she was wearing woolly fingerless gloves in bright red. 'Knitted by my grandson,' she said. 'Aren't they jolly?'

'You're Amanda Robinson?' Lydia flipped open her notebook. 'I wanted to ask you about what you've seen. I've been asked to look into it by the senior management so I want you to know you can be completely honest.'

'You mean, I don't have to worry that my boss will think I'm a nutcase.'

Lydia smiled. She liked Amanda's directness. 'In essence, yes.'

'I'm not one of those people who believes things. I mean, we've all had a funny feeling in a cold house or thought that someone seemed a bit off or thought about a person just before they've rung. It's just coincidence and our mind picking up on subliminal cues. Nothing super-natural.'

Lydia could tell Amanda was gearing herself up. Whatever reassurance Lydia had given, she seemed keen to establish her sanity.

'But I saw a figure in Churchill's bedroom. Clear as anything. I swear you'd think it was a customer trespassing under the rope. Only that's impossible.'

'The rope?'

'You know, the barriers to stop people getting too close to the exhibits, touching things. Only we don't have ropes. That was just a figure of speech. We have wooden barriers and sheets of glass. Nobody could get into his bedroom. It's just not possible.'

'Can you describe the figure?'

'It's a woman. Very beautiful. And young, I think. She's got dark hair and she's wearing a white dress. Something with lots of ruffles and lace. Old fashioned, but I couldn't tell you the time period for sure. Maybe Victorian or Edwardian?' Amanda sounded very certain and there was something practised in her delivery. This was not the first time she had told the story. She was also speaking in the present, not the past.

'You've seen her more than once?'

'Oh, yes. Every day for the last couple of weeks. Well, every shift. I'm off on Mondays. Usually Wednesdays, too, but I've been covering.'

'For who?'

'Liam.'

'And why is Liam off work?'

Amanda gawped at Lydia. 'Isn't that why you're here? Liam's dead.'

. . .

After interviewing another of the guides, one of the cleaning staff, and a curator from France who had been granted access for a research project, all of whom described seeing a dark-haired female figure in a white dress in Churchill's bedroom, Lydia spoke to the man who had given her coffee. It was half past nine and the first group of visitors were inside. The cafe was quiet, but a few members of the public had clearly bypassed the exhibits to come straight for some fortifying caffeine and sugar. Lydia couldn't blame them. The man rang up a chocolate muffin and a pot of tea for a customer and then turned his attention to Lydia's question.

'I don't wander about the place as a rule,' he said.

'So you haven't seen the ghost, then?'

He grinned at her. 'You've seen this place. It's full of them.'

Lydia wasn't sure if he meant the staff, the punters or whether he was being metaphorical. It was too early for that sort of nonsense, so she cut to the chase. 'The woman in white in Churchill's bedroom. Have you seen her?'

'Nah,' he said. 'I don't go that way.'

For a moment Lydia was stumped. Go what way?

He must have seen her look of confusion. 'To get out of here. I don't go past the bedroom and I don't go walk about at the end of my shift gawking at it all. Just want to get home, innit.'

'Fair enough,' Lydia said.

He turned away, but Lydia had one more question. 'Did you know Liam?'

'Nah. Not really. He was new. And the guides don't talk to us lowly kitchen serfs, do they?'

Lydia headed out into the corridor and hunted down the bedroom. She walked past the map room, with a group of visitors staring past the glass, audio guides plugged into their ears, to Churchill's bedroom. It was surprisingly austere for a leader, although there was a dingy carpet which, the exhibition guide informed her was a sign of his status as nowhere else in the complex had a carpet. One wall held a giant map, flanked by curtains which could be pulled across if Churchill was meeting with someone without clearance to view it. In addition to the single bed, the counterpane pulled primly up over the pillow, there was a desk and a couple of tub chairs. On the desk sat the original microphone the man had used for broadcasts via the BBC - something every hipster podcaster would kill to own. There were a couple of telephones, too, marking the space as clearly a place to work. It was more office than boudoir, that was for certain.

A couple moved next to Lydia, one of the men clearly more into the experience than the other. He was enthusiastically muttering facts to his partner. 'See the black telephone with the green receiver? Those were for private conversations. They played white noise so that anybody listening in couldn't hear. So cool.'

Lydia looked away, but not before she caught the tableau. One man staring intently at Churchill's bedroom, as if he could burn every detail of it into his mind, while his companion gazed fondly at his profile, ignoring the exhibition completely in favour of drinking in the sight of his beloved. Her eyes pricked with unexpected tears. The naked love on the man's face had stabbed her through to her core.

The things humans do for love. Everyday acts of kindness and consideration. Accommodating one another and compromising. She had been set the perfect example by her parents, but she didn't know if she could ever manage such a feat. Things were as real and true with Fleet as she had ever experienced, but she still spent so much time holding him back. And now, yet again, his work was threatening to drive a wedge between them. He was pulled by his duties and responsibilities as a proud member of the Met, while she was increasingly embroiled in her Family business. Business that was steadfastly murky, despite her very best intentions and efforts.

Lydia found Rebecca Collier in her small office. 'I'm heading off,' she said.

'Did you find everything you need?' Her voice was cool and the phrasing sounded automatic.

'Everything except the woman in white,' Lydia said and watched as Rebecca winced. 'The guides all said she appears after hours, once the punters have gone home. That's convenient.'

'I thought so,' Rebecca said, brightening up. 'So you agree it's most likely a prank they've cooked up themselves?'

'It's certainly possible,' Lydia said, thinking of the strangely identical stories. They all described the figure and the experience of seeing her in the same way. Either they concocted the story together or they had had recounted it to each other so many times that the story had become homogenised through repetition.

'Well, thank you for your time,' Rebecca said tightly.

Lydia recognised a dismissal when she heard one, but she wasn't quite finished. 'One more thing,' she said. 'Amanda told me about Liam. How did he die?'

Rebecca stared at her open-mouthed for a beat. 'Liam Dodds isn't dead. He stopped turning up for shifts and is in breach of his contract, but he's not dead. At least,' she paused. 'Not as far as I'm aware.'

'He's been phoning in sick?'

'No,' Rebecca became animated. 'He hasn't had the courtesy to contact me at all. Luckily he was on a temp contract, zero hours, so it's not difficult to replace him, but it is an inconvenience. It's a privilege to work in a historic location such as this and his behaviour has been extremely unprofessional.'

'So he just ghosted you,' Lydia said, regretting her choice of phrase as soon as it was out. 'You haven't heard from him. Not even an email? Text?'

'No,' Rebecca said, pinking up either through embarrassment or frustration. 'I've told you.'

'So what makes you so sure he isn't dead?'

Rebecca gawped at her before recovering. 'That isn't a possibility. I mean, I would know if that was the case. People do tend to be more laissez-faire when it comes to work responsibilities these days. We've had all kinds of problems with unreliable temps. But if it wasn't down to unprofessionalism. Discourtesy. If he is actually... Well. That would be very sad for his family, of course, but it would be no concern of mine or the trust which runs this facility. It happened off site.'

Well, Lydia couldn't argue with that. Still. 'Give me his contact details, anyway. I need to speak to him.'

'Why?'

'He might have seen the white lady.'

'I really don't see-'

'Best to be thorough,' Lydia said. 'When I told your boss I would gather witness statements, I meant all of them.'

Rebecca closed her mouth and nodded. There was nothing like a bit of police jargon to move things along. Not to mention invoking the powers that be. Hierarchies had their uses.

Lydia left with Liam's address, email and phone number. It was a relief to be outdoors after the stale air of the bunker and she thought about the months the staff had spent underground during the war, collating information, sticking pins into maps, seeing the same pale faces and sitting in front of the sun lamps so they didn't get rickets from the lack of vitamin D.

The man lived so far away from Whitehall it was practically no longer London. Lydia decided to leave interviewing Liam in person for another day, although she did send a quick email and call the number. The mobile went to voicemail and she left a message, asking Liam to call her back at his earliest convenience. She was doing the job under duress, but she would still do it properly. It was a matter of professional pride and, as always, the curiosity of an unsolved question had wormed under her skin. She could feel it lodged there, and knew it was an itch that she would have to scratch.

CHAPTER TWELVE

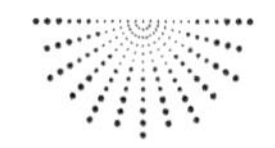

The next day, Lydia was at her desk with strong coffee in her Sherlock Holmes mug, trying to kick-start her brain after too-little sleep. Maria Silver's unwelcome voice did, at least, help to cut through her brain fog.

'What do you want?' Maria Silver had excavated the ground in Highgate Woods at the site of the cave-in and Lydia assumed she was calling to crow about it. Feathers knew how she got permission from the council, but that was the perk of being a Silver she supposed. Maria had probably only had to ask.

Lydia didn't know if Maria had found the Silver Family cup and hadn't cared enough to ask. While she had been recovering it had been enough that Maria hadn't been calling her or showing up making demands to cement their tenuous truce. The news story was very small and only reported in the Law Society Gazette. If Lydia hadn't had a Google alert set up on the firm she wouldn't have seen it. They were expanding, taking on twenty new staff. She assumed this phone call was Maria finally treating herself to a gloat.

'I heard you were in a bit of legal hot water. Thought you might need our help. I can send over our terms and prices today.'

'What are you talking about?'

'Mikhail Laurent. A suspect in the Rafferty Hill missing person case, died in police custody. And he implicated you.'

Lydia took a slow breath to stop herself from asking Maria how she knew any of that information. It was Maria's job to know things and she was the head of the Silver Family, which meant she was extremely good at it. 'How kind of you to think of me.'

'Isn't it?' Maria's voice was poison.

'I'm not a suspect in the case, however, so I don't require the services of your firm.' And would sooner die than engage them. Charlie had used Alejandro Silver for his legal needs, but Lydia had no such faith. She might have brokered a continuing truce between the Crows and the Silvers but that didn't mean she was stupid enough to trust Maria Silver.

'That's wonderful news. I must have misunderstood. I thought that the dead man named his killer and that the Murder Investigation Team had your picture pinned slap-bang in the middle of their murder board. I have an image taken within the office and I'm looking at it right now. I suppose I must be seeing things.'

'That must be it,' Lydia said, as evenly as possible. 'Perhaps you need more sleep?'

'Physician heal thyself,' Maria said and ended the call.

Lydia leaned back in her chair and thought for a moment. She might need legal representation and the thought of engaging Maria's firm made her skin crawl. But they were still the best of the best.

They weren't hurting. Twenty new staff was progress, but it wasn't stellar. It wasn't massive. Either they hadn't found the cup or they had and it hadn't given them as much of a boost as Maria hoped. Or, and this was a slim hope, Maria was concentrating on building her legit legal firm and was keeping the Silver Family stuff in the past. Alejandro was feathers-knew-where and the truce was in place. Maybe Maria had decided to put vendettas and Family squabbles on permanent hold. That was a pleasant thought. All the heads of the Families steering them into calm, legal, non-murderous futures.

Still, she had a more pressing concern right at this moment. She called Fleet. 'Tell me something straight.'

'Okay,' Fleet's voice was wary.

'Is there a photograph of me pinned to the murder board for the Mikhail death?'

A beat of silence. Which told Lydia the answer. 'Right. Thanks.'

'Lyds...'

She had already hung up.

THAT AFTERNOON, LYDIA WENT BACK TO THE bunker. She interviewed the last couple of guides who had reported seeing the white lady, ones who hadn't been working the day before. The facility was open to visitors and the cafe was packed, so she just spoke to them as best she could while they were going about their work. It was the same story repeated, with no variation or addition in detail, and Lydia felt the sense, again, that there was something very off about the whole thing. It seemed as if Rebecca Collier was going to have her wish and her report would say that this was some kind of weird prank cooked up by the staff. She just hoped that would be considered satisfactory by Sinclair and that she would honour her agreement to keep Aiden out of police custody.

The last guide on her list was called Ren Tanaka and she wasn't entirely surprised to find a Japanese man waiting for her in the small staff area. The room wasn't much more than a short corridor, the space taken up with a wall of lockers and doors leading to the staff bathrooms. Ren looked like he was in his early thirties, but it was hard to be sure. His luxuriant black hair was worn in a long, floppy style artfully held in place with product and he wore wire-rimmed glasses, both of which made him look young and student-ish. He greeted Lydia politely enough, but she could tell he was keen to get home. She ran through her questions, getting the same responses as she had already received.

'And you've definitely seen this figure?'

His eyes slid left. 'Just once.'

'Okay,' Lydia left it. This wasn't a criminal case and she only had to go through the motions. What did it matter if they were making up a story to freak out their boss? Presumably Sinclair was fulfilling a favour of her own by drafting Lydia in to investigate and would be happy whatever the outcome. Or perhaps she was just flexing her blackmailing ability, showing Lydia how powerful she could be?

'Can I go?' Ren was carrying a brown leather rucksack and he hoisted it onto one shoulder.

'Were you friendly with Liam Dodds?'

His eyes softened. 'Yeah. He was all right.'

'Are you still in contact with him? Now that he's left?'

Ren shook his head. 'He just went. Didn't say goodbye, just stopped showing up for shifts.'

'Amanda seems to think he's in some sort of trouble. Do you have any reason to think she might be right? Did he ever talk to you about his life outside this place?'

'No trouble that I can think of,' Ren said, after a moment's thought.

Lydia didn't know why she couldn't leave things alone. Liam wasn't her concern. 'Any idea why Amanda would be concerned about his wellbeing?'

Understanding dawned across Ren's face. 'She worries about everyone. More so about the guys, especially the young ones.'

Lydia frowned. Before she could ask if Ren was talking about personality or an anxiety disorder, he continued.

'She lost her son. Years ago, but I don't think it's something you get over. She told me about it. She tells everyone, wants to keep his memory alive. It was sad.'

'What happened?'

'He was an addict. Died of an overdose when he was twenty two.'

Lydia thanked Ren and headed back to the public part of the bunker. She felt a pressing sadness from Ren's story and it wasn't helped by the weight of the concrete and stone and metal above her. The ceiling seemed to be getting lower and she wanted to follow Ren out into the fresh air. Instead she forced herself to pay one last visit to Churchill's bedroom. The job was wrapped up, but there was no harm in doing a final check.

When Lydia watched David Attenborough documentaries with her parents, she had always hated the bit when the newly hatched bird was snatched up by the raptor. She couldn't understand why the film crew hadn't intervened. She knew the explanation, of course, that interference would alter the documentary. That it would no longer be a factual account or representative of what happened in the wild. And that it would make no difference in the big scheme of nature. As Henry pointed out, raptors have to eat, too.

One issue with being a battery, powering up the latent unseen power in the city, was that her presence observing the white lady ghost was likely to alter her patterns of behaviour and the rules of her existence. Case in point, Lydia was looking through the glass into Churchill's bedroom, ten minutes before closing time and definitely not on the ghost's usual schedule of appearances, when she saw a telltale shimmer just above the nondescript counterpane on Churchill's single bed.

The place was almost empty, just the last stragglers from the final tour wandering through. An outdoorsy-looking couple with a baby in a sling and a small boy had just stopped. The adults were deep in a discussion about whether little Seth should be allowed another biscuit to keep him going or whether it would spoil his tea and Seth had been joining in vociferously. Truthfully, Lydia had tuned them out, when she noticed that Seth was no longer speaking. She glanced down and saw that the little boy was now standing unnaturally still, his eyes wide and terrified as he stared at the semi-translucent lady that had appeared on Churchill's counterpane.

She crouched down. 'It's okay,' she spoke softly. 'She won't hurt you.'

The boy's eyes swivelled in their sockets, finding Lydia briefly before snapping back to the ghost. His tiny frame was shaking and Lydia hoped he was of an age that was still in nappies or the poor kid was going to be walking home in damp clothes.

He tugged on his mother's hand. 'Lady.'

She glanced at Lydia, smiling indulgently at this sign of genius. 'Yes, darling, that's a lady.'

'There.' The kid was pointing at the ghost, now, and Lydia could feel the waves of emotion rolling from him. He was willing his parents to look, to validate what he was seeing and to explain it. To make it normal and safe. Lydia knew that his lizard brain, the part that he had inherited from his caveboy ancestors, was screaming at him to run.

The mother was still arguing with the father and she barely looked into the room, where the boy was pointing.

'They can't see her,' Lydia said. 'Only we can see her, but that's all right. It's a secret.' Having gone to a fairly rough comprehensive in Beckenham, Lydia knew first-hand that it was better to blend in. Maybe this kid was only seeing the ghost because Lydia was nearby, but just in case this was a regular talent, Lydia felt a responsibility to pass on her best advice. 'Don't tell anyone else,' she said. 'But don't be afraid. They won't hurt you.'

'Excuse me?' The mother had stopped arguing about mealtimes and had noticed that Lydia wasn't stooped to tie a shoelace or retrieve a lost museum guide and was, in fact, engaging her small son in conversation.

'Don't speak to my child without my permission,' the mother was saying, 'you can't just do that.'

Lydia ignored her and stayed focused on the kid. 'She's just a picture, like on the TV. She can't touch you.'

The boy had large blue eyes and they were glistening with tears. Lydia considered herself basically immune to children, but she still felt a twist of sympathy in her stomach. If the tears fell, Lydia felt like she might join in. 'I promise,' she said and squeezed her coin.

He blinked and she saw him square his narrow shoulders. Giving the kid one last reassuring smile, she straightened up.

'Excuse me?' The mother wasn't finished. She made 'excuse me' sound like a threat and Lydia felt a flash of admiration.

'He's the same age as my nephew,' Lydia lied and watched the woman relax a little. Still, she ushered her family away a moment later. A guide walked past, telling the last stragglers that it was five minutes until closing and asking them to make their way to the exit.

It wasn't one of the guides she had interviewed and she watched to see if they seemed to see the ghost, but they didn't so much as glance into Churchill's bedroom. 'I have a pass,' she said, as a way of explaining why she wasn't following directions. The guide nodded and moved on.

Alone, Lydia looked back through the glass. The ghost was still there, unmoved from her position on the edge of the bed. She was shimmering in a way that was painful to focus on for too long and her face was turned away. Lydia would have laid money on a couple of facts, though. The woman had grey hair twisted up in a bun, and was wearing a knitted jumper and dark green slacks.

CHAPTER THIRTEEN

That evening, Fleet arrived with takeaway and a bottle of red wine. As 'I'm sorry you're a murder suspect in a case I hadn't even told you was being treated as murder' goes, it needed work.

'Can I come in?' He ducked his head and gave her the kind of small, hopeful smile that made her want to hug him. And then do many other, more vigorously physical things immediately after.

'What's the food?'

'Spring rolls, chicken chow mein, beef in black bean, wantons.'

'From Jade House?'

'Of course.'

Lydia stepped back. 'We can eat. I'm not promising to talk to you, though.'

'Fair enough.'

Fleet moved into the tiny kitchen and poured wine into short tumblers, the only clean glasses available, and began unpacking the food.

Lydia got a plate, loaded it, and retreated to her desk. She wasn't going to sit with Fleet on the sofa or the floor, dipping into the communal food and chatting like everything was fine.

After a few minutes, Fleet crossed to the sofa with a plate and began eating.

Lydia opened her laptop and pretended to work. The first forkful of food reminded her that she was starving. When had she last eaten? She couldn't remember.

'It's not my team,' Fleet said, after a while. 'They gave it to DI Lowry.'

Lydia swallowed her mouthful of food. 'Is that supposed to make me feel better?'

'A bit, I suppose.'

'Were you even going to tell me?'

'Only if it looked like anything was going to be done. Which is very unlikely. There is nothing to connect you to Mikhail. And you didn't kill him.'

'How would you have known they were going to make a move, if you're not on the team?'

'I'm management, I get reports.'

Lydia bit into a spring roll, trying to maintain her anger. It was harder when she was eating delicious food. Fleet was smart.

'So, they've opened it as a murder case? I'm surprised.'

'You thought it would be hushed up? To protect the Met?' Fleet's voice was mild, but there was heat in his eyes. Whatever the failings in the police as an institution, Fleet believed he and his colleagues were doing a difficult job to the best of their abilities and that, by and large, they were good people. He might rail against top brass, but she knew he felt every accusation of police corruption like a knife in his back.

Still. She wasn't going to lie. 'Yes.'

They ate in silence for a while after that.

Feeling a tiny stab of remorse, Lydia put her fork down, picked up her wine and went to sit next to Fleet. 'Am I under surveillance?'

Fleet finished chewing and swallowed before he answered. 'Not yet. There's no warrant.'

'No grounds for a warrant, either,' Lydia said. 'No reasonable grounds for treating me as a suspect, in fact.'

'Your name written by the deceased in his dying moments and past form, reputation...'

He was ticking them off on fingers, but it made no sense. Lydia said so. 'There is nothing substantial there and you know it. What is going on?'

'I don't know what to say. It's Lowry's show and as soon as it was set up, you were named as a suspect.'

'But I wasn't there. How am I supposed to have killed a man when I wasn't there and he was being watched by CCTV so everyone knows I wasn't there? I mean, the footage goes fuzzy for a couple of minutes, right? Was I supposed to break in and kill him in that time?'

'I shouldn't be talking to you about this,' Fleet said.

'Obviously,' Lydia replied. She sipped her wine and waited.

He sighed, just a little, before elaborating. 'Delayed poison of some kind. Ricin takes days to kill.'

'Was ricin found post-mortem?'

'No. As you know.'

'So they are working on the assumption that I used a hitherto unknown slow-action poison? That's far-fetched.'

'Not all poisons are detectable post-mortem. And they are working on connecting you to Mikhail.'

'Good luck to them. I never met the man. I told you.'

'I know.' A pause. 'But what about other Crows? Are you sure he didn't know Charlie?'

Hell Hawk. When would Charlie stop causing problems?

Later, once the empty plates were left abandoned on the desk and they had moved to the bedroom with the rest of the red wine and a mutual desire to make up, Lydia curled against Fleet. He was sleepy but Lydia still felt wide awake. More relaxed and no longer furious, but nowhere near sleep. 'What if they find something to connect me to Mikhail? What if Charlie did know him? Theoretically.'

Fleet shifted and curled an arm over her body, anchoring her close to him. 'You didn't kill him so you've got nothing to worry about.'

Lydia didn't feel like pointing out that wrongful convictions did happen. 'It would help if we knew more about Mikhail. What was he doing blackmailing Rafferty? It doesn't make sense.'

'I know.' Fleet's voice was quiet and his breathing was slow.

'So he really didn't say anything?'

A pause. 'Not a single word.'

'Talk me through the arrest again.'

Fleet breathed in deeply. When he spoke, his voice was more awake. 'We picked him up after a house got knocked over in Dulwich. Owner was on holiday and he had the code for the alarm system.'

'How?'

She felt Fleet roll away and she turned to look at him. He crossed his arms behind his head, seemingly resigned to not getting sleepy-time just yet. 'It was handily written on the chalkboard wall in the kitchen. Probably Mikhail didn't even need access to the house to see it. I stood in the garden and looked through the glass doors to read it.'

'Feathers.'

'Yeah. Not smart. I mean, I know I'm not supposed to blame the victim, but sometimes...'

'So how did you nab him?'

'Neighbourhood Watch. Couple next door were feeding the cat and the wife happened to pop round at the exact time Mikhail was upstairs. She saw a filled duffel on the kitchen floor and heard footsteps upstairs. She went back out to the street and called nine-nine-nine.'

'And cops responded in time?'

'Hey,' Fleet said. 'We're not entirely useless.'

Lydia patted his arm. 'I'm just surprised. You're stretched and that sounds like a low priority task. Was it just lucky timing?'

'Nah,' Fleet looked a little bit sheepish. 'The cat-feeding neighbour is Margaret Wainright.'

A pause. 'Well that clears that up.'

'Officially, as you know, there is no such thing as a two-tier service in the Met. But...'

'She was the last chief,' Lydia said. 'Must have caused a panic when her address came up on the call sheet.'

'Barely retired, too. Still a lot of clout. And you know police... We tend to trust our own.' He shrugged. 'I'm not saying it's fair.'

Lydia held up her hands. 'Human nature, innit.'

'So the uniforms arrived double-quick and got rewarded by Mikhail closing up the door neatly behind himself with two bags full of jewellery, electronics and cash. And, as it turned out, a notebook with torn sheets that matched the blackmail notes delivered to Rafferty Hill.'

'That was a good catch.' Lydia was wondering why a standard lined notebook had raised any kind of flag for a booking officer.

'A bit more luck. The detective interviewing Mikhail had been on the Rafferty team originally before the staffing got reduced. '

'Staffing's reduced on it?'

'No new leads. Grown man missing for weeks. It's looking colder by the day. Got to move the resources to where we might actually get results.'

'So the detective picked up on the notebook straight away?'

'Yeah. That and Mikhail's likeness to the figure caught on CCTV of Rafferty's building. It would have been logged on the system and the connection would have been made, regardless. Everything is cross-referenced in the database, but it still needs a human to see that connection and act on it. The detective knowing the Rafferty case expedited it.'

'What did Mikhail say about the notebook?'

'Same as he said about everything else.'

'Nothing?'

'Correct.'

Fleet visited his aunt every couple of weeks and now that Lydia had met her once, Fleet had issued a standing invitation. 'I know you won't be able to come very often,' he had said, which had pierced her heart. She had gone all in with Fleet. They were now a proper couple in every sense and that meant their lives were entwined. Family obligations and all. Fleet had visited her parents several times and she was overdue to join him for a trip to Auntie.

The flat was free of dogs and other visitors which was something of a miracle. The smell of cooking meat wafted through and Auntie fussed over Fleet for a while, sucking her teeth and telling him he was too thin. 'You're not sleeping enough,' she said, tilting her head to consider him. Her gaze slid to Lydia in silent rebuke.

'Work has been intense,' Fleet said. He talked about his team and recent cases and Auntie chipped in with pertinent questions. It was a practised duet and Lydia saw a new side to their relationship. They genuinely enjoyed each other's company.

Eventually, Auntie heaved herself up from her chair. 'It's time to baste the meat. Lydia will help me.'

Fleet was already half up from his seat but he sank back down at a glance from Auntie. Lydia got up instead and followed Auntie to the tiny kitchen where the cooking smell was deliciously intense, flooding Lydia's mouth with saliva.

Auntie pulled a tin out of the oven and lifted silver foil. She spooned cooking juices over the joint of beef and recovered it.

Once it was safely back in the oven. Auntie hung her floral oven gloves back on the hook on the cupboard where they lived and turned to face Lydia.

'So, you're not dead.' Auntie didn't look all that thrilled.

Lydia spread her hands, palm up.

'I hope you're not here to leave another message. You have something to say to Ignatius, you best tell him directly.'

'I know you don't trust me.'

Auntie tilted her chin up. 'Any reason why I should?'

'I love him, you know.'

'Doesn't mean you won't hurt him. Doesn't mean you're good for him. And it doesn't mean I trust you.'

'I won't hurt him.'

'You still head of your family? Still chief Crow?'

Lydia nodded.

Auntie folded her lips in until they all but disappeared.

'I'm glad you initiated this cosy chat, actually,' Lydia

said. Since Auntie had laid her cards on the table and made it clear that she didn't like Lydia, she felt like she had nothing to lose and there was a gap in her knowledge that had been bothering her for weeks. 'I wanted to ask you about Fleet's father.'

Auntie shook her head as if she couldn't believe Lydia's audacity. Luckily, she was used to seeing that expression and it didn't faze her. 'I know they aren't close, but I want to know more. Blood is important. Or it can be.'

'Ask Ignatius.'

'I did. He won't talk about him.'

'Then you should respect that, child.'

'I do. And I know you are only protecting Ignatius. I respect that.'

'Good then.'

'But it's getting stronger.'

Auntie went still.

'His gleam. You know what I'm talking about. The extra something that fizzes in his blood. I can sense it and it's got stronger.'

Auntie's face scrunched in disapproval. 'Since he met you.'

Lydia didn't try to deny it. 'Yes. But there's something new there. And he's not talking about it. He won't talk about it. I need to know more about where he came from. His lineage.'

'This is private.'

'I know. I'm not asking lightly. I want to be able to look after him.'

‘I think you’re saying words you think I want to hear, but you speak like it’s a foreign language.’

‘Maybe,’ Lydia said. ‘But it’s a language I’m trying to learn.’

Auntie nodded in acknowledgement of this.

Encouraged, Lydia asked the question she couldn’t ask Fleet ‘I need to know where his father is. What he is. I need to know if he’s a threat.’

Auntie let out a laugh that clearly did not come from a place of humour. It was like a release of tension. Of madness. ‘Of course he’s a threat, child. Why do you think his mother ran so far away?’

CHAPTER FOURTEEN

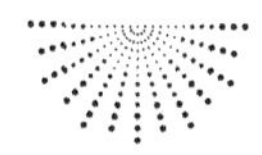

Lydia was sitting in The Fork, drinking some good coffee and looking through her work notebook. She had been thinking about Amanda at the bunker. She had lost her son to drugs, now she saw every young man as in danger, every change of behaviour as a warning sign. Lydia realised something important: she had been doing the same thing. She had known Charlie as dodgy and Maddie as a killer, so she was seeing every sign of her increased power as another step on a deeply criminal path. She thought she had learned not to be afraid of herself, but she hadn't reckoned on getting Maddie's power. And how that would make her feel. Lydia picked up her pencil and wrote 'power is a tool'.

Aiden pushed through the front door with an urgency that made Lydia look up in alarm.

'There's more trouble,' Aiden said, his face flushed.

'It must be Tuesday.' She kept her voice steady. Charlie had always seemed unflappable and now she was the leader, she felt she had to do the same.

'What?'

'Never mind. What's the problem? If people are still complaining about their profits, we could give them a bonus. There's plenty of money in the account.' That was one thing about Charlie's legacy, the Family weren't hurting for cash.

Aiden did a double take and Lydia felt a cold mass in her stomach. 'What?'

'You should speak to Jo.'

'The accountant?' The mass solidified and Lydia felt it pressing upward on her lungs, stopping her from breathing. 'What don't I know?'

He shook his head. 'Not my area, boss. You really need to check in with Jo. She knows the books.'

Lydia made a note. Then she wrote a number one next to it. She would get organised. Work through the problems one by one. Under number two she wrote 'Mikhail'. She looked up and realised that Aiden was waiting to speak. 'Tell me, then.'

'The pub on Church Street was hit last night. Trashed.'

'That's what insurance is for,' Lydia said, flooded with relief that it hadn't been something worse. 'Wait. Was anybody hurt?'

Aiden shook his head. He still looked deeply unhappy. 'They used to pay us for protection. Everyone knows it's a Crow pub.'

'We don't do that anymore. We're legit. They know that.'

'Yeah. Everybody knows that, too.' Aiden's frustration burst through. 'Which is why our places are getting knocked over. No repercussions.'

'But insurance,' Lydia said, feeling that if she repeated the words, they would begin to solve everything. 'And the police. That's the legal system. It's out of our hands, now. Not our business. Literally.'

'There was this,' Aiden unlocked his phone and tapped at the screen before passing it over.

It was a picture of the inside of the pub. The floor was a mess of broken glass and smashed furniture, and there were ripped-up cushions and artwork from the walls strewn about. It was like the pub brawl to end all pub brawls had just finished. Painted on the wall in red letters were the words 'Get The Crow'.

'Hell Hawk.'

'Yeah,' Aiden said. 'That's what I thought.'

Looking at the words in this new context made Lydia see them anew. It wasn't a cry for help or an attempt at incrimination at all. It was an instruction.

LYDIA DIDN'T PARTICULARLY WANT TO CALL PAUL Fox. She definitely didn't want to seem to be running to him for help, but there was the old adage: keep your friends close and your enemies closer. She wasn't sure which category Paul fell into, but the advice, handily, applied to both.

'I've got a bit of bother,' Lydia said, when Paul answered. 'Nothing I can't handle, but I wanted to ask you something.'

Silence. Paul was clearly still not over his bad mood.

Lydia carried on regardless. 'Do you know of anyone who might be launching a campaign against me?'

That got a snort.

'Apart from the Silvers. I'm disregarding the Pearls. The weak ones are too scattered and the strong ones are dead.' Lydia squeezed her coin as she spoke, hoping it was the truth.

'Don't forget the Foxes,' Paul said, finally speaking.

'Don't joke,' Lydia said.

'Who said I was joking?'

Well, she was just going to ignore that. 'Do you know the Half Moon in Camberwell?'

'Can't say I do. Pub is it?'

'Glad to hear it,' Lydia said, ignoring the automatic physical response that Paul's voice always set off in her stomach region. It was Fox mojo. Animal magnetism. Magical pheromones. And bloody inconvenient. 'Someone left a message there last night.'

A pause. 'What sort of message?'

'An incitement to violence, I think.'

'You think? Those are usually pretty clear.'

'It was ambiguous.'

'Ambiguous violence doesn't sound too bad. I wouldn't worry about it.'

The implication that she had enough other things to worry about was clear. 'Will you let me know if you hear anything?'

'I might. For a fee.'

'Of course I'll pay,' Lydia said. The words hung in the air just long enough for their meaning to twist.

Paul didn't say goodbye. One moment he was there,

listening silently and then he was gone.

LYDIA WOKE UP IN FLEET'S BEDROOM. HIS HEAVY blackout curtains blocked out the light and the sheets were smooth and clean. Everything was, in short, as comfortable and conducive to sleep as usual. The numbers on the alarm clock read almost five. And Fleet's side of the bed was empty.

She lay for a few minutes, listening for sounds of Fleet in the bathroom or kitchen. His side of the bedding was cold, so he had clearly not just got up, but she listened anyway, hoping. The silence of an empty flat was broken by stomping from above and a bin lorry reversing outside.

She padded through the flat, trying to keep a lid on her panic. It was a Sunday and Fleet wasn't doing overtime. If he had been called into work, she would have been woken up by his phone. She had to keep reminding herself that Maddie was dead and gone, no longer a threat to Lydia and her loved ones.

Finally, she found a note. 'Gone for walk.'

There was a single kiss and it was definitely Fleet's handwriting, but that was all the available information.

It hadn't started as a good evening, Fleet had seemed tense even before he'd asked about the pub on Church Street. Lydia knew she had been evasive in her response, but there wasn't much to say. She didn't tell Fleet that she had called Paul. That information would only worry and annoy him. And prolong the argument that she could feel gathering in the air. Plus, and she told herself this was the primary reason for her secrecy, she didn't want to dwell on the incident at the pub until she had worked out what she was going to do about it. There was no point incriminating Fleet, making him an accessory, if she could avoid it.

To avoid the conversation veering toward the trashed pub and the messages being left for the Crows, Lydia had asked Fleet about Rafferty Hill. No further leads, no sign of the man, and increasing pressure from his family. All in all, it hadn't improved Fleet's mood. In the end, though, they had watched Netflix, eaten some takeaway and had an early night together. Fleet had seemed fine. Relaxed, even.

Fleet used her phone's GPS when needed, but had his own switched off. She had asked him about it ages ago and he had said it was Met policy. Basic safety and security. What he didn't know was that Lydia had attached a tracker to his car. Yes, that was the kind of untrusting thing that paranoid partners and underhand debt collectors did. But it was also standard-fare for private investigators who also happened to be heads of dodgy families which included professional killers. She had added the tracker when Maddie had been ramping up her intimidation tactics, in case she decided to take Fleet for an unscheduled road trip.

Lydia opened the app on her phone, praying that the tracker was still functional. She didn't know how long the battery would last. She was in luck and it showed up immediately, a little blinking red dot on a satellite map view of the city. The postcode was in North West London, next to Hampstead Heath. What the hell was Fleet doing there? Early morning run? She called his mobile again and counted the rings to keep calm while she waited for him to answer. Twenty-five before the voicemail kicked in. Had it always been set for that many? Lydia couldn't remember. Fleet usually answered quickly. She stood still with the phone in her hand, caught in indecision. Finally, she shoved the gadget into her jacket pocket and headed out of the door.

Fleet's car was parked in a side street near to Hampstead Heath. She had spent the drive racking her brain for plausible explanations. His note said 'gone for a walk' but maybe that had been shorthand. Maybe he had joined one of those outside exercise classes or a friendly five-a-side team. There were plenty in Camberwell, but perhaps he had a friend from work who lived in this area and had roped him in.

Lydia had come up with a detailed scenario that explained Fleet getting up out of bed without waking her, leaving a cryptic note and heading to North West London early in the morning. Problem was, she didn't believe a word of it. Friendly five-a-side teams didn't meet to train at five in the morning. Something was wrong.

Lydia was standing next to Fleet's car, frozen with indecision. She wanted to start combing the area but if he saw her, he would know she had followed him. That wasn't a good sign for a trusting relationship but, on the other hand, they had always had to deal with a more heightened version of reality. He could be in danger. He would understand her concern. Surely.

Her phone buzzed. Her heart stuttered when she saw the name on the display.

'Sorry I missed you,' Fleet said. 'Everything okay?'

'You went out,' Lydia said.

'I left a note.'

Fleet did not sound like himself. His voice was flat and strangely thin. An image of the ghost at the bunker, translucent and vibrating, leapt into Lydia's mind. She pushed it aside. Fleet wasn't a ghost.

'Where did you go?'

'Just around.'

Lydia moved away from his car, in case he was heading back as they spoke. Her own car was parked further down the road and she got in.

'Where are you?'

'Just getting into my car. I'm going to head home. Where are you?' Lydia didn't lie. Fleet might assume she meant her car outside his flat, but she hadn't specified.

'Heading back, now. Did you want to meet for lunch? Pub?'

'Sure.'

It wasn't until Lydia was halfway back to Camberwell that she realised: Fleet had been just as evasive with her.

CHAPTER FIFTEEN

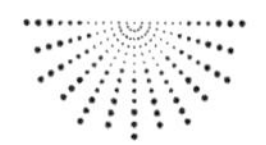

Lydia had a ghost sighting at the bunker that appeared to be entirely bogus. And an actual ghost who didn't match any of the descriptions but who was, nonetheless, definitely in residence. The job which Sinclair had sent her to do involved the 'white lady' so she could, perhaps, call it 'job done'. But there was a ghost. And Lydia hadn't recovered from her obsessive nature overnight. Luckily, Jason was up for a field trip.

'It might be busy there,' Lydia said, thinking of the weird energy of the place. All those frightened workers, the massive stakes of the world war, bombs dropping up above. Not to mention, people dying in situ from stress or heartbreak. It was possible that the place was stacked to the ceiling with restless spirits.

'I don't mind,' Jason said, stretching his arms above his head. The floppy sleeves of his jacket fell down and bunched around his shoulders. 'I'm going mad knocking around here. Can't you give me some more work to do?'

Jason had given her the address for Mikhail's ex-girlfriend, but she hadn't had a chance to follow up on it, yet. Bloody Crow business taking up her time. Bloody Sinclair and her demands.

She regarded Jason. He was fully corporeal, not looking even slightly ghost-like and she couldn't remember the last time he had randomly disappeared. It seemed to be another side effect of her increased power. 'Do you think you can still do it?'

Jason reached out and took her hand with his. It was cold, but very solid. Flesh against flesh.

After a few seconds, Lydia moved away. 'Let's go outside.'

In the lane running along the back of The Fork, Jason still looked solid and Lydia felt a shiver of panic. Would this work? Was Jason now free to move wherever he liked? Untethered from The Fork? And what would that mean?

They walked down the alley, past the wheelie bins and a pile of rotting cardboard. When they were almost at the entrance, where the alley met the main road, Jason doubled over, retching. When he straightened up, there was a slight vibration around his edges. He held up his hand and the light passed through it. He smiled crookedly. 'Looks like this is my new boundary.'

'Okay,' Lydia took both of his hands in hers. 'Hop on.'

She was halfway through a preparatory deep breath when Jason flowed into her. It was like jumping into an ice-cold swimming pool and for a second she was frozen, unable to finish her breath. And then she felt Jason tuck himself into a corner of her mind. Like a visitor who knew the way to the spare bedroom.

The terrifying cold retreated to a manageable chill and Lydia made her way onto the main street to find her Audi. She had never felt confident enough to drive while carrying Jason before, except in extreme circumstances, but at this moment she felt fine. In control and hardly nauseous at all. Either it was because her and Jason were a well-practised duo, or it was another facet of her increased power.

LYDIA PARKED AT A MULTI-STOREY IN WESTMINSTER and walked past the abbey to Whitehall and the bunker. Jason was a considerate passenger and she felt almost normal. There were definite advantages to absorbing Maddie's power. It turned out that strength felt pretty damn good.

The sky was darkening above the imposing white edifice of the treasury building and she knew it was about to chuck it down in one of London's brief but barbaric rain showers. Thankfully the last cohort of tourists were safely inside so she didn't have to squeeze past an angry queue to get to the entrance. She was wearing her visitor pass lanyard and she waved it at the man on the front desk and descended to the lower level.

The corridors were lined with gloss-painted brick-work and girders which stretched above, reminding you that you were beneath street level with a few tons of government building above. They were well lit, but it was so easy for Lydia to imagine them with strobing light or bathed in emergency red as bombs dropped above, shaking the ground.

She didn't know if that had ever happened or whether bombs sounded like muffled bangs and the men and women in the war rooms just carried on, typing notes on noiseless machines, sitting in front of sun lamps, and moving coloured pins on the gigantic map which dominated the command centre of the bunker. How did they feel? Were they happy to be doing such vital work, so close to their leader? Or were they crushed by the responsibility and the ever-present threat?

The final stragglers had already been herded to the exhibition room, where the life and times of Churchill were detailed with the use of diary pages, objects and photographs, and the corridor housing Churchill's bedroom was empty.

The ghost was sitting on the bed, hands still folded in her lap. Lydia felt a rush of relief that this hadn't been a wasted trip. It might be easier to carry Jason as a passenger, but it still wasn't exactly fun. 'All right,' she said out loud. 'Time to disembark.'

She closed her eyes as Jason left her body, thankful that she didn't have an audience.

Jason's form was shimmery and insubstantial, but Lydia could see him clearly enough. 'I like 'disembark'. Very professional.'

Lydia was busy sucking in air and trying not to vomit, so she didn't answer the ghost.

He put one hand an inch above the glass which sealed Churchill's bedroom and then moved through it as if it wasn't there.

The figure on the bed didn't move. Lydia couldn't see the woman's face, it was bowed down to her lap, as if studying something there. Her hands were loosely clasped and Lydia couldn't tell if she was holding anything. Partly because the figure was half-turned away from the viewing window, her body shielding her lap, and partly because her image wasn't very clear. It vibrated at the edges and flickered in and out of existence, the way that Jason's had done before Lydia had powered him up. For a moment, Lydia could only make out a faint amorphous shape of light, and then the seated woman became clear for a few seconds. Just as Lydia was taking in the details, fixing it in her mind, it would shimmer and blur, or blink away completely, leaving Lydia staring intently at the counterpane on Churchill's bed.

'Hello,' Jason was saying, his voice barely audible through the glass. 'Don't be afraid.'

The figure didn't react and Lydia wondered whether it was at all sentient.

He crouched down in front of the figure. 'I'm here to help. My name is Jason. Can you tell me your name?'

The woman was still flickering, but it was clear to Lydia that her previous impression had been correct. She wasn't wearing a white gown of any kind. Trousers and a knitted jumper, sensible shoes and hair in a neat bun. Jason was still speaking in a low, soothing voice, and it occurred to Lydia that in another life he would have made a wonderful therapist or nurse.

The ghost wasn't responding, although the flashes when she was clearly visible were becoming longer and the times she disappeared shorter. Her head was still bowed, but she got a glimpse of jawline and a mouth. Just an impression and a quick one, but she didn't think it was a young woman.

Jason had his head tilted, as if listening. After a few minutes he turned back to Lydia. 'She's very sad. Feels wronged,' he glanced back at the ghost, as if for her confirmation. She didn't move. 'It's okay,' he said to her. 'You don't have to talk if you don't want to.'

Another minute passed. Jason stayed crouched in front of the ghost, looking into her face, waiting. Eventually, he looked to Lydia. 'Shall I stay? Keep trying?'

Lydia's heart contracted. It was pure kindness to make the offer. She knew the prospect of disappearing terrified Jason, and the longer he stayed this far from The Fork, the more likely that became. 'Not this time. We'll try other avenues first.'

She saw the tension in Jason's shoulders ease. 'I'm going to leave, now,' he said to the ghost. 'If you want me to stay, give me a sign.'

The figure didn't move.

'I think she's holding something,' Jason said over his shoulder. Turning back to the ghost, he said, 'may I see that?'

The figure disappeared. Not with a shimmer or a fading, but in an instant. A light that had been extinguished with the click of a switch.

'She's gone,' Jason said, unnecessarily. His expression was bleak and it sliced through Lydia's heart.

'It's okay,' she said, although she wasn't sure who she was reassuring.

Jason frowned at the bed, reaching out a hand. 'There's something here.'

He stepped back to the window and held up a small object so that Lydia could see it. A brass button. It was embossed with the British crown and an eagle. It looked like the kind of thing that belonged in the exhibition portion of the museum. A stray artefact that had been carelessly left in the wrong place. Jason tapped it against the glass. His hand passed through the glass and the button fell to the floor, just inside the room. If she wanted to touch the thing, she was going to have to get corporeal help.

Lydia took Jason home before going back to the bunker. He sank onto the sofa and opened his laptop. The blue light from the screen illuminated the slight translucency of his features and she wondered if she should leave him straight away.

'It's fine,' he said, tapping away on the keys. 'And you'll be back tonight, right?'

'Absolutely,' Lydia said. She had charged up a bracelet with her Crow power and now she went and retrieved it from its location under her bed. 'You could wear this if you need topping up.'

He flashed her a smile and then continued tapping at the keys. She understood. He hated going outside The Fork because it reminded him that he wasn't alive. Hitching a ride with Lydia didn't just make him physically weaker, it reminded him that he was a ghost. And being close to the living, to the world, but not being of it, was the worst thing. He wanted to be back in the world where he was the same as everybody else. When he was a stream of characters on a computer screen, it didn't matter that he didn't breathe.

Rush hour was in full force and she didn't want to risk getting stuck in traffic, so Lydia rode the underground back to Whitehall. She stood with a man's armpit pressed close to her face for half of the journey and wasn't in the best of moods when she arrived at the bunker. It was just after closing time, but there was a security guard in the reception area and a desk attendant shutting down the computer system. Lydia tapped on the glass door, holding up her pass. The guard unlocked the door. 'Forget something?'

She walked the echoey passages, made more eerie in their quiet desertion, and tracked down Amanda. She was in the staff room, picking up her coat before leaving for the day. Between the tube ride and the fake ghost, Lydia didn't have any patience left, so she dispensed with the niceties. 'Why did you want me to find Liam?'

Amanda blinked. 'He just disappeared. Not so much as a goodbye.'

'That doesn't seem particularly unusual. I mean, people leave jobs all the time.'

'He just stopped turning up, though. I was worried.'

'Why didn't you call him?'

'I didn't have his number. And Collier wouldn't give it out. Said it was data protection.' Amanda pulled on a mustard-yellow jacket and began fussing with a scarf, winding it around her neck one way before unwinding it and trying again.

'You knew I was an investigator so you thought you would ask me?'

'No,' Amanda's eyes widened. 'I thought that was what you were here for. I mean... Why else?'

'The ghost,' Lydia said slowly, starting to wonder if Amanda was playing with a full deck of cards.'

'Oh, come on,' Amanda said, resuming fussing with her scarf. 'Who is going to pay someone to look into that? A ghost story. I assumed it was a cover.'

'A cover?'

'So that they could pay an investigator to find Liam. He's only young. He might be in trouble.'

Putting aside that slice of naivete, Lydia felt herself soften again. 'You're really worried, aren't you?'

Amanda nodded. 'We need to look out for each other. And he's just a kid, really. Boys that age, they can get into all sorts of trouble.'

Lydia thought about Aiden. About all of her young cousins and the gangs who were causing mayhem around town. Most of them were in their late teens or early twenties. It was a life that had an early expiration date. It hit her, Amanda's experience of loss might be making her more paranoid about Liam, but that didn't guarantee there was nothing sinister in it.

'I'll check up on him,' Lydia promised. 'And I will let you know.'

'Thank you,' Amanda said, genuine emotion in her voice. 'The others think I'm being silly.'

That was enough caring and sharing. Lydia wasn't a counsellor, she was an investigator and she had a job to finish. So that she could attend the thousand other jobs on her list, she thought, suppressing a sigh. 'About the ghost. I do need to know if you've got anything to add to your story?'

Amanda's cheeks flushed pink, but she shook her head. Suddenly silent.

'Have you seen the figure again? Since I've been here?'

'I need to get home. I'll miss my bus.'

Lydia considered producing her coin. She was tired and more than a little fed up. Then she remembered, she didn't need to produce her coin, she could just stop trying to hold back her Crow mojo, let it run free. 'Did you really see a ghost?'

Amanda's eyes had glazed over. 'Not really. Well. It was a bit of fun, wasn't it?'

Right. 'I need you to let me into Churchill's bedroom.'

Amanda took a step back, suddenly completely serious. 'I can't do that.'

Fed up with being sent on a wild ghost chase, Lydia pushed a bit more Crow behind her words and repeated the request.

Amanda's hands began to shake and tears began streaming down her face. 'I can't do it. I don't have a key.'

Lydia immediately tried to turn off her whammy. She imagined turning a tap and hoped that would work. 'Who does?'

'We have specialist cleaners that go in,' Amanda managed between sniffs. She scrubbed at her face with the end of her scarf. 'They work across all the facilities run by the Imperial War Museum. I don't know when they're next due.'

This was a pain. Lydia would just tell Rebecca about the button and consider the job finished. She had more than enough trouble to be dealing with above ground.

'And Ms Collier, of course.'

CHAPTER SIXTEEN

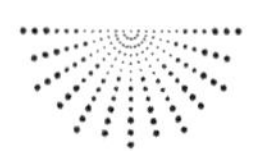

Walking down the passage, Lydia tried not to look at the displays in the rooms of the bunker. The mannequins with their dead waxwork faces, overly red lips and staring eyes. She heard a whooshing sound, quiet and sinister from one of the overhead pipes and felt her coin in her hand, squeezing it for reassurance. There was something wrong with this place. Some residual energy that had become twisted and dark over the passage of time. Or Lydia was just sick of being underground.

She found Rebecca Collier in her tiny office. She had a large pink plastic bottle on her desk, with measurements printed on the side, and a tiny succulent plant which was either totally fine with zero sunlight or also made of plastic.

'Will this take long?'

'Not at all. I'm almost done.' Lydia sat down without being invited. 'When is Churchill's bedroom due to be cleaned?'

Rebecca frowned. 'At the end of the month. Why?'

'One of the guides told me that nobody accesses the room, which was why they knew they had to be seeing a ghost. That it was impossible for any other figure to be inside, but that's not true, is it? Some people must go in.'

Rebecca clicked her mouse and then adjusted her gaze from her computer screen to Lydia. 'The curators, of course, and specialist cleaning staff.'

'And you,' Lydia added after a beat.

Rebecca stiffened. 'Not really. No.'

'But you have access.'

'Of course I have access. This entire facility is my responsibility.'

'Excellent,' Lydia said, 'I've got something to show you.'

AT CHURCHILL'S BEDROOM, REBECCA COLLIER seemed unduly anxious. Her eyes kept darting to the room, looking into every corner, the floor, the ceiling. It was as if she was deliberately avoiding looking at the bed. 'I can't let you inside. We have to preserve the exhibit.'

'I've been in older rooms,' Lydia said briskly. 'It's not going to disintegrate if we breathe on it.' Before Collier could object further, she added. 'I don't have to go in. I just need you to fetch that.'

Collier followed the direction of her pointing finger. The brass button was on the floor next to the glass where Jason had dropped it.

. . .

Back in Rebecca's office, the button on the desk between them, Lydia was the first to speak. 'Did you put it there?'

A tiny crack in Rebecca's façade. Lydia wasn't sure if anybody else would have noticed, her expression remained the same – annoyed, but she had picked up a pen and was fiddling with it. 'Why would I do that? It doesn't belong there. It was clearly dropped by a member of staff. I will speak to the cleaning team-'

'It's okay,' Lydia said. 'I'm not here to hang you out to dry. I solved the problem I was asked to solve. I don't think I need to provide ancillary information in my report. It's not as if this is the kind of thing that will be repeated.' She wasn't intending to ever set foot inside the bunker again, for starters.

Lydia touched the uneven surface of the brass button with one finger. 'This is yours, I presume.'

Rebecca's gaze flicked down and to the side.

'I don't know if it belongs to a relative or...'

'Why do you ask?' Rebecca's mouth was a thin line, her eyes a mixture of fury and fear.

'The ghost. The white lady.'

The thin lips curled into a sneer.

'More accurately she's a sad-looking woman in sensible slacks. Could be your grandmother, judging by the age.' Lydia examined Rebecca for a moment. 'Although maybe not. I don't see much family resemblance.'

Rebecca's sneer disappeared and she swallowed hard, not meeting Lydia's gaze.

'I do know she feels seriously wronged. Which isn't a surprise when it comes to ghosts. They usually have something to make them restless spirits, otherwise they'd be taking a long nap... Well, wherever spirits do that. I don't know. I'm not a theologist. I'm just an investigator.'

'Can I rely on your discretion? Outside this facility? I know this would make a good story, but...'

'Of course,' Lydia said, placing her hands onto the desk to stop them curling into fists. Why did so many people equate 'investigator' with 'venal scum who would sell their own granny to the tabloids'? 'That's part of the service.'

'Thank you.' It was like the words had been dragged from her lips. No wonder she was in a back-office role. Rebecca Collier wasn't a people person.

'Right, then,' Lydia stood up. She had been going to ask Rebecca why she had left a military button in an exhibit or whether it had been accidental, but she discovered she no longer cared. She just wanted to get out. 'I'll leave you to it. I won't mention your role in my report, but I do ask you to return that to wherever you got it.'

Rebecca looked back at the button. 'Is she in here, now?'

Lydia glanced around, although she was already pretty sure the ghost wasn't with them. It was too warm in the office. 'No.'

Rebecca's shoulders went down a notch.

'I'll be off,' Lydia said, suddenly filled with the wild happiness which meant she was going to be getting out of the bunker. Again, she wondered how the workers had managed during the war. Months underground with nothing but artificial lights and their duty to keep them going.

She had started to stand up when Rebecca spoke. 'It's not mine.'

'I'm sorry?'

'That's not mine,' Rebecca nodded at the button. 'And I didn't know it would do what it did. I was just following orders.'

It took Lydia a beat to catch up. Then it hit her. 'This was a set up?'

Rebecca pushed her chair back, as if suddenly very keen to put some more space between them. Smart woman.

SHE WENT TO THE STAFF ROOM TO COLLECT HER jacket. The cafe worker was pulling a bag from his locker. 'You're here late.'

'I'm just leaving.'

'See you tomorrow, then.'

'I'm done, actually.'

He didn't pause on his way to the door. 'Ah well. Good to meet you. Take care, innit.'

The door banged shut and Lydia looked around the empty room. She wondered how many ghosts were floating around, not strong enough for her to see. How long would she need to stay before she powered them up enough? And would it happen all at once? She imagined a crowd of grey shapes, pressing in from all sides. Their mouths moving, trying to communicate, hands grasping.

. . .

Outside in the corridor, it was Rebecca Collier who appeared like an apparition.

'There's someone here to see you before you go. They're in the switch room. The cafe. Don't forget to leave your pass at the desk when you leave.'

'Who?'

Rebecca shook her head, lips tightly pursed, and then stalked away as if Lydia's presence was still a personal affront.

'I'm heading out,' Lydia called after the retreating figure. 'I'm done.'

Rebecca waited until she was at the door to her office before turning back. 'I was never your client,' she said and then disappeared into her office.

The cafe lights were on but the counters were cleaned off, the coffee machine silent and the display cases empty. The chiller cabinet had a grey thermal blind pulled down, hiding the brightly coloured cans of fizzy juice and posh lemonade.

Sinclair was sitting at one of the middle tables. Her chair was set away from the table and she was leaning back, head tilted and eyes closed as if relaxing on an outside terrace somewhere sunny. One leg in tailored black trousers was loosely crossed over the other and her cream shirt was made of something silky. Probably silk.

'So this wasn't a favour,' Lydia said, throwing herself into the chair opposite. 'It was a test.'

Sinclair opened her eyes. 'One you passed with flying colours. Well done.'

'Why all this?' Lydia waved a hand.

'You had to believe it was a case. I could hardly pop you into a lab, you would never have cooperated.'

'I'm still getting paid.' It wasn't a question.

'A favour. Yes.'

'Say it.' Lydia leaned back in her chair. Her fingers were itching to hold her coin, but she forced the feeling down.

'That unfortunate death in Camberwell? Very sad that there are no leads.' Sinclair lifted one hand from her lap and waved it in a dismissive gesture. A murder case wafted away like it was a tiny fly. 'But that's not what I want to discuss.'

'We're done,' Lydia said. Her anger was a dull thing. Contained and muted, but it was still there. She enjoyed the sensation and felt almost grateful to Sinclair for inspiring it. Anything to peel away the clouded layer which had settled between her and the world. 'Our transaction is complete. I left the button on Rebecca's desk if you want it back. I assume it came from your personal stash.'

'You think I have a collection of haunted objects?' Sinclair raised an eyebrow.

Lydia spread her hands. 'What else should I assume? I'm not judging. It's nice that you have a hobby. Probably good for stress relief. Something to calm you down after a day spent doing whatever it is you do for queen and country.'

A small smile appeared on Sinclair's face. 'I like you.'

Lydia shut her mouth. She did not need a new secret service operative pretending to be her friend.

'And this wasn't just a test for you,' Sinclair said.

She looked surprised, as if she hadn't expected to speak. Although, Lydia knew well, that could be part of her carefully calculated act. Still, Lydia couldn't resist giving Sinclair her personal theory. 'Someone told you it was haunted and you wanted to see if they were full of shit.'

Sinclair looked pleased. 'Exactly so.'

'Glad you're happy,' Lydia said with absolutely zero sincerity. She put her hands on her knees, preparing to stand up.

'You know that Gale's department has been closed?'

Lydia stilled, waiting.

'I am not him. I have no personal crusade, no particular interest in your family or the myths and stories about the Pearls, Silvers, and Foxes. Only the places where they might threaten national security which, it must be said, doesn't seem to be a real danger. You are all too busy fighting among yourselves.'

'What was this about, then?'

'Whether I have a personal interest or not, I still inherited his projects. And all his assets...'

Sinclair left the sentence hanging. Assets left by Gale. She could only mean Charlie. Which meant he wasn't dead.

Lydia swallowed. 'Did Charlie tell you the button was haunted? Was he part of the test?'

'I need to make certain decisions,' Sinclair said. 'I wanted to have all the data first.'

A cold chill ran down Lydia's neck. She forced an unconcerned tone into her voice. 'Glad I could help.'

CHAPTER SEVENTEEN

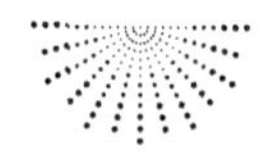

Lydia was pretty sure that Liam was fine and that Amanda was reacting poorly to his abrupt departure on account of her personal history. Still, he hadn't returned her messages or answered his phone, and that itch was still there. Besides, the job was complete as far as Sinclair was concerned, but that didn't mean Lydia was done. She was aware that she was probably being stubborn, working on something when she didn't have to as a minor 'fuck you' to Sinclair, one that made little sense, but she was going to do it anyway. Having opened a small mystery, she had to close it for her own satisfaction. Fleet called it a compulsion, but he had the same inclination so he couldn't talk.

Lydia took the Audi into Kingston upon Thames and parked in a pay and display by the river. It was an expensive suburb with signs of affluence like upmarket floristry and a branch of The White Company, and Lydia wondered how Liam could afford the rent on a guide's salary. All became clear when she arrived at his address and found a Victorian terrace in a leafy street and a middle-aged woman answered the door. 'Yes?'

Lydia plastered on her most innocent-looking smile. 'Are you Liam's mum?'

An expression flickered across her face. Weariness. 'Yes. Is there a problem?'

Lydia noted the question. 'I'm a detective. May I come in for a moment?' If she said 'detective' rather than 'investigator', lots of people assumed she was with the police without her having to claim it. Sometimes 'investigator' was better as people thought it had something to do with an insurance claim. Lydia had picked one on the spur of the moment and was gratified when it worked.

The woman stepped aside and Lydia entered a tiled hallway with an oak console table clustered with framed family photographs and an overflowing coat rack.

'This way,' Liam's mother said, leading the way to the back of the house. That was surprising. People usually stayed near to the entranceway, feeling psychologically safer, even though they had just opened the only barrier between themselves and the possible threat. Lydia wondered if Liam's mother was always this trusting or whether it was a case of mistaken identity. Perhaps Lydia looked like someone she knew? Or it was her Crow whammy flowing freely, coercing everybody to bend to her will. The thought wasn't quite as distasteful as it should have been.

It turned out to be one of the ubiquitous extensions with an open-plan kitchen and living room, but of a more moderate variety than Charlie's. There was an iPad and a mug on the kitchen island, potted herbs on the windowsill and a chopping board with diced carrots on the side. It was homely and wholesome and it reminded Lydia of her mum's kitchen. If you shrunk the whole room and changed the painted Shaker-style units for nineteen-seventies pine.

'Please have a seat.' Liam's mum took one of the stools around the island, and Lydia did the same.

'How has Liam been recently? His mood?'

The woman frowned. This was definitely not the line of questioning she was expecting. 'Fine, I think. Why-'

'And he's working at the Churchill Bunker, I believe?'

She nodded, happier to be on firm ground. 'Yes. He's a guide.' This was said with pride.

'He's getting on well, there?'

The woman jumped up. 'I haven't offered you tea. Would you like some? Or I have juice.'

'No, thank you. I'm fine.' She wanted to tell her that she didn't need to offer drinks to a random visitor and that she shouldn't, in fact, be so quick to allow a complete stranger into her home. Watching the woman smiling nervously she felt a surge of protectiveness and wondered whether this was why Amber had been so trusting, too. Perhaps people were accepting her story and inviting in because her Crow whammy was running at full strength all the time, now. 'Are you expecting to see Liam today?'

The woman's face relaxed. 'I should think so. He's only popped to Tesco, he'll be back soon.'

'Great.' Lydia was still battling the urge to warn the

woman against letting people into her home. She had a job to do, but what if this wasn't her Crow power? What if this woman was always so naïve?

As if reading her mind, Liam's mum gave her a strange look and then shook her head lightly. 'Who did you say you were, again? A friend of Liam's?'

'A detective,' Lydia said. Was the woman unwell? Was this why she was feeling protective? Was she sensing her vulnerability?

The sound of the front door opening and a man's voice called through. 'They didn't have sourdough.'

Liam appeared with two cloth shopping bags. He dropped them the moment he saw Lydia and bolted back out of the doorway.

Lydia was on her feet in seconds, but Liam was fast. He was out of the front door by the time she made it there and halfway down the street. She wouldn't catch him at this distance. She needed to speak to him and had come all this way, out to the suburbs, to check in on the little bastard. She didn't have time for this. *Stop running.* The thoughts flicked like lightning and, almost at the same moment, Liam stopped moving. It happened immediately, like he had run into an invisible brick wall.

She caught up to him easily. His eyes were wide and terrified and his mouth worked without sound. Then, as the shock seemed to wear off, he began swearing, loudly. Eventually, a question emerged from the stream of panicked expletives. 'Did you see that?'

Lydia could feel his consciousness. It was a glowing pulsing thing, delicate and so close she felt she could reach out and pick it up. She had stopped him running.

Liam's body had obeyed her thought as if it had been his own. *Lift your arm.*

Liam's arm drifted upward. 'Oh God! I'm having a stroke.'

'You're too young for that,' Lydia said, releasing her hold on his arm and, mentally, stepping away from his consciousness. She felt fuzzy with shock. *It had been so easy.*

'You need to call an ambulance,' Liam said, his eyes wild with panic. 'That's not... That's not normal. Something's wrong with me. My arm just moved-'

'You're fine,' Lydia said, pushing Crow behind her words. Her coin was in her hand, but she pocketed it. She didn't need to spin it in front of Liam, could see he was visibly calmer already. 'Come on, let's talk.'

She walked back toward his house, Liam trailing with a faintly dazed expression. 'I've got a couple of questions. You're going to answer them and then you can go back inside, have a cup of tea with your mum. She's very nice, by the way.'

He nodded automatically.

Outside the front of the house, Liam tapped a cigarette from a packet and began patting his pockets for a lighter. His motions seemed automatic, although his eyes were becoming more focused.

'First off, why did you run from me?'

'I recognised you,' Liam said. Then he looked faintly surprised as if he hadn't expected to answer her so readily. 'Collier showed us your picture, said we needed to cooperate.'

Sinclair had been thorough. 'You haven't been at work.'

'Yeah. I'm done with that place.' He glanced at the house, as if checking that his mother wasn't in earshot and lit his smoke.

'May I ask why?'

Lydia telling him that he was fine really seemed to have landed. Or he was more relaxed now that he had a lit cigarette in hand.

He blew smoke from the side of his mouth. 'Why do you care?'

'I'm an investigator. I've been asked to look into the ghost sightings at the bunker and I wanted to interview you. If that's all right.'

'I don't work for them anymore.'

'I understand. I need you to talk to me, anyway. It won't take long.'

Liam took a long drag on his cigarette, looking into the middle distance. 'Why do you think I left?'

'I'm sorry?'

'That ghost carry on.'

'You saw the white lady?'

Liam made a noise halfway between a snort and a laugh. He was definitely calmer. 'I left the bloody job. I told you, I don't want anything to do with this. Whatever it is.'

'You must feel strongly about it,' Lydia said.

'Yeah, well...' Liam shrugged. 'I was going to leave, anyway. I couldn't stand it underground. Gave me the creeps.'

She felt a burst of empathy for Liam.

He dropped his cigarette and ground it out with one toe. His eyes met Lydia's for a second. 'Is it about the cash?'

'Not as far as I'm aware,' Lydia said evenly. She had stopped herself from saying 'what cash?'.

'I've spent it.' He was being defensive. 'And there's no paperwork. If they're after it, tell them I'll just say it was a bonus. A gift. They can't prove anything else.'

'All right,' Lydia nodded. 'I'll let them know there's no point trying to collect it.'

His shoulders relaxed a notch. 'Right. Good.'

She took a punt. 'The cash was for the ghost?'

'Stupid bloody idea. I mean, attendance has been down, but it's Winston bloody Churchill.' He had become truly animated for the first time in their conversation. Lydia didn't know if it was because she had managed to dial down her Crow whammy or whether he just really cared about Winston Churchill's legacy. 'You can't be running around with a sheet on your head. That's not what people want.'

'They asked you to...'

'Nah. Just a... Figure of speech type thing.' He waved a hand. 'We all had to say we'd seen the white lady. If you asked, I mean. I assumed they were working it up so that they could make it part of the official tour. Use you as a 'ghost authority' or whatever. I guess they could say it had been professionally investigated and that would be enough. Stupid bloody idea. It's embarrassing.' He caught her eye. 'No offense.'

'None taken.' Liam really did seem to care about the integrity of the bunker. 'Shame to leave the job, though,' she began, wondering if she should explain to him that it had all been a set-up, that the bunker had no intention of making it part of the exhibition. That Rebecca Collier would probably murder Sinclair before she allowed such a travesty.

'I'm going to uni,' he said, in a rush. Like it was a shameful secret. 'Doing history online. Don't say anything.'

Lydia had no idea who she would tell, but it absolutely wasn't what she had been expecting Liam to say. 'Good for you,' she managed. 'And thank you.' She fished a twenty from her pocket and handed it over. She didn't need to, she already had the information she had come for, but there was an undeniable lump of guilt in her stomach. Not only had Liam opened up to her because she had pushed Crow whammy behind her questions, but she had reached out and stopped his body. She had physically controlled him, whether she had intended to do so or not. Did a cash payment make magical coercion okay? Probably not, but what else could she do. Hell Hawk.

He pocketed the money. 'At some point you've gotta do what's in your heart, innit?'

CHAPTER EIGHTEEN

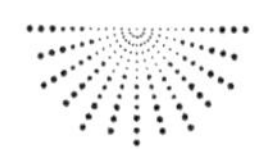

Lydia was glad she wasn't seeing Fleet that evening. She needed time to process what had happened. The way that Liam's eyes had widened in panic, the ease with which she had slipped inside his mind. She could sense his thoughts, not as anything she could describe in language, but a sense of his consciousness as a living thing. It was akin to when Jason hopped on board and she was aware of his presence in a more intimate and immediate way. But the difference was stark in one way. She could reach out Liam's arms as easily as her own. She hadn't even intended to do it. She had been frustrated that he was getting away and had thought 'stop running'. Liam's body had obeyed instantly. She hadn't meant to do it, but she had slipped under his surface and taken over the controls to his body. Which made her a monster. She shook her head, as if that would deny the truth. Not a monster. But with monstrous power.

Half a bottle of whisky later and Lydia was feeling a little better about the situation. She lay on the floor of the living room while Jason made a series of hot drinks, leaving them in a row on top of her desk. He stopped short of moving the whisky bottle away from her, but she could see he was concerned. 'I'm fine,' she said. 'I'm more than fine. Turns out Maddie left me her stuff.'

'In her will?' Jason frowned.

His face looked funny viewed from her angle on the floor and she almost laughed, letting out a small burp at the last moment. 'Excuse me.'

'Are you drunk? I don't think I've ever seen you drunk.'

'Sadly not,' Lydia said. She could feel the whisky warming and relaxing her but, as usual, it seemed to stop short of making the world fuzzy. It was annoying.

'Is it Fleet?' Jason sank to the floor, sitting cross-legged next to her head.

'Nope.' That wasn't entirely true. How could she tell him this? He accepted her, he accepted her magic and her criminal heritage, but this felt like another step along the path. A huge step.

'What then?'

She couldn't say it. A wave of nausea appeared from nowhere and she pushed herself from the floor. She made it to the bathroom in time to throw up in the sink. Rinsing the basin and then her mouth under the cold tap she knew the reason. She had been re-running the moment she took over Liam's free will, the moment she had made his limbs move just by thinking. She had been re-running it for the last few hours, trying to isolate the mechanism. If she could understand it, she could control it. Make sure it never happened by accident again. She could choose never to use it, never to be like Maddie or the Pearl King. Never be a monster.

She spat into the basin and swallowed some water before washing her face. Pressing the towel to dry her skin, the looped surface soft and comforting and her eyes closed, she let herself admit the truth. The thought that had sent the whisky on its return trip. She had felt powerful. She had liked it.

Paul took several rings to answer his phone and, when he did, he sounded distracted. There was background noise and Lydia assumed he was out somewhere. It was half past ten on a Thursday night and, she supposed, that's what other people did with their lives. Not everyone was working at their desk in their living room by the light of a single lamp.

'Just checking in. Have you heard anything about an anti-Crow campaign?'

'I'll call you if I get anything worth trading for.'

Lydia pinched the bridge of her nose. She had a headache forming. 'How long is this going to last?'

'What?'

'The big freeze.'

'I'm not in the mood for riddles. And not everything is about you. I told you, I'm distracted with other matters. And you made it clear that our relationship is purely business.'

'Is there anything I can do to help?' The words were out before she could stop them.

A short laugh. 'No.'

She tried a different tack. 'So, nothing to report? That's disappointing. I thought you could find out anything.'

'Transparent flattery doesn't work on Foxes. We invented that play.'

'Worth a try.' Lydia was about to hang up when something occurred to her. 'Can I add something else to my commission?'

'You can try.'

'Rafferty Hill.' Lydia didn't know how much of Fleet's terrible mood was related to his missing person case, but she thought that solving it might go some way to repairing relations. The pressure of dating a chief suspect couldn't be helping his stress levels.

'What about him?'

'He's a missing person. Suspected foul play. I'm taking an interest.'

'Makes sense.'

'You heard that I'm a suspect in the case?'

'I am aware.'

'So,' Lydia had started pacing the floor without realising it. She slowed, trying to calm her breathing. 'I will pay extra for any information you can provide. Anything that leads to...'

Paul interrupted her. 'That boy has been living it large. He's been seen in a couple of our more discreet venues.'

'Wait.' Lydia stopped walking. 'You've seen Rafferty Hill? The man who is all over the news for being missing, presumed dead?'

'I heard that the police were assuming it was a kidnapping situation.'

'And you didn't think to go and tell them that you'd seen the man in question alive and well and throwing shapes at Club Foxy?'

'No.'

'I don't get it, why wouldn't you-'

'Think for a second, Little Bird. Why would I go out of my way to help the police? And he's not at Club Foxy. He's been at the smaller dens. The exclusive places.'

Understanding dawned. 'You know that Fleet is heading the case. You're punishing him.'

'That's neither here nor there. There's never been a lot of love between my family and the law. We don't run around doing the police's jobs for them. Besides, someone wants to lose themselves at one of my clubs, it's not exactly good business to tell tales.'

Lydia could see his point. Part of the allure the exclusive clubs sold was anonymous oblivion. Places where everyone kept their mouths shut and their wallets open.

A sudden burst of thumping bass, let Lydia know that Paul was in one of his establishments at this moment. He must have gone outside or to one of the back rooms to take her call.

'I'm doing a walk through,' he said.

Lydia waited. She put the phone on the desk so that she wouldn't be deafened and listened to the sounds of music and raised voices. After a few minutes, they became muffled again. 'Yeah,' Paul drawled. 'He's here.'

'Rafferty Hill is in a club right now?'

'My club. Yeah.'

Lydia paused. 'You want to call the police or shall I do it?'

'I don't know why you care,' Paul said. 'Don't you have enough to deal with doing your own job and handling your own family? Why do you have to do Fleet's job, too? Is he not up to it?'

'I got a read off Rafferty,' Lydia said. 'I watched a clip of him being interviewed and I got a Pearl vibe. I'm a bit jumpy about that Family at the moment. I told you about the necklace...'

'From your jackdaw henchman, yeah. I remember.' A pause. 'You've really gone all in with your precious Fleet, haven't you? Head of the Crow Family, running to the police with information. It's not like this guy's murdered anyone. He's just a citizen enjoying a night out. It's not a crime. And this is supposed to be a free country.'

'People are worried about him. And the Police have it down as suspected murder. I'm a suspect in Mikhail's death and Mikhail has been linked to Rafferty. I don't like the way this is heading.'

Paul clicked his tongue against his teeth. 'What's your boyfriend doing about all this?'

Lydia ignored the jibe. 'Rafferty's family are deeply concerned. And he's going to lose a prestigious job if he doesn't come out of hiding and show up on set next week. You'll be doing him a favour by giving him a push.'

'It doesn't look good for my establishment if the boys in blue come bursting through the front door.'

Lydia thought for a moment. 'What if I came to get him? Quietly.'

'You're known around here,' Paul said. 'Giving the chief Crow a free pass won't go down well, either. Could incite a riot.'

He spoke with complete seriousness and Lydia felt a chill. 'Feathers.'

'I'll speak to him,' Paul said. 'Persuade him to give himself up voluntarily. He will walk into a station by midday tomorrow and reassure the police of his status as a non-murdered individual. Good enough?'

'Yes. Thank you.'

'Just trying to keep the peace,' Paul said, sounding tired. 'It's not for your benefit, Little Bird.'

'Got it.'

CHAPTER NINETEEN

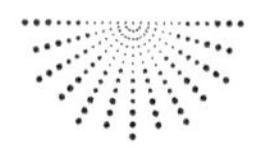

Lydia had fallen asleep in her desk chair again and she woke up before five, her neck screaming. The necklace from the jackdaw was sitting front and centre on her desk, although she could've sworn it had been buried by drifts of paperwork. She opened her top drawer and used a pencil to shove it inside. She wasn't going to be bullied by inanimate objects.

Jason walked in from his bedroom, his laptop tucked under one arm. He didn't just look more alive day-by-day, he acted that way, too. He was so sharp and clear that Lydia could see the fine lines around his eyes which deepened when he smiled and the heart-shaped mole which was just under his jaw. She had the impression that if she laid her head on his chest, she would hear his heart beating.

She rubbed a hand over her face and stretched her arms above her head. The muscles of her shoulders and neck complained but she told them to suck it up. The row of mugs was still in situ across her desk and she selected a herbal tea as being the least offensive to drink cold. She was rewarded with a pleased look from Jason. He probably thought his health advice was starting to land.

'You know Mikhail has an ex-girlfriend? Did you know he had a kid, too?'

Lydia spat the mouthful of orange blossom and lavender back into the mug, as discreetly as she could. 'I think I'd heard something about that.'

'They live in Camberwell. You know that, because I gave you the address.' The faintest whiff of reproach in his words.

'It's been hectic,' Lydia said. She straightened up, showing Jason her full attention. 'I'm listening.'

'I found her online. Thought I would poke about in her emails, just while I was waiting for you.'

Lydia nodded encouragingly. When Jason still seemed to be waiting for something else, she added a noise of approval.

Looking mollified, Jason perched on the edge of the desk. 'Well. She's in the process of looking for a flat. She's been emailing agents about viewings and I know she really liked the one she saw yesterday on Warner Road because she emailed the agency about it this morning.'

As ever, Jason's hacking skills were both impressive and scary. Lydia reminded herself again to never put anything in email she wouldn't mind being read by a random stranger.

Jason sighed, seemingly out of patience with Lydia's

slowness. 'It seems like she just came into some money. Enough for a deposit on buying a place, if she decides to go that way. She's been renting an absolute shithole on the border with Peckham and the places she's looking at are significantly nicer. My point is, where did the money come from?'

Lydia digested this. 'A pay out for Mikhail's death? The timing fits.'

'That's what I was thinking.'

'In payment for what? Scrawling me a message? Or implicating the Crows in his death? But why?'

'To make trouble for us?' Jason shrugged. 'That might be enough of a reason for some. And are we assuming Mikhail was poisoned?'

'I can't think of any other explanation. Apart from Family stuff.'

'Magical means?' Jason waggled his eyebrows.

'Got to be.' Lydia hadn't wanted to admit it, given that it didn't help her position as a person of interest, but it made the most sense. The only delayed-action poisons she knew involved plenty of vomit and diarrhoea and convulsions. They didn't leave a person feeling perfectly fine before killing them instantly and stiffening their body so that they remained seated. Mikhail had frozen in place.

'You said he looked peaceful when he died,' Jason said. 'That sounds super-creepy.'

'Yeah. It's another note against it being poison. Strychnine leaves the victim with a rictus grin, but you would never mistake it for peaceful happiness.'

'Maybe he just welcomed the end. We don't know

what was going on in his life, but I'm guessing there were some stresses there. I don't know many career criminals, but I'm guessing it's not a relaxing life. Did he work alone?'

'As far as we know.'

'And he'd been doing this for a while?'

Lydia's phone buzzed and she moved to check it. 'One sec,' she said to Jason. He nodded and moved to the sofa with his laptop. It was a message from Fleet. 'I have news. Can you meet me?'

Lydia had a pretty strong idea what Fleet was going to tell her, but she typed back anyway. 'Rafferty Hill?'

'Yes. He just walked in. Right as rain.'

Paul had come through on his promise.

LYDIA WASN'T GOING ANYWHERE NEAR Camberwell nick, but she agreed to meet Fleet a couple of streets away. She had barely parked the car when she saw him striding along the pavement. He wrenched open the passenger door and threw himself into the seat.

'Are you okay?' Lydia said. She had expected Fleet to be happy and relieved. Instead, it looked like something had seriously freaked him out.

He stared out of the windscreen, clearly not seeing anything. 'I had that dream, you remember?'

Fleet had dreamed that Rafferty Hill was alive. It seemed it had been another premonition. 'Of course.'

'And then he just walks into my station. Bold as brass.'

Lydia let her head fall back against the seat. 'That's good, though. He's alive.'

'Very alive.' Fleet turned to look at her. 'Obscenely alive and well. After the weeks of worry for his family, the hours of trouble, the manpower, the cost to the taxpayer. He just strolled in.'

Fleet was angrier than Lydia would have expected. 'What did he say?'

'Memory loss, apparently. He seems fully recovered, now. He has agreed to a health check as long as it doesn't take long.'

'That include a psychiatric assessment?'

'Just a light one,' Fleet said. 'Box ticking, really. We don't need to spend any more resources on the happy, healthy, financially solvent grown man.'

'You are angry,' Lydia said. She didn't add 'this isn't like you'. It seemed like Fleet needed to lash out at something. His job was stressful so it made sense that he would hit his limit at some point. She just hadn't seen him like this before. Fleet was usually supernaturally calm and sympathetic. She put a hand on his arm.

'He was just so... I don't know. There was something...' Fleet trailed off. He had resumed staring to the front and it looked like he wanted to smash the windscreen. 'And everyone else was just falling over him. I've never seen Lowry simper before and I hope I never see it, again.'

'I'd like to meet him,' Lydia said. 'Is that possible?'

He didn't look at her. 'Why? Let me guess... Because he's on TV.'

Again with the bitter tone. Fleet's gleam was

painfully bright and, was it her imagination, or was it a colder light than it used to be? 'No,' she said. 'Because I was helping to look for him. Because I questioned his flatmate. But mainly because he seems to have really pissed you off and I'm curious as to why. I've seen you after a day spent with a mass murderer and you weren't half as angry.'

Fleet turned to look at her. The lines on his forehead were deep, his brown eyes flat. 'What are you saying?'

'I don't know, that's the point.'

He stared for a few moments, not speaking. Finally, he drew a sharp breath in through his nose. 'Fine. He's at King's. I was going to let him make his own way from there, but I can spare a uniform to escort him home. You can tag along and talk to him on the way.'

'What does this mean for us?' She didn't like the pleading tone that had crept into her voice. She wanted Fleet to stop being weird and distant. She wanted to lean into him and tell him about what had happened with Liam, the way she had accidentally hijacked his body and his will. She wanted Fleet to tell her that everything was good and that she had nothing to worry about. That he wasn't going anywhere.

'The Rafferty Hill case is closed,' Fleet was looking out of the windscreen, his expression serious.

'That's not what I asked.'

'Mikhail's death is still unexplained. But there is nothing, save his message, that points to you. And that isn't conclusive. You're not the only Crow.'

'And yet...'

Fleet nodded. 'They really want to get you in for something. You need to be careful.'

'Is that an official warning?'

Fleet smiled sadly, finally looking at her. 'No. A friendly one.'

Lydia declined Fleet's offer to let her tag-along on Rafferty's lift home. She had no desire to deal with a copper and their probable hostility. Not to mention that she felt sure that the paparazzi would have got wind of Rafferty's return. There was a good chance that his exit from the hospital would be mobbed and Lydia had no interest in getting her picture snapped in conjunction with Rafferty Hill.

That night, Lydia waited until eleven o'clock and then went for her nightly run. It only took twenty minutes to run to Rafferty and Amber's flat past Burgess Park. She was definitely getting fitter which was one upside of the insomniac night-time running. There was a drizzle falling as she pounded up Old Kent Road. She slowed to a jog as she approached the address. There were solid rows of parked cars and Lydia saw at least one with an occupant. At the end of the street, she saw the glint of light on a camera lens and knew that there was another pap huddled under the porch of the small block of flats opposite Rafferty and Amber's building.

She paused, wondering whether it would matter if they photographed her going in. Deciding it wasn't ideal for her line of work to have her picture in the tabloids, she reached out her senses, finding the consciousness of the nearest pap as easily as spotting a candle flame in a dark room. There were the threads. She tugged experimentally, feeling herself slip inside the man's mind. He was tired. And he needed a piss. She suggested that he should go to sleep and, after a brief resistance, the light of his consciousness dimmed.

Walking closer to the converted school which housed Rafferty, she looked for the second photographer. It was easier this time, and she heard a dull thump as his prone body hit the floor. She hoped they were asleep and not unconscious.

Once inside she hammered on the flat's door. After a while, it opened on the chain. Amber's eyes widened when she recognised Lydia.

'Let me in,' Lydia said. It was late and she couldn't be bothered with the niceties so she pushed a little Crow behind her words. Amber froze. A prey animal's instinctive response.

'Now, please, Amber,' Lydia said, making her voice a little gentler. Amber was no good to her if she couldn't move. Although, she remembered an instant later that it wouldn't matter. She could move Amber's body for her. Luckily, she didn't have to test her own patience as Amber lifted the chain and stepped back to let Lydia inside.

The flat was a mess. The artwork that had been on the walls when Lydia had last seen the living room was now in a haphazard stack in one corner, and every surface was covered in empty wrappers, magazines, drifts of paper, and used crockery.

'Get Rafferty,' Lydia crossed to the sofa and then

changed her mind about sitting down. A half-full pizza box was open on top of a pile of its fallen brethren. 'And what happened here? Welcome home party?'

Amber opened her mouth and then closed it again without making a sound. Her eyes had gone strangely glazed.

Lydia didn't know what she had done to Amber, was worrying that her Crow whammy leaking out had somehow scrambled her brain, but then she was distracted by something else. A wave of sensations rolling through her body and mind. Her skin tingled and she felt warmth like the flush of desire. Beautiful music was just on the edge of hearing and she strained to capture it. She saw Amber's glazed expression, her lips parted as if caught in the moment of desperate longing and knew that her own face mirrored it. She snapped her lips shut, clenched her jaw. But still, her whole body was betraying her. It wanted. It had to have... Her head was filled with colour and warmth and desire, no room for ordered thought. She squeezed her coin and the room snapped back into sharp focus. The red fog of desire retreated a little, leaving her whole body empty and her nerves jangling.

And then Rafferty was there. In the room, his face impossibly handsome. Cheekbones that seemed sculpted from marble, bright eyes shining with intelligence, and the sort of hair that begged to be touched. Lydia caught herself two steps away from reaching for it. Her finger-tips itched with the urge to feel those silky strands, to touch, to feel, to own.

Rafferty Hill smiled, his gaze holding hers. In that

moment, Lydia would have done anything he ordered, given him anything he asked. Then, mercifully she tasted feathers on her tongue and felt the edges of her coin pressing into her palm. And she knew something very important. Rafferty Hill wasn't a descendent of the original Pearls. He was a full-blooded Pearl. Which was impossible.

CHAPTER TWENTY

'To what do I owe the pleasure?' Rafferty Hill was wearing black sports trousers and the waistcoat from a smart suit. His bare arms were pale and corded with blue veins. He was slim with defined muscles and, somehow, his unconventional outfit didn't look ridiculous.

'Just checking in on you. You gave us all quite the scare.'

Rafferty moved to a shelving unit which was made to look like it had been fashioned from packing crates and had probably cost more than Lydia's car. He picked up a bottle of whisky and tilted it to his mouth. Lydia was pulling on every reserve of her Crow power, but she still found the sight of his throat moving as he swallowed mesmerising.

He wiped his mouth and tilted the bottle in her direction.

Yes. Anything you want. Anything you say. 'No,' Lydia managed.

'Put some music on, darling,' Rafferty said to Amber.

'Don't,' Lydia said. Amber looked from one to the other, her head swivelling slowly and her mouth hanging slackly open.

'Interesting.' Rafferty paused. 'What are you, then?'

A Crow, Lydia said in her head. She managed not to obey him out loud, but only just.

Rafferty's gaze intensified as the silence lengthened. Eventually, he broke eye contact to tip some more whisky down his throat.

'Where have you been hiding out?'

'Not hiding,' Rafferty said, wiping his mouth with the back of his hand. 'Evolving.'

'What does that mean?'

'Six weeks ago I was reborn. I had been sleepwalking through my life and I woke up fresh and new. There was this,' Rafferty paused, looking uncertain for the first time. 'Electricity. Energy. I don't know, something running through me. Something that hadn't been there before.'

'It just appeared?'

He nodded. 'While I was sitting there. On the sofa with my hand on my balls.'

Lydia was beginning to have a thought. 'What time was this?'

'I don't know. Late-ish. Eleven, maybe? I was watching something. Can't even remember what. Everything from before is kind of grey.'

'Grey?'

'Not important.' More hand-waving. 'Washed out. Dull.'

'And everything after?'

He smiled dazzlingly. 'Technicolour dream coat, baby.'

Oh marvellous. Religious mania.

'Let me show you.' Rafferty spun on his heel and left the room.

Unsure whether she was making a huge mistake, Lydia followed. Before she could examine that thought, she found herself walking into Rafferty Hill's bedroom.

The bed was covered with drawings. Sheets torn from a large cartridge pad and spread out in an overlapping blanket of jagged black sketches, highlighted in places with bright colour. Marker pens were scattered over the bed and floor. 'It's come to me.'

Lydia didn't need to ask what.

'Creativity,' Rafferty said, gesturing around. 'True creativity. I thought I was on the right path as an actor, but I've realised I'm an artist. A real artist.'

EVERY INSTINCT THAT LYDIA POSSESSED WAS telling her to get far away from the Pearl. She was squeezing her coin tightly in one hand to stop her brain from flooding with X-rated thoughts of curling around Rafferty Hill and staying there until she died, happily. Through the advancing mental fog, she knew that she had to get Amber out of the flat and far enough away that she could make her own decisions. That glazed look in her eyes wasn't drugs, she was drunk on magic and, for once, it wasn't just Lydia's power that was at fault.

She left Rafferty in his bedroom with an act of sheer

willpower and, not trusting herself to hold on for much longer, grabbed Amber's arm as she passed through the open plan living room and dragged her toward the door. 'Let's go for a drink,' were the first words which jumped out.

Amber was stronger than she looked and she grabbed hold of the back of the enormous sofa, digging her heels in and leaning back to break Lydia's grip. 'I can't leave. He needs me.'

The threads of Amber's consciousness were there, Lydia could feel them. She stopped trying to physically pull Amber and closed her eyes, retreating to the dark world of power and instinct. The beating of wings and pulse of blood, the scrape of claw on bone. She followed those sensations until she could feel her own wings spreading wide, crowding out the fading impulse to run back to Rafferty. When she had a firm grasp on Amber and was no longer in danger of heading back to Rafferty's bedroom to bask in his magnificent presence, she opened her eyes. 'Come with me.'

Amber followed.

Outside on the street, the streetlights seemed brighter than before and the noise of the cars scraped her ears. She was momentarily disorientated, feeling as if she had to manually adjust to the new sensory input. Her shoulder blades itched, the muscles moving along her back with the desire to take flight.

'I don't...' Amber's speech was slurred, but she straightened up. She had been leaning heavily against

Lydia as they'd left the building and Lydia had been half-dragging, half-carrying her, thankful that she was a slight woman.

In the glare of a streetlight, Amber was blinking like a heavy sleeper awakening from a dream. The Pearl effect. 'It's you,' she said. The light from the streetlamps illuminated her drawn face. She wondered if Amber had remembered to eat or drink anything since Rafferty had reappeared.

'Yep.' Lydia led Amber down the street, away from the building. There was a parade of shops and take-aways, including a twenty-four-hour store which was proudly, and somewhat optimistically, called 'Best Supermarket'.

The further they got from the building, the more awake Amber appeared. She was shaking, though. Lydia hadn't thought to pick up a jacket, so she pulled Amber into the shop. The harsh lighting made Amber look even worse, but there was a heating unit blasting hot air and she put Amber in front of it while she bought water and chocolate.

The cashier was watching something on his phone and barely looked up. She decided to stay inside the almost-deserted shop to speak to Amber. Warmth seemed more important than privacy, if she was going to get any sense out of Amber.

She opened the water and passed it over. 'Drink.'

Amber did, her limbs moving slowly as if underwater.

While Amber drained the bottle, either her thirst kicking in or Lydia's Crow power lending weight to the instruction, Lydia tore open the chocolate bar. She swapped the empty bottle for the snack. 'Eat this, it'll help.'

As Amber mechanically worked through the chocolate, her eyes becoming steadily more alert, Lydia wondered what would happen when she went back to the flat. Would she remember to look after herself? To eat and drink and wash? Would Rafferty notice if she was starving to death and make sure she stayed alive? Lydia pushed her concern for Amber's welfare down. Before she could get distracted, she had to get answers.

'You weren't surprised to see a debt collector. When I came before. What trouble was Rafferty in? Drugs?'

Amber had ploughed through the chocolate and was rubbing her thin arms, while she chewed the last piece. Her growing awareness was accompanied by a wariness to her expression, the shutters coming down.

Lydia repeated the question, keeping her voice gentle and her stance relaxed.

'Not really,' Amber said, her voice thick. She swallowed and ran her tongue over her teeth. 'He had an open tab but he paid his bills on time.'

'And you were the go between for that side of things? Keeping him clean and protected?'

Amber glanced away, looking for a way out of the conversation. 'I got a cut.'

Lydia shifted so that her body was squarely between Amber and the exit. 'So why weren't you surprised? If he was so in control?'

'He'd started gambling.' Amber folded the chocolate wrapper, not meeting Lydia's gaze. 'I didn't know the half of it, apparently. Anyway, we'd had a couple of heavies round, threatening to break stuff.'

'Stuff?'

'For starters,' Amber grimaced. 'Raff told me it would be fine when he did his next job. It was a big pay out and he'd have more than enough to settle the debt.'

'Were they from a casino?'

'Nah. Some shithole club in Camberwell. I told him to stick to the legit places in future.'

'You didn't think about advising he got help? Addiction therapy?'

'You ever successfully advised an addict?'

It was a fair point.

Lydia unlocked her phone and showed Amber a picture of Mikhail. 'You seen this man hanging around?'

'Not hanging around. That's one of the men who came to break stuff.'

Mikhail wasn't a heavy, but it was possible he had done the job as a favour. Or because he needed the money. Fleet had said that he didn't have a fixed address, that his ex-girlfriend guessed he was sofa-surfing, that suggested he might be desperate for cash. Maybe he was taking any jobs that paid.

'How worried was Rafferty? I can imagine the threatening letters wouldn't have helped his state of mind.'

'He didn't even see them,' Amber said. 'I opened them and burned them first. All except the last one. He was missing by then and I had a feeling I should hang onto it. Evidence.'

'Why didn't you tell the police he hadn't even seen them?'

'I wanted them to search for him, not sit back like he was off on a cruise somewhere. I was worried about Raff.' Amber straightened, her body swivelling unconsciously in the direction of home. 'I should go. He might need something.'

She shoved past Lydia with more speed and strength than Lydia had expected, leaving her to follow a step behind. Out on the street, Amber was fast-walking back toward her building.

'You don't have to stay there,' Lydia said, walking with her. 'I can help you find somewhere else to live.'

Amber stopped moving as if stunned by the proposition. Her eyes, when she looked at Lydia, were bright and her cheeks were flushed red against her pale skin. 'Why would I want to live anywhere else?'

Lydia passed Amber her card. 'Call me if you need anything. If you decide you want to leave. I'll help you.'

Amber shoved it into her pocket, but was already turning away, her feet carrying her back to her beloved Rafferty.

WALKING BACK FROM RAFFERTY HILL'S FLAT, LYDIA tried not to think too hard. She wanted to be blank, just for a few peaceful minutes.

Jason passed her a hot chocolate minutes after she arrived home. 'You look worried.'

Lydia opened her mouth to deny it, but then changed her mind. She told Jason about Rafferty Hill and his strange transformation. The influx of Pearl mojo that had transformed him from hotshot young actor with a sprinkling of inherited glamour, to full-strength Pearl, with all the attendant power and sway that conferred. Question was, what did that mean? What was Rafferty going to do?

'You think it's your fault?'

Lydia nodded at Jason. 'I think the Pearl court energy went into Rafferty. It had all been caged underground and I opened the door.'

'And turned him from a pretentious actor into a pretentious artist.'

'We don't know if he was pretentious before, to be fair.'

Jason briskly began measuring flour into a bowl. 'I'm making you pancakes.'

'I'm okay,' Lydia said. 'You don't need to feed me.'

'I have a query,' Jason cracked an egg into the flour. 'Was it just Rafferty that got the Pearl mojo? Are there other Pearls having life-changing epiphanies? I mean, we only know about Rafferty because he went walkabout.'

'And we only really know about that because he's famous. Most missing adults don't get the same kind of police attention.'

Jason added milk and began whisking the batter. Lydia got the frying pan she had stolen from the cafe kitchen out from its hiding place.

'I think it's a good thing,' Jason said. 'I mean, physics says energy can't be destroyed, right? It can only be transformed. Kinetic into heat and all that.'

Lydia's physics knowledge was hazy at best. 'I'll take your word for it.'

'Well, you couldn't stop that from happening. And if it's been transformed from an evil person-snatching king to an art-loving actor, that's a good result, right? One shady court of immortal bastards transformed into a sprinkling of arty-crafty types waking up with new talent or charisma or whatever. Doesn't get better, really.'

Lydia watched Jason pour batter into the pan and swirl it with a practised, professional tilt of his wrist. She wanted to believe him. She wanted this to be a sign of the peaceful and harmless dissipation of the Pearl power. There had been something about Rafferty, though. Something horribly familiar. He hadn't spoken to her like she was a new acolyte ready to worship at the altar of his artistic talent and oh-so-hotness. He had spoken to her like she was a subject. And he was royalty.

CHAPTER TWENTY-ONE

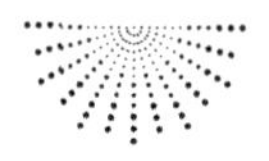

It crossed Lydia's mind that she ought to warn Maria Silver and Paul Fox about Rafferty Hill. But she hated the former and was irrationally annoyed with the latter, so she shelved the thought for a later date. Besides, she had something more important to deal with at that moment.

She had texted Fleet and her phone buzzed with his reply. He could spare a half hour for his lunch break and she was welcome to join him. Sitting on a bench in Ruskin Park with the flowerbeds in bloom, deckchairs arranged around the bandstand and the Shard and the Gherkin in the distance framed against a bright blue sky, it almost felt like a pleasant picnic. Fleet's shoulders were hunched with tension, though.

She unwrapped her cheese and ham toastie and popped the ring on her can of cola. Fleet swigged from his water bottle and opened the lid of a Tupperware filled with salad. The man's body was a temple.

They had been a little out of step and Lydia decided

that she was going to be a grown up and lay it all out. Communication was the key to a healthy relationship, according to Emma, and she would know. Between bites of lunch, Lydia told him about what had happened with Liam and the strong Pearl vibe she had got from Rafferty.

As they talked it over, she could feel the old ease growing and her sense of wellbeing along with it. 'I can't believe I did that,' she said. 'To Liam. I mean, I didn't *mean* to do it, but still. It's like with that man. Felix. I didn't intend to kill him, but that doesn't...'

Fleet put an arm around Lydia and pulled her close. 'It's not your fault. And that was self defence.' He spoke into her hair. 'It's going to be okay. You'll learn to control it. It's just something new. And it's good that you're stronger. I want you to be as safe as possible.'

A knot loosened in Lydia's stomach. She wrapped both arms around Fleet, enjoying holding him and being held on a beautiful warm day in the city she loved.

After a few minutes, they disentangled in order to finish eating. Fleet was definitely more relaxed, so she risked asking about his reaction to Rafferty, the unusual anger.

Fleet drank some more water and tilted his face to the sun. He seemed to be deliberating his words. Finally, he said 'It bothers me that he just showed up.'

'I could see that.'

Fleet ducked his head, looking embarrassed. 'It was... I dreamed you were with Paul Fox.'

'I wasn't.'

'It was very real. Like my premonitions.'

Lydia smiled, trying to make light of it. 'So you believe in those, now? When they're showing you something that makes you jealous, that's when you decide they are sacred truth.'

'That's not it... I'm just saying.'

'You've got nothing to worry about. I love you.' *I killed my own cousin to protect you.*

'I love you, too,' Fleet said. He rested his forehead against hers, putting one hand on the back of her head. 'I'm sorry. I'm all over the place at the moment. I'm... Out of it half the time. Don't know what I'm thinking.'

'What's going on? You can talk to me.'

He sat back, shaking his head. 'I'm just not sleeping well. Tired.' His lips turned up at the corners but it was a faded version of his usual sunlight smile.

Lydia had a sudden, visceral understanding of how hard it must be to be in a relationship with her. Of how Fleet must have felt every time she had evaded his questions, hidden parts of herself and her life. If this was karma, then it truly was a bitch.

'I'm in this for every part. Everything. I know you don't want to talk about Sinclair or your father and I'm not pushing, but it might help.'

Fleet clicked the lid on his lunch. 'I'd better head back. Paperwork waits for no man.'

Lydia wanted to stop him, but she had an appointment back at her flat. One she couldn't miss.

THE WOMAN WITH A SHAVED HEAD CROUCHED IN front of Lydia's bookcase was apparently the best tattooist in the city. Or the only one that the Crows of Camberwell would use, at any rate. Tor, also known as The Artist, certainly had more ink over her skin that any human being Lydia had ever seen in real life. 'I love this,' Tor pointed to a book, her finger not touching the spine. Whether out of respect for Lydia or for literature, Lydia couldn't tell.

'I have a meeting at five.' Lydia didn't want to be rude, but her schedule for the next few days was completely packed. Aiden had done a good job rooting out those who were feeling disloyal, as well as outside interests who were looking to make some easy cash or score some rep points. So many ruffled feathers that needed smoothing, so many smooth feathers that needed to be plucked.

Tor straightened up and looked Lydia in the eye. 'You'll have to cancel that.'

It was probably good for her to interact with people who weren't cowed by her position and reputation, but it was also annoying.

The tattooist must have seen something in Lydia's expression, because she added: 'I just mean you'll be tired after. Really tired. Like, you'll kind of pass out.'

'I have a very high pain threshold,' Lydia said. She shrugged out of her hoodie.

'It's not a question of pain.'

Tor had arrived with an impressive-looking aluminium case. She abandoned the bookcase, now, and crawled over to open it. The tools of her trade were held reverentially in moulded foam and Lydia lay down on the sofa, using her right arm and folded hoodie as a pillow.

Tor took her left arm, the one which had been broken, and laid it onto a cushion. 'It's easier if I show you.' After swabbing down Lydia's skin, she picked up her gun. It was cylindrical and wireless. The kind which cost over a grand. And Lydia had seen at least five in the case. She wondered if Tor worried about her stuff getting nicked when she paid house calls and then she didn't think anything else because the needle was biting into the skin of her forearm. Her mouth flooded with saliva and a shudder of nausea chased through her body. It wasn't pain, exactly, but there was something else. Something plucking at her power, or to the unnamed place it came from and stitching it with white hot stabs. Okay, so it was pain. Her vision cleared and she saw Tor holding the tattoo gun clear and regarding her with a serious expression. 'It'll get worse.'

'Carry on,' Lydia said. She closed her eyes and concentrated on breathing steadily. Black wings flapped and the thousands of tiny heartbeats which were, now, just a blink away, filled her. She could feel cool air and sunshine on her feathers, see the curve of the earth below. Then she was on the ground, something warm caught between her talons. Something was tearing at her wing but she tore at the small thing she had caught. Blood and flesh in her beak. Hunger satisfied.

When she came back to herself it was dark. The curtains were open and the streetlights glowed orange through the windows. Her arm was on fire and she almost didn't want to look. It would be a charred mess, surely. There was no other possibility, judging from the level of heat and pain. She had never felt anything like it. When she forced herself to look, she discovered that her arm was covered in a clear bandage, but otherwise intact. There was no sign of Tor or her suitcase of torture. Just an envelope which Lydia assumed contained her invoice.

The proximity alarm sounded and then the main door to the flat opened. It had to be Fleet or Aiden as they were the only people with a key, but she didn't have to reach out her senses to find out which. The sunshine gleam was flooding her eyesight even before he passed through the hallway and into the main room. She closed her eyes against the light.

'Holy shit,' Fleet said.

'You like?' Lydia didn't open her eyes. Since when did Fleet's gleam hurt?

'I don't know... I don't know what to say.'

Cautiously Lydia cracked her eyelids. Fleet was looming above her, his expression stricken.

'It's just some ink,' she said, forcing herself to look at her arm. The clear bandage was clogged with blood, but through the mess Lydia could see that Tor had done a good job. The crow was in flight, just the way she wanted and, more than that, Lydia could feel its joy as she looked at it. She could smell the ozone and feel the wild freedom of flight. And there were the three black feathers falling down toward her wrist, each one burning as if they went all the way through to her just-healed bone. One feather for each life she had taken.

'Why?'

'To remember,' Lydia said. She had killed Felix by accident. The regret she had felt for that had been short-lived and had been almost entirely focused on her loss of control. Felix had been a professional killer and she had been defending herself and Fleet. The second was for Maddie. Her blood kin. Her cousin. Yes, Maddie had also been a psychopathic assassin, and she had acted out of good intentions, to protect those she loved, but she had acted with, as Fleet would write in a report 'with malice and aforethought'. No accident. She had planned to kill Maddie. The third feather was for Ash. And the others who had died on her watch. Not murders. Not by her hands directly, but deaths she felt a responsibility for. Ash, Yas Bishop. Even Mr Smith. Gale. It might have been the Pearl King who had snapped his neck like it was a Twiglet, but Maddie had been right about his death. Lydia had walked him into that underground court and hadn't intended for him to walk out again. Now that she had inherited Maddie's power, added it to her own, she felt it was more important not to lie to herself. And she was done lying to the world, too.

Fleet was shaking his head, like he was trying to deny the evidence of his eyes. 'Remember what?'

'Who I am.'

He swallowed hard. 'It's like...' He trailed off.

Charlie. She realised he had been going to say it was like Charlie.

Fleet met her gaze. 'Is this because of what happened with that guy. Liam?'

'It's because of everything. I'm not turning into Charlie, but I thought this might help me control my new abilities. And they send a signal.' She had to project strength.

He nodded, still looking faintly nauseous. 'I understand.'

Fleet went and fetched her a glass of water and planted a cautious kiss on her forehead. 'I'll leave you to rest, if you want?'

Lydia felt a stab of relief. 'I'm not going to be good company tonight.' She didn't want to tell him that his gleam was hurting her.

Fleet left after that and Lydia just felt a sense of relief that he had taken his painful gleam away. She didn't just feel as if her arm was on fire, her whole body was burning up. She stumbled to the bathroom, feverish and sweaty and took a couple of paracetamol. She fell asleep again, and when she woke up it was late and her stomach was rumbling.

She swallowed some more pain killers and checked her food supplies. They were woefully inadequate, which wasn't exactly a shock. She headed down to The Fork to raid the kitchen, but found Angel sitting at one of the middle tables.

The cafe was shut, and Angel would usually have left by this time. It occurred to Lydia that Angel must have been waiting for her, not realising that she was asleep upstairs. Angel would usually leave her a note or call her mobile. That she needed a face-to-face meeting didn't bode well. Lydia prepared herself for a wage increase or staffing request. Or, given her current run of luck, the news that Angel's beloved eight-ring burner was haunted.

'Everything all right?' Lydia said, crossing to the table and sitting opposite. Her arm felt significantly better than earlier, but it was still tender through to the bone.

'I need help,' Angel said. She had taken off her apron and hairnet and was sitting very straight in her chair. 'You know Nat left?'

Lydia nodded. She was slightly ashamed that she hadn't given the matter much thought. It had been busy and she and Angel weren't exactly close, but still.

Angel's hands were tightly clasped on the table. 'I didn't tell you why. I've been getting threats. I mean, I was getting threats. That was the problem.'

It took Lydia a beat to process her words. 'What?'

'To the house. Posted through the door. It freaked Nat right out. That's why she took off to stay with her mum. I thought it would blow over. She'd calm down, her mum would drive her batty and she'd come back. But she hasn't. Says I have to speak to you and get it sorted.'

Hell Hawk. 'She's right. You should have told me about this earlier.'

Angel's eyes widened slightly.

Lydia forced her expression to soften. She reached out to pat Angel's clasped hands, but withdrew at the last moment. They didn't have that kind of relationship. 'I'm sorry. Tell me about the threats.'

Angel leaned down and retrieved a squashy leather tote bag from the floor. Inside were several letters. Notes, really. Block capital letters on torn lined paper, each detailing in short and guttural sentences what was going to happen to Angel's wife if Angel didn't stop working for The Crow.

Lydia stared at the black letters and then up at Angel. 'Why didn't you tell me?'

Angel shook her head very slightly. 'I worked for Charlie for years before you took over. This isn't my first... Experience.'

'And what did Charlie do?'

Angel held her gaze, but didn't answer.

Feathers.

'So you thought you'd wait them out?'

'I was waiting to see if it was serious. People say shit. It's mostly just piss and vinegar. I'm a curvy bisexual multi-ethnic woman. If I jumped every time someone threatened me, I could be in the Olympics.'

Lydia paused. 'But this was enough for Nat to hide. To leave.'

Angel's eyes flashed with anger. 'Which is why I'm talking to you now. She says she won't come back unless you know about it. Unless you do something.'

'I'm going to sort this.' Lydia was holding the note, still. Something was tickling at the back of her mind. 'Is this all of them? The notes?'

'No, I burned a couple. They said the same stuff.

About how I was a traitor and I had to stop working for the Crow blah blah.'

'A traitor to who? To what?'

Angel shrugged. 'No fucking clue. They never said.'

So far, so generic. The only specific part of the letters was 'stop working for The Crow', otherwise the letters could have been copied from The Ladybird Book of Intimidation. 'They were shoved through your letter-box, right? You have a main front door?'

'Yeah.'

'When did the last one arrive?'

'A week ago.'

'What day?'

'Wednesday night, I think. I found it on the mat the next morning and that's when I had that little mishap in the kitchen. I had hoped they were just going to stop and was going to tell Nat that there hadn't been any for nearly two weeks and she could come home and then that bloody one arrived and that's why I burned the hash browns.'

Lydia was only half-listening. The paper looked like the stuff that was used in the note left for Rafferty Hill, as did the handwriting. It was block capitals, but there was a preciseness to the penmanship. And the last letter had been delivered the night before Mik the Jekyll had been taken into custody.

CHAPTER TWENTY-TWO

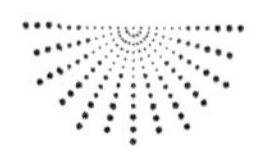

Tower Hill isn't named for the famous prison, but for the hill on which people were executed. The last man killed at the Tower of London was a German spy. He was probably forced to provide information as part of a deal which kept him out of prison or from being killed, but he died for his crimes, anyway. The British didn't care about his motives or whether he had been coerced. They only cared about his actions. Lydia flipped her coin and let it hang in the air, rotating slowly. Actions mattered. Not legality. Not intentions. She had deaths on her conscience and though not all of them were by her hand, they were a consequence of her actions.

If she allowed illegal betting and someone got into more trouble than they could handle, it wouldn't end there. An illegal debt would be collected in an illegal way. And before she knew it, the Crows were back to knee-capping and worse. Dumping bodies in the water in the dead of night.

Lydia's head hurt. There was no way out. She couldn't do no harm, so she was left trying to do the least damage possible. Did that mean she should step down? But there was no guarantee that whoever took over would do a better job. Uncle John was set in the old ways and he hated Lydia. That meant he would be motivated to remove any truces she had struck, any gains she had made. Not because he disagreed with them, necessarily, but because they were her legacy. Aiden wasn't a bad man, but he was young and easily led and had spent many years looking up to Charlie. Plus, Aiden was a good soldier but he wasn't the smartest or the most strategic thinker. When faced with a problem, he would take the shortest route through. That meant violence.

Aiden was slouched in the chair she used for clients, keeping quiet while she thought. She straightened up, putting her feet on the floor. 'Tell me you've got something.'

He passed a hand across his face. 'It's the Brixton Mob. They painted the wall of the pub. I don't know how they are linked to Mikhail, that part doesn't make any sense.'

'Okay. Why is the Brixton Mob coming for us? Because we're pushing back on the gambling?'

'That. And some old business. A vendetta against Charlie.'

Lydia rolled her eyes. 'If they can find him, they should feel free to have a go.'

'This is serious,' Aiden said. 'Charlie killed their father and they're after Crow blood to settle the score. Yours, specifically.'

Lydia leaned back in her desk chair and contemplated the ceiling for a few moments. The stained white paintwork didn't offer any answers, but it did give her space to digest Aiden's words. She had put Charlie away in a box and locked that lid tight, but he was still causing trouble. Even if she threw him off a roof, his legacy would endure. Too many years doing too many bad things and all of those problems coming home to roost. To her home, specifically.

'Boss?'

Aiden had been speaking, she realised. 'I know,' she said, automatically. 'So, they want blood, but at the moment they're splashing red paint around Camberwell establishments?'

'They're calling us out. I don't think they really expect to incite action, but it's cheeky. Public. Makes it impossible for us not to respond.'

'I agree.'

He looked relieved. 'You'll authorise direct action?'

There was no good outcome. No way for her to carry on without spilling some blood. If she didn't step up, innocent people would get hurt. And Crows. 'Arrange a sit down. I'll meet with them.'

Aiden's relief was replaced with fear. 'You can't do that. They'll kill you.'

'I don't think so,' Lydia said. 'And don't tell me what I can't do.' She spoke mildly but Aiden flinched.

. . .

Lydia was just getting ready for the meeting when Fleet called. He sounded upset. 'Where are you going?'

'Right now?' Lydia said, playing for time. 'Why?'

'I saw something.'

'A premonition? I thought you didn't believe in those.'

'I don't,' Fleet's usually calm tone was panicked. 'I don't. But I saw you in a hotel. A nice one, I don't know it. There were a lot of guns.'

'I'm just settling down with Jason. We're having a film night. Maybe you caught a glimpse of Casino. We're starting with that. Have you seen it? Sharon Stone is a revelation.'

Lydia had the restaurant of the Ruskin Hotel cleared and was sitting with her back to the wall in the largest booth in the room. She had wanted to use The Fork, but needed to give the appearance of neutral ground. Oscar, the leader of the Brixton Mob, wasn't to know that she had taken a chunk of money from the Crow accounts to buy a controlling share of the hotel. If the Brixton boys wanted to continue running their poker games out of the hotel, they were going to have to pay a cut to the Crows.

Aiden opened the door and five men streamed in. They were all carrying concealed weapons or moving as if they were. Lydia was neither impressed nor concerned by their display. There were three Crows visible and another five hidden in the restaurant kitchen. Besides, she knew she could sew up the mouths and steal the muscles of any man there without moving from her chair.

She gestured to the chair set opposite her. 'Drink?'

'Not with you,' Oscar said, but he sat down.

Lydia held his gaze. His pale blue eyes weren't giving anything away. Eventually she asked. 'What about your colleagues? They look hungry. Famished, in fact.'

'We're here to talk terms.'

'Very wise. We killed your...' She pretended to forget. 'Father, was it?'

One of the men standing on either side of Oscar shifted his weight. His right hand had begun to drift up as if he was going to reach for his weapon but he stopped himself in time. It confirmed for Lydia what she suspected. The Brixton crew were not here to play nicely. 'So you went for one of ours. I gather that didn't work out so well. Forgive me,' she spread her hands. 'I'm getting all the details second-hand. I've been very busy.'

'We want to settle things,' Oscar said stiffly. 'Stop it escalating.'

Lydia nodded. 'Escalation is bad for business. You take a single feather, I break both your arms. That kind of thing. Gets nasty very quickly.'

'On both sides,' Oscar said with heavy emphasis. '

'Your dad is dead, and your foot soldier, and now you are here, sitting in my restaurant and refusing to take a drink.'

'You shouldn't be so sure of yourself,' Oscar said and reached for the gun or knife or Kalashnikov or whatever he was hiding in his coat and was giving him the balls to challenge a Crow in her own roost. His expression froze as he realised he couldn't move. Lydia could understand why Maddie had always been so bloody cocky. Knowing that she could snip the strings which connected body to brain, knowing that she didn't have to listen to a single second more of this petty thug's posturing. It was a blessed relief. A little bit of hush whenever she wanted it.

The man's eyes were bulging and his cheeks puffed as he tried to speak. Lydia hoped he could still breathe, but she felt a chill over her mind which didn't seem to care that much one way of the other. 'Charlie Crow killed your father. It was a long time ago but you've been nursing that grudge and letting it fester and grow. I don't blame you for that. I don't even blame you for wanting revenge, even though you know that if Charlie Crow came for your dad, there was probably a reason. Maybe not a good reason, but dear old papa wasn't a civilian. Wasn't an innocent. The way I heard the story, your daddy had a few nasty predilections of his own and wasn't keeping to much of a code. Not a code I recognise anyway.'

She paused, took a sip of her whisky. 'But you feel you've got to save face. To be seen to want revenge. Or maybe you really loved him and this goes deep for you. Either way, the outcome is the same. You die. Your colleagues die. We take whatever piss-poor little operation you are running.' Another beat. 'You have a moment. Right now. An opportunity to change the story.'

Lydia reached into her pocket and withdrew a bundle of cash. She put it on the table between them. 'You work for me. You can keep your gang name and run your streets, but you pay the Crows ten per cent for the privilege. And if we call, you come running. As employees, you are entitled to financial reparation for the loss of your soldier.' Lydia tapped the money with one finger.

She released the hold she had on the man from the shoulders upward. 'What do you say?'

He took in a loud and ragged breath as if he hadn't had enough oxygen and licked his lips. His eyes went from the bundle of notes to Lydia's face. 'Yes.'

'I'm sorry, I didn't quite catch that.'

The man was like a shrew scurrying for cover. Prey. Lydia felt the power running through her, could hear a thousand wings, a thousand hearts beating. There was blood on her tongue and the urge to swoop down, claws open.

His gaze was stuck to the table, the words dragged from him with obvious pain. 'I agree.'

'Good. Now tell me something... Why now? This thing with Charlie, it's from back in the day. Why not pursue it then? You can see Charlie isn't here,' Lydia spread her hands.

His eyes widened.

Lydia leaned in close. 'Just between us. Did I do something to hurt your feelings?'

'I didn't know before,' he said, quietly. 'Got a tip.'

She released his body, and he slumped a little before catching himself and straightening up.

'Who from?'

Oscar swallowed.

'I can make you tell me.'

'A note. Hand delivered by a kid. They said a woman paid them twenty quid to do it.'

'Do you still have it?'

He shook his head. 'It used details that made me believe... It had information that proved it was legit.'

'Who was the note from?'

Oscar's expression twisted for a second. 'I don't know why he decided to come clean, now, after all these years, but it was signed by Charlie Crow.'

Lydia nodded, keeping her expression neutral.

His hand was reaching for the cash when Lydia said, 'One last thing.'

His hand stilled.

'No civilians. And no children.'

After a beat, he nodded.

'Now get out.'

After the men had filed away and the Crows were in the kitchen, warming up food from the freezer and having a celebratory drink, Aiden sat down in the chair vacated by Oscar. He poured Lydia another whisky and one for himself. 'I thought you wanted us to go legit?'

'And, as you pointed out on more than one occasion, that was never going to work.' Lydia lifted her glass in a silent toast. 'Not without casualties. Not without a struggle.'

Aiden opened his mouth to argue but Lydia kept

going. 'Look, whatever party trick I can pull out in front of the locals, we're not strong enough for a struggle. We're not fighting fit. We don't have the numbers.'

'Yeah, but... Gang stuff. I mean, that's...'

Lydia looked Aiden in the eye. 'You killed one of them. Someone, maybe even Charlie himself, told them that Charlie killed a key player back in the day. What was I supposed to do?' The possibility that Charlie had got a note to the head of the Brixton Mob was a disturbing one. How would he manage such a thing? And why?

Aiden looked down at his drink.

'Besides. This way, news will get around. You come for us, you die. You join us, you live.'

Having placated her Family and calmed a potentially lethal situation with one of the biggest gangs in South London, Lydia was feeling pretty pleased. Fleet was waiting outside The Fork, his shoulders hunched.

The relief on his face as she got out of her car was instantly replaced with fury. 'Film night? Jesus, Lyds.'

'Don't start,' Lydia said, moving toward the entrance.

Fleet's hand on her arm stopped her cold. She turned to face him.

'Guns. We had reports of armed men entering the Ruskin Hotel about an hour ago. Anything you want to tell me?'

'I don't know,' Lydia said, looking at Fleet's hand on her arm pointedly.

He moved his hand, shoving both into the pockets of

his coat. 'When did you start lying to me? What is going on with you?'

'Are you still DCI Fleet, proud member of the Metropolitan Police?'

He nodded. Sharp and angry. 'We're past this. You know I'm on your side... You know I choose you. You can tell me anything, you know that-'

'Are you going to tell me where you went? Who you met? What deals you've made with Sinclair?' It was on the tip of her tongue to ask him whether Sinclair ever spoke about Charlie.

Fleet's expression closed down.

The silence stretched between them for a minute.

'I thought so,' Lydia said, and turned to The Fork.

She didn't watch as Fleet walked away.

CHAPTER TWENTY-THREE

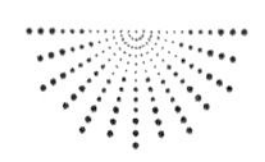

Lydia woke up the next morning and peeled away the bandage from her arm. The skin was tight and itchy, but the burning sensation had subsided. Tor had warned her that the tattoos would look fuzzy until the healing process was complete, but the black shapes had crisp edges and she could see every filament of the feathers. Was it her imagination or had the crow's wings moved slightly? The skin around the ink was red and felt like she'd been out in the sun for too long. She washed her hands and applied the healing gel Tor had left, waiting for it to dry before she pulled on a t-shirt and jeans.

Her phone sat on the duvet, silent. While Lydia hadn't expected Fleet to be in touch, she had hoped. She picked up the device and unlocked it, just to check. Nothing. She didn't know how to breach this new gulf between them. She had to lead her Family. She had to be the new Charlie in deed as well as name. Fleet had said that he understood that, but being faced with the realities was clearly more of a challenge. She would give him time. And maybe clear up the mystery of Mikhail's death while she waited. If she could exonerate herself, even if only privately to Fleet, that could only help.

So, why had Mikhail been sending threatening letters to Angel? Assuming that it wasn't a coincidence that the letters had been arriving while Mikhail was active? He had worked for the Crows in the past and, as far as Aiden had been able to find out, there was no bad blood between them.

She called Aiden. After he had assured her that all was quiet and there were no fires that required her urgent attention, she asked about Mikhail. 'What did people say about him?'

'He was the best for cracking cribs. If you needed somewhere turned over, he was your man. Built like a brick shit-house, but not violent. Looked good and intimidating but don't ask him to do any actual work in that area.'

'All good between us? No reason why he would be sending threatening letters?'

'Letters?' Aiden shook his head. 'That's definitely not Mikhail. Word around is that he wasn't London's greatest thinker. I'm not even sure he *could* write. And he had a real one-track mind, you know?'

Lydia shook her head, waiting for Aiden to spin a tale of womanising or drinking.

'If Mik wanted to get back at you, he'd nick something. That was his thing. His go-to move, you know? Or he'd show you photos of his kid. Apparently he could talk about his kid for hours. Stu said he was stuck on a job with Mik once and he nearly killed him just to shut him up.'

LYDIA WENT FOR A RUN. SHE NEEDED TO THINK. As she pounded the paths of Burgess Park, she pictured Mikhail. The faithful soldier. He had been chatty about his kid. Proud of his son. On good terms with his ex-girlfriend, despite a rocky family history of his own. Despite being an adult-size criminal, working for the Crows, since he was barely thirteen. The anger at Charlie flared again. Mikhail had been *a child*.

What else? He wasn't known for big thoughts, strategic thinking, or being especially literate. Aiden said he wasn't sure if the man could write. That could be hyperbole or people talking shit about Mik, but that didn't mean there wasn't a grain of truth. The man wasn't considered a scholar or a leader, that was certain.

What was he considered? An excellent housebreaker. A skilled lock-picker. Good at following orders. A dependable employee of the Crow criminal empire. There was no reason for him to start sending threatening letters of his own volition. Not to Rafferty Hill and certainly not to Angel.

So who had given him the orders to do so?

. . .

Lydia didn't expect Mik the Jekyll's ex-missus would be too keen to open the door to a random investigator and she couldn't afford to add 'impersonating a police officer' to her list of crimes. Not now that she knew the full extent of the ongoing Crow enterprise. She had accepted that she was the head of a still-quite-dodgy organisation and that meant keeping her nose as clean as possible. After all, they eventually picked up Al Capone for tax evasion. A good lesson for crime bosses through the ages.

Lydia also knew that the way her Crow mojo seemed to be continually streaming, whether she wanted it to or not, the poor woman was likely to do as she was told. She felt that approaching her in a public place would be less coercive and frightening than strolling into the woman's home. And she wanted to make sure the kid wasn't anywhere near. She couldn't claim to do no harm, not anymore, but she was going to do her best to keep the cuts shallow.

Fleet had passed on the information that Mikhail's kid went to Camberwell Grove Primary just off Peckham Road. His ex-girlfriend, Stacie, was renting a second-floor flat in an uninspiring building only two streets away. Lydia was standing at the corner, pretending to speak on her phone at quarter past two. At twenty to three, Lydia watched Stacie leave the main front door and head toward the school. Lydia slipped her phone into her pocket and followed a few paces behind.

Lydia knew they were close to the school when she saw an orderly line of parents on the pavement ahead, waiting for the gate to be unlocked. The road was chock-a-block with parked cars, with more parents waiting inside. Stacie had been moving at a good clip, but she slowed down as they got closer. Lydia touched her shoulder when they were still several paces behind the queue of parents. She didn't want to give her a chance to meet a school-run friend and start chatting. 'Stacie?'

'Yes?' Stacie turned around. She was prettier than Lydia had expected. No, that wasn't quite right. The woman was more beautiful than anybody would expect to see in a purple hoodie and jogging bottoms on a drizzly Thursday afternoon in Camberwell. Her face belonged to a Greek goddess and Lydia could suddenly understand why Mikhail would kill himself in order to leave her with a payday. It was the kind of beauty that was a power all of its own. The kind that could launch a career. Or ruin a life.

'Are you all right?' Her accent was pure south London, but her tone was gentle. The goddess was, quite possibly, a nice person to boot. The best thing that had ever happened to Mik the Jekyll, that was for certain.

'I need a quick word. About Mikhail.'

Stacie was carrying a scooter with one hand, the back wheels rolling on the pavement, and it clunked down as her whole body sagged. Her glossy dark hair hung around her face in curtains, not quite hiding her radiant looks.

'It's nothing bad,' Lydia said quickly, feeling awful. The face visible between the locks of hair was wary and resigned all at once. Like the bad things had just kept coming and she knew they would never stop. Her shoulders were rounded, like she was trying to disappear into herself. It made Lydia want to protect her. To spread her wings wide and shield the woman underneath. Then it hit her. She was the head of the Crows and this was Camberwell. Her manor. She could protect Stacie and women like her. Yes, she might not be walking the right side of the law in the conventional sense, but she could do right by the civilians of Camberwell. A small itch at the back of her mind told her that Charlie had probably started out thinking the same way, but she pushed it away.

'Who are you?'

'Lydia Crow,' Lydia said. 'I just want to ask you about Mikhail. About the work he was doing.'

Stacie frowned, but her posture had relaxed slightly. The name 'Crow' didn't seem particularly unwelcome. Or surprising.

'How much do you know?' Open questions. Lydia wasn't trying to use her power, but she knew it was probably flowing out, anyway. She hadn't yet found a way to block it. And she didn't know if she wanted to.

Stacie glanced toward the waiting parents. 'I can't talk here.'

'Leo will be out in a minute. You prefer to talk in front of him?'

The woman paled, her face suddenly tight and vulnerable. She shook her head.

'I don't want to cause any trouble,' Lydia said. 'I am here to look out for you. And your son. I promise I mean you no harm.'

Stacie's perfect lips turned inward as her eyes darted around, looking for escape or rescue.

'It's okay,' Lydia said. She pushed as much Crow as she dared behind her words. 'It's safe to speak to me, I swear.'

Stacie's head was shaking before she'd finished the sentence. 'I'm never supposed to talk about his work. When we were together, that was the rule and I always followed it. Always. I still do. I never speak to anyone. I don't.'

Lydia nodded her understanding. 'That's very smart. But I'm not just anyone.'

'We weren't together anymore. Mikhail is Leo's father... Was his father, I mean. And we were friends. That's it. I don't know anything. I'm not a part of...' She trailed off, gesturing helplessly to encompass a nameless world.

'You're not in any trouble. You won't get in any trouble by talking to me. And I know you weren't with Mikhail,' Lydia said. 'You hadn't been for a while. I know that.'

'He's always been good to me. Even when he was having problems. But I swear we weren't together.'

It seemed to be vitally important to Stacie that she get across that she was no longer romantically involved with Mikhail. Lydia wondered how many situations the woman had dealt with in the past as a result of living with a man like Mikhail. What debts had people come looking to collect? Scores to settle? Stacie might want to leave everything to do with that life behind, but it wasn't going to be possible. Not without help. 'You know the

Crows, right? Mik used to work for Charlie. I've taken over from Charlie and I want to make sure you're looked after. You and Leo are considered part of the family and with Mikhail gone... Well. It's not right that you should be left in the cold.'

Stacie's frown deepened. 'You don't owe...' She caught herself. 'I mean, I don't mean to be rude. You've already been so generous. There's no need...'

Lydia wanted to ask what Stacie meant, but kept the words back, letting her mind catch up. Stacie was talking about the money that had arrived in her life, the money that was enabling her to look at buying a home. Stacie thought that money was from the Crows.

'Mik worked for us,' Lydia said, playing along. 'He was very loyal. We're very pleased.'

Stacie glanced toward the school again. She didn't look exactly happy, but less like she wanted to run. 'That's good. So this is, like, a courtesy call? You're checking in on me?'

'Yep,' Lydia attempted a warm smile. 'And to pass on our condolences.'

'You know we weren't together anymore?'

'You said. But still...'

'Yeah, well. Thanks.' Stacie had been looking toward the school, but she turned to face Lydia. Innate politeness overcoming her reticence, Lydia guessed. With a full view of her face, Lydia felt a cold block appear in her stomach. Stacie had a livid bruise on one side of her face. She had styled her hair to cover as much as possible and was wearing enormous sunglasses, but the wind lifted her hair and exposed the mottled black and purple skin. Something had cut her, too. There was a nasty gash in the process of healing. It was on her temple and, if Lydia had to guess, she would say it was caused by a heavy piece of jewellery, like a signet ring.

The words came out more harshly than Lydia intended. 'Who hurt you?'

The fear that flashed across Stacie's face stabbed Lydia through the middle. At that moment, the school bell rang and she glanced anxiously toward the gates. 'No one. An accident.' She pulled her hair back around her face, trying to hide her injuries.

There was no discussion, no dissent. Every part of Lydia wanted to use her new abilities to make Stacie tell her exactly who had hurt her and where they lived. But that was no way to help a terrorised and terrified young mother. Instead she smiled blandly as if accepting the blatant lie. 'Well, if you ever need anything, anything at all, you call me.' She passed Stacie her card, letting her sleeve ride up as she did so, revealing her new tattoos. Stacie glanced at them, her eyes widening quickly. It could have just been because they were moving – Lydia was upset – or it could be that they reminded her of Charlie, which would mean she had met the man. Lydia was past caring. She just wanted Stacie to know that she was strong enough to help her. 'I mean it,' she said. 'Anything.'

The kids were streaming out of the school, now, parents peeling off with tiny people in their branded blue sweatshirts and colourful backpacks. Stacie was looking toward the gate, moving almost unconsciously toward the children.

'See you,' Lydia said and walked away. The skin on her arm was burning, again. The pain was bright and sharp and it made her thoughts clear.

CHAPTER TWENTY-FOUR

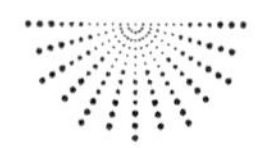

Lydia walked around Camberwell until her rage had subsided to a manageable level. This was her manor. *Hers*. She couldn't solve all the problems, she knew that, but surely she could look after people one-by-one. Suddenly she realised that the trail of souls traipsing into The Fork, cap in hand with their issues and their concerns hadn't just been a power trip for Charlie. Whatever his faults, he had been trying to look after his community. A vision of him sitting in a cell, like the one Mikhail had died in, or maybe worse, flashed into her mind. She had done an excellent job at pushing thoughts of Charlie down, but she allowed this one. Just held it for a few moments and let the guilt and sorrow wash through her body. She hadn't wanted it to end the way it did. He had tried to kill her, but still. He was her blood.

Fleet called as Lydia approached The Fork, in a conciliatory mood. 'I'm sorry about last night.'

'Me, too,' Lydia said, stepping around a patch of something disgusting on the pavement.

'I was just... Thrown, I guess. And concerned. I'm still concerned.'

Lydia felt the pulse of a headache behind her eyes. 'Can we do this in person?'

'I'm outside your place. Where are you?'

Lydia pushed the door to the cafe open. 'Here. Let yourself in.'

A minute later, Lydia rounded the corner of the stairs which led to the short hallway in front of the main flat door. Fleet hadn't used his key and was waiting outside the flat. He was dressed in joggers and a t-shirt and was carrying his gym bag. 'I'm sorry. I'm so glad you're okay. That's what matters. I don't care about...'

Lydia didn't let him finish that sentence, just walked up close and put her hands around his neck. His arms wrapped around her and they stood like that for a beat. Lydia inhaled his scent and ignored the burning brightness of his gleam. She would adjust. It would be fine. As long as his hands were on her back and her body was pressed against his, her eyes closed.

She felt him inhale deeply and then he moved away. His gaze flicked to her left arm, the tattoos.

Lydia moved past him and unlocked her door. 'Have you eaten?' She stepped inside and turned back to look at Fleet.

He hadn't moved. His expression was pained and, in that moment, she realised that he wasn't going to.

'Sorry,' he said, rubbing his hand on the back of his

neck. 'I can't come in. They formed a task force today. Your name is on the list.'

'Because of last night?'

'That. And other gang activities. The Crows are linked or implicated in several incidents over the last few months. And the Mikhail death has been absorbed by the investigation. They're anxious to blame it on an outside force. You can imagine.'

'Makes sense.' Lydia had known they were pursuing an outside conviction. They didn't want the blame to fall in-house. She just didn't think they had any real chance of doing so. Mikhail had died alone in his police cell.

'There's nobody here,' Lydia said. 'Nobody to see. Angel isn't going to shop us.'

'That's not the problem.' Fleet took a breath, and she realised there was worse to come.

'I'm being sent to Coventry.'

'Like the expression?'

'Only literally.' He nodded. 'Training course.'

'You're a bit busy for that,' Lydia said.

'Yeah. Well. It's...'

'Optics,' Lydia finished. 'We've been here before.'

'I know. I get the feeling that they don't trust me to stay away from you, and this course is a way to force it.' He gave her a crooked smile. 'At least for a few days.'

She forced herself to smile back. It wasn't Fleet's fault that he was being sent away. He'd been warned to stay away from her many times before, had chosen her instead, it made sense that his superiors were resorting to more direct action. It just didn't feel like the best timing. She needed him. 'I'll miss you,' she said.

'Me, too.' Fleet wrapped his arms around her and they hugged.

Lydia buried her face in his neck and breathed deeply. His gleam was still too bright, but she was adjusting. She hoped that once her tattoos were fully healed, everything would be back to normal. And Fleet would be back from his stupid course. 'You don't have to leave straight away,' she said, her voice muffled.

'I do. I need to pack and get up north. It starts at nine tomorrow morning.'

She pulled away to look into his face. 'They're really hustling you out of London. Is it bad this time?'

'Seems that way,' he said, his eyes sliding away from hers. 'But it won't be for long. I'll do this, keep the peace, but it doesn't mean anything for us. I'm all in.'

'I know,' Lydia said, pushing aside the part of her that was insisting that something was wrong. 'So am I.'

He smiled, a small private smile that was all hers. 'And I'll make it up to you.'

LYDIA'S INSTINCTS TOLD HER THAT STACIE wouldn't have filed charges against whoever hurt her, but that didn't mean there wouldn't be some kind of report in the system. She got Jason to hack into the police database and look for domestic disturbances at Stacie's address. It wouldn't throw anything up if it had happened elsewhere, but it was worth a punt.

Nothing came up. Sitting in her car on Stacie's street, Lydia could understand why. It was the kind of place where the locals didn't trust the coppers. The people who didn't want the police anywhere near had made it abundantly clear to the rest of the inhabitants that calling them would not end well. The strongest and the scariest made the rules. Which, at this moment, suited Lydia just fine.

She watched Stacie leave for work, making a silver puffy coat over old leggings and gold hoop earrings look like a million dollars. Once Stacie was out of sight, Lydia was out of the Audi and at the shared entrance to Stacie's building. She was on the first floor and Lydia was hoping that whoever lived below would have some insight into her life.

She had to knock on a couple of doors before she got an answer. A man with a stained green jumper and wispy white hair asked if she was from the council. 'I've had no hot water for a week.'

'Just checking on you,' Lydia said, not answering him directly. 'May I come in?'

'I can boil the kettle if you want tea. No milk, I'm afraid. Fridge is on the fritz. Things always go wrong in threes, don't they? Have you noticed that?' The man was wearing fingerless woolly gloves and checked brown slippers. He shuffled into the flat, not breaking to take a breath. Lydia followed, wondering if this was her Crow power leaking out or whether he was always this hospitable to strangers. She had to assume it was the former or it seemed unlikely that he would have survived on this street. Although, Lydia reassessed as she entered the room which served as living room and kitchen, it was more likely that he was left alone because he had absolutely nothing left to take.

There was carpet on the floor and a single sagging chair which looked like it had been taken from a skip.

'Did you say yes to tea?'

'I'm fine, thank you,' Lydia said.

His face fell. 'The cups are clean. I've been boiling the kettle to do the washing up.'

'Tea would be lovely, thank you.'

'Are you going to look at the immersion? It's in the bathroom. Just through there,' the man nodded back to the tiny entrance hall.

'Of course,' Lydia said, and went in search of the bathroom. She was expecting small and grim and that's what she found. It was clean, though, and smelled of pine disinfectant. A cupboard above the sink housed a variety of prescription tablets and a single well-used toothbrush. There was a floor-to-ceiling cubby in the corner, the front covered with a roll up blind. Lydia knew nothing about plumbing, but she looked dutifully at the hot water heater, hoping that there might be a handy 'fix it' button on the front that she could press. She imagined, just for a moment, walking back into the kitchen, triumphant. It would be nice to play the hero.

'I'll need to send someone out,' she said as she walked back in. 'It's beyond me, I'm afraid.'

'That's all right, dear. Thank you for trying.'

The tea was weak, but served in a dainty cup with a matching saucer. The china had pink flowers on the side and had a worn gold rim. 'This is very nice,' she said, after taking a sip.

'I didn't complain,' the man said. 'I called about the immersion heater but I didn't complain.'

Lydia nodded, although she wasn't sure what he was talking about.

'I don't want it marked down. I don't want it...' He trailed off, faded blue eyes gazing into the distance for a moment. 'On file.'

'What didn't you complain about?'

'You don't know?'

Lydia shook her head. 'Not my department.'

'No, you're a heating girl.'

'Sure.'

'The noise,' he said. 'I definitely did not complain about the noise. It was really loud, though. And late. I don't sleep much, but still.'

'Upstairs?' Lydia could hardly believe her luck. This flat was directly below Stacie's.

'There was a ruckus.' The corners of his mouth turned down. 'There's a kiddie there. It's not right.'

'The resident is known to us. She has a small boy, I believe.'

'I'm not saying anything. Don't write it down,' the man said. He looked distressed. Lydia didn't want to lie outright, but she wanted to reassure him, too. She wondered whether the Crows had any contacts at the council, whether there was any way she could check on this man's welfare.

'I heard shouting. And she screamed. She was crying, begging him.'

'Begging who?'

His gaze shifted. 'The girl who lives there. She's nice. Takes my bins out for me when it's icy. She did that once. And there was a leak coming down into the kitchen, over there,' he gestured into the corner. 'She made the phone calls. They came and fixed it. I don't know what she said to them, but they came and fixed it.' His face brightened at the memory. 'I wanted to ask her to call about the hot water, but that didn't seem right. She's got enough on her plate and I don't like to take advantage. That happens with kind natures. Some people take liberties.'

'That's true.' Lydia put the teacup and saucer onto the counter. 'Do you know what happened?'

'Upstairs?'

'I'm worried about the scream you heard. I want to help.'

He shot her a look which wasn't in the least bit vague and Lydia had the uncomfortable sensation of being truly seen.

'I believe you do.' He took a long slurp from his own cup, smacking his lips together. 'Even though you're not from the council.' He raised his bushy eyebrows in response to her unspoken question. 'They never stay for tea. And you don't have a-' he gestured to his chest area. 'Badge necklace thing.'

Lydia tried to look reassuring and friendly. 'Busted.'

'Can you help?' He raised his eyes to the ceiling. 'It's a new man. I don't think he's good for her. I heard the name Ryan. When they were... I heard her shout it. She didn't sound...' He shook his head. 'Her old one was quiet. No screaming. I hope it doesn't last.'

'Have you seen him? The new man?'

'Out front. He got out of one of those noisy cars. Souped-up. He's a nasty piece of work. You know that just by looking at him. Even if you hadn't heard... What I didn't hear.'

Lydia wasn't generally a fan of people making snap judgements about others based solely on their appearance but in this case, the old geezer had it bang on. 'I'm not from the council,' Lydia said. 'Or the police. Nothing is written down and nobody will ever know that you spoke to me.'

'I didn't speak to you.'

'Exactly.' Lydia moved toward the front door. 'Thank you for the cuppa.'

'Don't be a stranger,' the man said.

CHAPTER TWENTY-FIVE

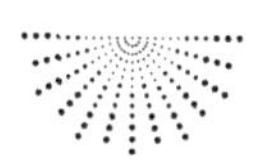

On reflection, Lydia decided it wasn't a bad thing that Fleet had left London. It was easier to be the person she needed to be when he wasn't around. And there were certain activities that, while he might not disapprove of personally, were definitely not legal.

It was late evening and Lydia was back on Stacie's road. This time she brought the Audi and was settled in the front seat with a travel mug of coffee and a family-sized bag of salt and vinegar crisps. It was past dusk, but the sky was a surprisingly light blue above the dark buildings. Lydia never knew if this was the ambient light from the city or some other phenomenon she didn't know about, but it was strangely comforting. The never-dark of London was vastly preferable, in her opinion, to the starlit shadowland of the countryside or the pitch black of underground.

She had watched Stacie moving around her living room until she had closed her blinds against the gathering night. Her son had bounced into view on occasion, but was mostly too short to be seen from this angle. He had been wearing a dinosaur onesie that Lydia made a mental note to hunt down for Maisie and Archie. She knew she would likely forget or fail to follow through, but she was awarding herself points for having the thought. She tapped out a quick message to Emma while she was thinking of her. Emma came back almost immediately to say that it was a horror-film-level bedtime and did Lydia want to adopt two children? Lydia tapped a reply with several laughing emojis and then turned her phone upside down and returned her full attention to watching Stacie's home.

It wasn't the best street and she understood why Stacie was looking to move. That and the fact that she was renting and was now in a position to buy a place. Have a secure roof over her head for her son. She had already formed an idea of the new man in Stacie's life and was not at all surprised when he appeared looking exactly as she expected. Thick neck, skinny jeans, mean little eyes set in a face that might have been handsome otherwise.

He got out of a souped-up Honda with a noisy exhaust growling and grime blasting through the open windows. A brief lean down on the driver's side to talk shit with whoever was dropping him off and then, after a farewell fist bump, pimp-walked toward Stacie's building.

Lydia was out of the car before she had even formulated an opening line. The growling Honda had barely peeled away when she caught up with Ryan. She almost didn't bother with a greeting, just reached out with her power to stop him in his tracks, but good sense cut in just in time. She had to check she had the right man, even though every sense she possessed, both as a Crow and a woman who had lived in the world, told her that it was him. And that he was a dangerous bastard.

'Ryan?'

He turned instinctively before plastering on an insouciant look. 'Could be, darling. What's it to you?' And then, there it was, the long look up and down as if assessing a cow at market.

Lydia's coin was in her hand and she gripped it with all her might. Not to draw strength, but for restraint. She could make the man walk in front of a truck right now and not even break a sweat. Could make him throw himself with all his might through the window of the downstairs flat. The possibilities flashed across the back of her mind like a flicker book of horror. Satisfying horror.

'I'm a friend of Stacie's.'

'Is that right?' He was still looking lascivious, still had no idea what was happening.

'I'm Lydia Crow.'

A beat. He had heard of the Crows.

'You're not welcome here,' Lydia said. 'Time for you to go.'

'What are you talking about?'

'Stacie,' Lydia gestured to the house. 'This part of London. You're not welcome. Not after what you did.'

He crossed his arms, tucking his hands into his armpits in a pose that was straight out of the hard-men films he probably watched late at night with a spliff and a lager. It was a pose that was meant to show off his biceps, to make him look serious. A real villain. But Lydia knew real villains. And Ryan was just a nasty little man. It wasn't difficult to control his body. It was as easy as deciding what he was going to do, just as if his body belonged to her. If she wanted to squeeze her own arms tightly around her body, she would just decide to do so. Now, she decided that she wanted Ryan to do the same.

His eyes narrowed in confusion as he felt his arms tighten around his chest without his volition. The hands that had been tucked into his armpits in a Jason Statham gangster impression were now reaching around his shoulder blades in a painful stretch, his elbows jutting out toward Lydia in an almost-comical way.

'Are you left or right-handed?' Lydia asked, conversationally.

'What? What are you doing? How are you-?'

'I'm guessing right. You punched Stacie on the left-side of her face. Or was it more of a side-swipe? That could've been with your left, I suppose.'

'Is that what this is all about?'

She could see the genuine irritation underneath his growing fear.

'That was just...'

'No talking,' Lydia said. She had the instinct that he had been about to sing the song of domestic abusers around the world 'she was asking for it, she wound me up, she made me do it'. And she was suddenly certain that if this weasel began to justify his actions she couldn't be held responsible for her own. His thin lips compressed so firmly that they rolled inwards, became invisible.

'I know you think that Stacie is alone and that you can do whatever you like. You think you're the big man and you're taking advantage of a sweet opportunity, but I'm here to explain that you are gravely mistaken. Camberwell belongs to the Crows. That means Stacie and her family are under our protection. You'd better get out of Camberwell by dawn and never set foot inside our boundary again.'

His eyes bulged with pain and fear, but Lydia wasn't sure it was enough. She pulled his arms a little further. 'You didn't tell me which side you use the most. So I'll dislocate them both, I think. Just to be sure you've got the message.'

Sweat was pouring down his face, now. That was better. Part of Lydia wasn't sure if she could follow through, but another part of her knew that his type could sense weakness like a shark finding a drop of blood in an ocean. If she backed down, he might come back. Might take out his rage and humiliation on Stacie or her son.

He was screaming behind his closed lips. Lydia felt a lick of referred pain and she instinctively channelled it away. That was interesting. The link that she had created, the link that allowed her to control Ryan's body, seemed to have a two-way functionality. She would have to watch that. Control it. 'Unless you've had enough? Perhaps you have received the message?'

She unlocked his lips and released the pressure on his arms by a fraction. Ryan began sobbing.

'Off you pop,' Lydia said, making a little shooing

motion. 'Trip to A&E is probably a good idea. Anywhere outside Camberwell.'

He began staggering away.

'And, Ryan?'

He looked back, terror and confusion and snot all over his face.

'You had better pray that nothing happens to Stacie or her son or any member of her family, because if it does I'll be paying you another visit.'

CHAPTER TWENTY-SIX

The next day, Lydia's run took her to the river. She had to keep busy and moving and to avoid, if at all possible, thinking too hard about what Fleet was going to say when she told him about Ryan. Her instinct was to keep it to herself, but the feeling that Fleet was keeping things from her and the agony it was wreaking on her psyche, had given her an entirely new appreciation for open communication.

The sun was out and the pavement was packed with tourists in bright summer clothes, carrying backpacks and holding out their phones to photograph everything. A street performer had gathered a crowd and Lydia cut down the steep steps in the embankment to the muddy foreshore to avoid the noise. She didn't get an answer on Fleet's mobile so she called his office to ask them to pass on a message. 'He's not in the office today,' the man said. He was a civilian administrative person and Lydia knew he wouldn't be authorised to give out any information on Fleet. Which was quite right. But she wasn't asking for information, she was giving it. 'I know, he's on that course in Coventry. Can you pass a message on, though? I can't get him on his mobile and I don't know if he's checking email while he's away.' Fleet had frequently complained about the black hole of his inbox.

'Did you say Coventry?'

'Yes. The course goes on until Friday I think.' Lydia walked down to the edge of the river. Down here the mud bank was exposed and she could see a couple of people walking hunched over, digging in the ground. Mudlarking. The word came to her, dredged up from a news story on the Thames.

'Hang on,' the voice said.

One of the hunched figures straightened. They were wearing multiple layers of green-coloured waterproofs and some serious-looking wellies. The face deep inside the green hood was attractive, blonde wisps of hair escaping from a woollen headband. The mudlarker wasn't paying attention to Lydia or to anything at all except for the object in her hand. She brushed mud from it reverentially.

'There's no course at the moment. Not in Coventry.'

'Right,' Lydia said automatically.

'DCI Fleet is on holiday this week. I can take a message for him, but if it's urgent then I can pass you to DI Lowry.'

'That's all right,' Lydia said. The words still coming on autopilot. 'No worries. It's not important.'

Hell Hawk. Lydia walked up and down the stretch of river for a few minutes, trying to ease the adrenalin from her system. There would be an explanation. She wasn't one of her own clients, jumping to conclusions and mistrusting their partners. Running to a PI when a good sit-down conversation would have saved them the trouble and cash.

The mudlarker was crouched down, rinsing their prize with a bottle of water. She glanced up and saw Lydia, smiling in a friendly way which was most unusual in London. Lydia instinctively took a step back and checked behind her for the pickpocket or mugger.

'It's a clay pipe,' the mudlarker said, her voice full of excitement. 'Look.'

Lydia peered at the object politely.

'Eighteenth century, probably. I've got a whole collection, now, but this one is in really good condition. Look how long the stem is.'

Where was Fleet? The fact that he had lied to her seemed to be hitting her in stages. The initial shock was giving way to a clenching pain in her chest.

'Are you all right?' The mudlarker held out the remains of her water bottle. 'Do you want some?'

Lydia shook her head. 'I'm fine. Thank you, though.'

The mudlarker beamed. 'We look out for each other down here. We're the weirdos, sifting through history, but everyone is welcome.'

Lydia wondered if that was why the woman was being so friendly. She had marked Lydia as a fellow weirdo. Another thought hit her, overtaking her internal monologue about Fleet for a moment. 'Do you ever find coins?'

'Sometimes,' the woman's expression dimmed a little. Disappointment that Lydia was jumping immediately to valuables, perhaps. Or maybe she thought Lydia meant modern currency.

'Ever find anything like this?' Lydia produced her coin.

The mudlarker's eyes widened. 'No. I don't think so. Is that gold?'

Lydia nodded. 'Look at the engraving. The crow. If you find anything like this, anything that feels like this, you call me.' She pocketed her coin and passed the woman her business card. As an afterthought she added. 'Or anything pearl or mother-of-pearl. Or silver.'

She didn't know why, but there was something about that clay pipe. Something was tugging on her arm, but she didn't know what. Stupid intuition. If only it would speak directly. And if only she knew whether it was her own instincts or an invisible spirit whispering into her ear. Or, worse still, something from Maddie lodged inside and manipulating her from beyond the grave. Feathers. That was a bit dramatic. And crazy. If she wasn't careful, she would end up babbling in the Maudsley. She had to pull herself together. And maybe Fleet hadn't lied. Maybe the course had been cancelled and he just hadn't updated her, yet. Or the person who answered the phone at his office had been messing with her. So many good explanations. There was no need to panic.

LYDIA HAD LEFT A COUPLE OF MESSAGES ON FLEET'S mobile, but he hadn't replied. She distracted herself, as she always did, by working. She knocked on the flat below Stacie's, just to say 'hello', but there was no reply. Upstairs, Stacie opened the door holding the front half of a fairy princess castle. She had a tube of glue tucked under one arm and the situation looked precarious.

Stacie stepped back and invited her in. 'Careful, I've got to hold these pieces together or they won't stay stuck.'

Lydia helped to carry the craft project back to the living room, and declined a cup of tea. Then she cut to the chase. 'Ryan won't be back.'

Stacie's eyes were wide. 'What do you mean?'

'I've warned him off. He won't bother you again.'

She shook her head. 'He said he'd kill me if I left.'

'And I told him I'd kill him if he steps foot in Camberwell.' Lydia gave Stacie a steady look. 'Which of us do you believe?'

Leo bounced in at that moment. He stopped in the doorway when he caught sight of Lydia. Instantly still and on his guard. It stabbed Lydia through the heart, but she managed a smile. 'Hey, there.'

'This is my friend.'

'Lydia,' Lydia said.

Stacie had jumped from the sofa and gathered Leo in for a hug. 'You want some TV time? Use your headphones, okay?'

She settled him on the sofa with a flip-top bottle of water and a bowl of crackers.

'That'll keep him busy for a bit,' Stacie said, motioning to the kitchen area with her head.

They moved as far away from the child as was possible in the small area, and used lowered voices.

'What do you mean 'gone'?'

'I sent him on his way,' Lydia said. 'I know he was hurting you.'

She shook her head, but not denying Lydia's words, more with a sense of wonderment. 'He wouldn't leave. Wouldn't give up that easy.'

'I made him.'

Stacie closed her eyes for a moment. The bruise on her face was still puffy and it must have still been painful. When she looked at Lydia, her mouth had a determined set. Like she had decided something. 'He had always been interested. Making comments, standing too close, you know?'

Lydia nodded. She knew.

'But everyone knew Mikhail was on the scene. Even when we split up, blokes were respectful. I mean, to a point. But if I said 'no' they listened.'

'Because they thought Mikhail would've killed them.'

'Yes.' Stacie's voice wasn't more than a whisper and she was looking over at Leo, reassuring herself that he hadn't heard.

'So this is a recent problem?'

'Very,' Stacie said. 'It was like Ryan had his alarm set.' She tried a smile, which made Lydia want to go and dislocate Ryan's arms all over again. 'Soon as Mik was pronounced dead, he came round. Said he was my new man. I went along with it because I didn't want him to get nasty with Leo. I thought if he just had... You know... He would leave. Some of them are like that. It's the conquest. Or a power trip. I thought there was a chance he'd just finish and go.'

'But he didn't.'

She shook her head. 'The money didn't help. He had his mates keeping an eye on me and one of them saw me go to the estate agent. He went ballistic. Said I was trying to leave him. And the money came out.'

Lydia didn't want to picture Ryan terrorising Stacie, badgering her with questions until she broke down and revealed that she had enough money to move out, but the images flashed up unbidden. She swallowed her nausea and her rage. Those feelings weren't going to help Stacie. And the last thing Leo needed was another scary person in his home.

'Why did you help me?' Stacie squared her shoulders. Her face was carefully neutral. 'I mean, really?'

'I told you. Mik worked for the Crows. We look after our own.'

She shook her head. Lydia could see a tentative wonder beginning to overtake her fear. 'I thought you would be angry.'

'I'm definitely not,' Lydia said, wanting to be perfectly clear. 'Why would you think that?'

'Mik... He did that thing. With the actor. That wasn't... I don't think that was what he was supposed to be doing.'

Lydia didn't know how much to reveal. She wanted Stacie to keep talking openly and, usually, it was best to appear as if you already knew everything. As if the interviewee was just confirming what you already had gathered. She nodded in agreement. 'He wasn't a blackmailer by trade. And it wasn't part of his instructions. What made him do it, do you think?'

'I told him not to. He was better following a plan, you know? Things always went wrong when he had his own ideas.' Her mouth turned down. 'I mean, he did jobs for your lot. But his other work, he never did around Camberwell. Didn't steal from his neighbours, went for well-off places over the river. People who wouldn't hurt too much. People with insurance and all that. I don't know what he was thinking with that Rafferty. I really don't know...' She shook her head.

Lydia waited.

Stacie was staring over at Leo. 'I'm not an idiot. He wasn't a saint. But he wasn't a bad person, you know? He wasn't violent.' She looked wistful as she spoke, as if 'not violent' was a rare and precious commodity in her life. 'He always made sure people weren't home when he knocked them over. I know it was still bad. But the people he was hanging out with, they would drag him down, give him ideas...' She trailed off as if realising that she might be talking about close members of Lydia's family.

Lydia smiled to show she wasn't offended. 'Oh, I know. You can't choose their friends for them, though. And people change depending on who they're with. Nobody likes to admit it, but it's true.'

'Yes,' Stacie nodded. 'I was listening to this podcast. This American businesswoman was saying that you are the sum of the five people you spend the most time with so you need to choose those people wisely.' Stacie trailed off again, the spark dying in her eyes. Lydia assumed she was taking a quick tally of her own social circle and finding it wanting.

'Did he talk to you about blackmailing Rafferty?'

Stacie shook her head. 'He knew I wouldn't approve. Would've given him an earful. I heard him on the phone, though. Boasting about it to one of the big shots. Trying to impress them. He was always just on the outside, you know? Even though he'd known them all for years, worked for them, with them. He was still like the hired help. Not on the inside.' She paused, twisting the thin gold band on her right hand. 'I'm not making excuses. I'm not blaming anyone else.'

'It's okay.'

'Is that why he died? Because he did something he wasn't supposed to?'

'His death is unexplained,' Lydia said. 'That's the verdict. I don't know how hard the police are going to push. As long as they're not being blamed, they probably don't want too much of a fuss.'

'Do you know what happened to him?' Stacie's voice was barely a whisper and she didn't meet Lydia's gaze.

'I think he didn't want to go back inside.' Lydia didn't know if this was going to cause more or less pain to the woman, but she felt she owed it to her to be honest. She had been thinking about Mikhail a lot and this was the only explanation that made sense. 'I think that he agreed to finish himself if that looked likely. And I think someone sweetened that deal with the means and a request to implicate the Crows. In return for a posthumous payment to be made to you.'

'What do you mean? Implicate the Crows? You're the ones who made the payment.'

'No, not me,' Lydia shook her head. Why did Stacie think the Crows were responsible? 'You said that before. Why do you think the payment came from my Family?'

'Then who?' Stacie looked genuinely mystified. Either Mik really hadn't worked for anybody else over the years, or he hadn't told her about it.

'I'm going to find out.' Lydia stood up to leave. Leo was still watching CBeebies, bright blue headphones safely over his ears and the enraptured but relaxed expression that Lydia recognised from Maisie and Archie.

Stacie walked her to the door. 'Is it really over?'

'Absolutely. Good luck with the move. Have you found somewhere you like, yet?'

'I still can't believe I can buy a place.' Stacie's eyes were shining. 'I want to stay near my mum and my Yaya.'

'You can,' Lydia said. 'Camberwell is your home.'

At the door, Stacie cast an anxious look back toward the sofa. 'I knew he wasn't supposed to be leaving those letters for the actor. I knew it wasn't a job from the Crows.'

Lydia paused, waiting.

'Little pieces of paper.'

'What did you say?'

Stacie closed her eyes briefly. When she opened them, her expression was resolved. 'I'm trusting that this is okay. I'm trusting you.'

'You can,' Lydia said. 'I'm going to protect you. You and your son.'

Stacie nodded. 'Right, then. He always heard from your lot in writing. I told you he wasn't that good at strategic thinking? He'd had a knock or two in his life and I don't think he was entirely all right. Maybe a bit slow with certain things. People don't realise how dangerous it is to hit your head, but it can be really bad. Long-term effects.'

Lydia tamped down the urge to hurry Stacie.

'Anyway, the Crows always gave him instructions on paper. He had to read them and then eat the paper.' She pulled a face. 'Disgusting, really, but I don't suppose it did him any harm.'

Lydia thought of Mikhail eating paper before he died. It could have been one of his last acts. She needed to know more. 'Is there anything else you can tell me? Do you know when he did his last job for the Crows? Or when he got his last written instructions?'

Stacie shook her head. 'He kept all that stuff at his place. Didn't want his work anywhere near Leo.'

'His place? Didn't you tell the police that he was essentially homeless? Just staying with friends?'

Stacie gave a small smile. 'I told you. I'm discreet. I don't blab about his work. And I definitely don't talk to the police.'

'Quite right,' Lydia said, giving her a reassuring smile. 'But you'll give me his address.'

Stacie nodded, looking sad. 'I don't suppose it matters, now, anyway.'

CHAPTER TWENTY-SEVEN

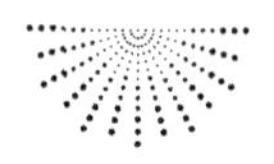

Lydia was on her roof terrace, a line of assorted corvids watching her with their bright, intelligent eyes. Her phone rang and she answered it, her heart lifting despite its sudden weight.

She made her voice breezy. There was a chance that the person she had spoken to at the station had alerted Fleet that she had called for him. If so, he would know that she knew it didn't exist. Or, he might have no idea. 'How's the course? Hope you're not too bored.'

'It's fine,' Fleet said.

Lydia closed her eyes.

'Tell me about you. How is the Mikhail investigation?'

'I've made some progress. Can't talk about it on the phone, though.'

A pause. 'Fair enough. That sounds promising, though.'

'Yeah.'

'That's good. How is everything else?'

'Fine,' Lydia managed. She felt sick. There were no traffic sounds on the line. No hints as to where Fleet might be. 'What's on the schedule for tomorrow?'

'More of the same.' Fleet's voice faded a little, like he was looking away from his phone. 'You know what these things are like.'

'I don't, actually.' Lydia was gripping her coin. She hadn't meant to conjure it but there it was. Solid in her palm and lending weight to her words. 'Talk me through it.'

'Hang on, Lyds...' He broke off and she heard his voice muffled, speaking to another person. She thought he said 'in a minute' but couldn't make it out.

'Sorry, I'd better go.'

'Where are you?'

A slight hesitation. 'The pub. Just ordering food. I'm bloody starving. Speak later, yeah?'

AIDEN WAS AT CHARLIE'S HOUSE USING THE training room. Lydia joined him for the last part of the session and was pleased to see that he looked a little healthier than the last time she had seen him. Either he was getting more sleep and drinking his OJ or Lydia's calming of the gang trouble had eased his stress levels considerably.

Once they had finished, they convened in the kitchen for a post-workout brunch. Lydia filled Aiden in on her visit to Stacie.

Aiden nodded approvingly, but had opinions. 'You

should have killed him,' Aiden said. 'He'll come back. With his mates.'

Lydia picked up her espresso cup.

'I don't mean no disrespect,' Aiden added. 'I just know the type. I reckon...'

'You weren't there,' Lydia said. 'He won't be heading back to Camberwell. And he won't take a step toward Stacie. Not a single step.' She hoped she was right. She knew that Aiden had a point, but she also knew that she wasn't in a hurry to add another tattoo for another death.

'I'll keep an eye on her, if you want,' Aiden offered.

Lydia felt a wash of relief. Aiden wasn't lost. 'On her mum, too. And her boy.'

Aiden nodded.

'This is what we're about,' she said. 'Using our strength to look out for the ordinary people in Camberwell.'

Aiden grinned suddenly, looking like a gangly young man, again. 'Like superheroes.'

'Exactly.' Lydia formed finger guns and pointed them at him. 'With great power, et cetera. And, before I forget, I've got another little job for you. Actually, delegate it to one of the others.'

'What?'

'Get a plumber around to the flat below Stacie's. Number three. There's a nice old geezer there with a duff immersion heater.'

Aiden opened his mouth, but if he was going to complain, his brain caught up before he did anything so stupid and he closed it again.

. . .

The address that Stacie had given was on the edge of Camberwell, just before it became Peckham. Mikhail had stayed with her and Leo two nights a week, so that he could have quality time with his son, and for the rest of the time he stayed 'off books'. He sub-let a maisonette under a false name, cash in hand, which was why the police investigation hadn't found it. Mikhail might not have been a big strategic thinker, but he had been in the life a long time. He had picked up plenty of tricks along the way.

It was dusk as Lydia approached. She had no idea how security conscious a career burglar was likely to be, but had hopes that human laziness would win out over professional knowledge. Her luck was in. Mikhail's place was one half of a nineteen sixties' semi and she couldn't see any sign of an alarm system. She went straight down the side of the house, which didn't even have a gate to deter intruders, and found only a single-glazed wooden door between her and the inside of the property.

She was already wearing thin gloves, but she pulled on some thick protective ones and took a hammer from her rucksack to smash the glass. Yes, it was noisy, but she knew Mikhail wasn't home and she wasn't too worried about Neighbourhood Watch. This felt like the kind of street where everyone minded their own business on the assumption it was for their own protection. Besides, she was on home turf. A Crow in Camberwell.

The shadowy kitchen smelled of ripe bin, but was surprisingly clean and tidy. Clicking on a small torch, she moved through the rest of the house. A first sweep, just to confirm the place was empty and then a slower walk-through. The lights from passing cars played across the walls of the bedroom. Lydia spun slowly, letting her instincts guide her. She didn't know what she was looking for, but she had a gut feeling that she needed to check. The bed was very low to the ground and there was nothing tucked under the mattress. Mikhail didn't have bedside cabinets. On the floor next to the bed was a charging station for his phone, an empty can of Fanta, and a well-thumbed copy of The Da Vinci Code. When Lydia opened the book, she found notes written in the margins of the book. Some street names, which could have been related to his work, a Christmas list for Leo, and a recipe for cassoulet. The writing was cramped, but surprisingly neat. Perhaps the dexterity which made Mik the Jekyll such a good lockpick also gave him excellent pen control.

The handwriting looked identical to the letters sent to Angel. Lydia ripped out a couple of pages from the book and stuffed them into her back pocket. The chest of drawers opposite the bed was filled with neatly folded clothes and socks rolled in pairs. On the top, a few more paperbacks, an engraved silver lighter that looked like it had been nicked from a country house, and a heavy brass ashtray with the remains of a spliff.

The house had two bedrooms. The second was clearly not often used for its original purpose. There was a single mattress leaning up against one wall, but the room was dominated by a weights bench. As well as the bar weights, there were a couple of kettle bells and a pair of boxing gloves. Lydia could feel the skin on her arms itching. She directed the torch beam at her forearm and saw that the tattoos there were moving.

Every hair on her body raised. There was something in this house. Something important. Then she heard it. The sound of the front door opening downstairs.

Lydia froze. The door to the spare bedroom was open and she was just inside the room. The sounds from the front door travelled clearly up the stairwell and Lydia could hear a rustle and then the soft sound of the door closing again. Steps in the hall, muffled by carpet.

She forced herself to take a slow quiet breath. Being oxygen-deprived wasn't going to be an asset if this became a physical confrontation. Please don't come upstairs, she prayed silently, and then sent up thanks to whatever spirits were watching over her when the figure moved into one of the rooms downstairs.

Lydia moved onto the small landing. The front door was in direct line of sight at the bottom of the stairs, the entrance to the kitchen and the living room were both on the right. To the left was the shared wall with the next-door house. She measured the distance. Regardless of which room the intruder had gone into, they were no more than a handful of steps from the front door. This wasn't a large house.

Still, if she got more than halfway down the stairs quietly, she could take the last steps and out the front door at a run. Then she would be in the open, on a quiet dark street. With the kinds of neighbours who weren't likely to pick up the phone to dial nine-nine-nine in a hurry. Or ever.

Her skin was prickling with cold sweat and she had

stopped breathing again. She inhaled softly through her nose, keeping her senses alert for more sounds from downstairs. All was quiet. If the figure had gone into the kitchen, they would have found the broken glass in the back door. Lydia would expect an expression of surprise at the very least. Unless the intruder was a pro, in which case they were likely standing very quietly and listening out for her, just as she was doing.

A thought hit Lydia. She had left her rucksack in the kitchen. It didn't contain anything that would identify her. Just the tools of the trade. A hammer, spare gloves, and a set of lock picks. Still. That hammer would be reassuring right about now.

You can control their body, a small voice in the back of her mind. You know you can. You just don't want to. Ryan had deserved it. She had been sure. She wasn't about to start reaching for that ability like it was nothing, like every person was a puppet waiting to have their strings pulled. She wasn't a monster.

There was a rustling sound and Lydia unlocked her muscles. She had to make a decision. Find somewhere to hide upstairs and hope the intruder only had business downstairs. Or make a break for it, now, while they were occupied.

There was a third option. The one that Charlie or Maddie would have taken. Confrontation. Lydia could feel the tattoos on her arms, the skin still tender and itching. The ink didn't make her Charlie. The power didn't make her Maddie. It hit her with the force of a blinding epiphany. She was still Lydia. And she was going to have to find her own way of doing things.

Right now, that meant creeping down the stairs as quietly as humanly possible.

She was almost to the bottom when there was movement from the right and, without real warning, the intruder was standing in the doorway to the kitchen.

Everything froze for a second. Lydia felt her lungs seize. Then the figure shifted slightly and the shadows resolved. 'Aunt Daisy?'

CHAPTER TWENTY-EIGHT

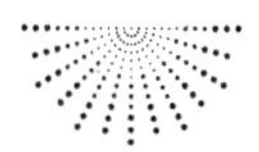

With the lights on and a piece of cardboard taped on the broken door to stop the air howling through the kitchen, Lydia watched as Aunt Daisy filled the kettle. Tea. The great soother of social awkwardness. Meeting your boyfriend's parents for the first time? Had a nasty shock? Bumped into a family member unexpectedly while conducting a criminal offence? Have a cup of tea!

Daisy put a mug within reach of Lydia and then retreated the few steps to lean against the opposite counter. 'There's no milk.'

'How are you feeling, now?'

'What?'

'Uncle John said you were unwell. I take it you've made a full recovery?'

Daisy coloured slightly. Stark pink circles on her pale complexion. 'Yes. Thank you.'

'So, what's this outing all about?' Lydia assumed that Daisy knew Mikhail, but she would prefer to hear it from Daisy. She had been trained in investigative skills and the most important principle of a suspect or witness interview was not to lead them down a particular path. Not to assume anything.

'I was...' Daisy trailed off.

Lydia almost felt sorry for her. She waited, though. Not moving, not picking up the mug of tea.

Daisy straightened her shoulders. 'I knew Mik. Back in the day. I wanted to get something back from him. Something I gave to him a long time ago.'

The other principle of interviewing people was this... They often lied. Lydia played along. 'You and Mik were romantically involved?'

'Only briefly. It was stupid.'

'There's quite an age difference.'

'Yes, well. That's not a crime. He was...'

Lydia waited while Daisy worked out how old Mikhail would have been during their fictitious affair.

'Of age,' she finished.

Lydia didn't say anything.

Daisy put down the mug she had been holding, giving up the pretence that she was relaxed enough to drink tea. 'What are you going to do?'

'I'm sorry for your loss,' Lydia said. 'For Maddie.'

The older woman's body jerked convulsively. 'You can't say that.'

'Even if it's true?'

'If it wasn't for you, my girl would be alive.'

Now they were getting to it. Lydia felt a rush of relief. She had been dreading this confrontation, dreading looking into a mother's eyes and seeing her grief. Lydia knew she hadn't had a choice, knew that Maddie had chosen her path a long time ago, but that didn't mean she felt nothing for Daisy and John. They had lost their child. 'I didn't have a choice,' Lydia said. 'You know what she was doing. It was never going to end well.'

'Not that,' Daisy bit out. 'She never had a chance. You were out. You were nothing. It gave our girl the chance to shine. She had everything, was going to follow Charlie, going to be the leader. Then you came back. You took everything from her.'

That wasn't exactly how Lydia remembered it. 'She ran away. I came back to find her. Have you forgotten?'

Daisy's jaw snapped shut. Her eyes were still blazing with anger but she was clearly done talking about Maddie. That was fine with Lydia. 'So, what are you picking up? I can help you look for it. You must know your way around so I'll follow you.'

Daisy made to move away from the counter but didn't complete the manoeuvre. 'It's okay. It doesn't matter.'

'You broke in to get it, so let's get it. Although,' Lydia pretended to have a realisation. 'You didn't break in, did you? You let yourself in. With a key. I take it the affair was ongoing?'

Daisy flinched. Then, after an internal struggle which she wasn't hiding very well, nodded. 'Yes.'

'Shall I call Uncle John and tell him or do you want to do it?'

Daisy shook her head.

'Or you can just tell me the truth.'

Silence.

'We're still family,' Lydia said gently.

Daisy stiffened.

'You obviously have a connection with Mikhail. I just want you to tell me the truth about that.'

Daisy didn't speak.

'Okay, I'll tell you what I think. I'm here looking for anything that will confirm that Mikhail was being given instructions from a Crow. He used to work for us, back in Charlie's day, and he was always given his jobs written down on slips of paper. He ate these pieces of paper, apparently. Not sure if that was to hide the evidence or because Charlie had some way of enchanting the words, making it so that when Mikhail ate the paper, he would carry out the instruction with no hesitation and no deviation. I don't know.'

Daisy's lips were compressed and she couldn't meet Lydia's gaze.

'Mikhail died with paper in his stomach. And now you're here. Which makes me think that you're the one who was giving him instructions. Or at least dropping them off for somebody else.' Lydia wondered whether it was Uncle John. Working behind her back to run Crow operations that Lydia would've vetoed. 'Was it a dead drop? You let yourself in, leave the paper for him to find? Did you make a delivery before he was arrested and now you want to clear the evidence away, just in case this flat comes to the attention of the police? Am I close?'

Lydia was watching her aunt's face very carefully and she saw the moment Daisy made a decision. A shutter slammed down behind her eyes. She shrugged almost imperceptibly. She wasn't going to talk. Any hopes that Lydia had harboured about a caring and sharing session evaporated. She would either have to use her power to compel her aunt or she would have to wait. After a moment of internal debate, Lydia settled on a course of action.

'You'll tell me eventually. When you need my help which, I'm guessing, will be pretty soon. Mikhail's story didn't end well. You should think about that.'

Slamming through the door to the flat, Lydia threw down her bag and jacket and went to find Jason. He was standing in a corner of his room, motionless. That didn't seem like a good sign. 'I need you,' Lydia said, and watched him come back to life, like a robot re-booting. 'Can you follow a bank transaction? Find out where it came from?'

Jason brightened. He looked more human by the second. 'I can try.'

Lydia went to make a coffee, while Jason sank onto the sofa, laptop open and a frown of concentration creasing his brow.

After she had finished the mugful and was considering making another, Jason called through to the kitchen.

'You're not going to like this.'

Lydia looked over his shoulder and listened as Jason explained, in way too much detail, how he had followed the transaction made to Stacie's bank account, back to its source.

She pressed call on her phone. Aiden answered after a couple of rings. 'Send Jo round to see me. Now.'

LYDIA MET THE ACCOUNTANT IN THE CAFE. SHE WAS at her favourite table and was halfway down her coffee when Jo walked in. The woman was somewhere north of sixty-five, was wearing stone-washed jeans, silver platform wedges and a gold puffy cropped jacket, and had a cigarette wedged in one corner of her mouth. If Lydia had pictured a particular person when thinking the word 'accountant', Jo was not it.

Lydia had taken her jacket off. She was wearing a t-shirt and wanted Jo to be able to see her tattoos. The crow was standing at the moment, its wings folded. It looked like black ink on skin. Innocent and still.

Jo's kohl-rimmed eyes were drawn to her forearm, just as she had planned, but when her gaze moved to Lydia's face, the woman looked singularly unmoved. Lydia supposed you didn't work closely for Charlie Crow for thirty-five years without developing a high tolerance for intimidation.

'The Crow business account. You have access to it?'

Jo nodded. She emptied the bowl of sugar packets onto the table, and used it as an ashtray. She clearly didn't expect the smoking laws to apply in The Fork. 'I have access to all the key accounts. I have read-only access to your business and personal accounts, too. That way I can make sure I'm filing returns in the most tax-efficient way. I've got to look at the whole picture for the

Family accounts, otherwise mistakes are made. I assumed you knew?'

'Of course,' Lydia lied. 'A payment went out two weeks ago. To Mikhail Laurent's ex-girlfriend. Did you make that transfer?'

Jo stiffened. Just for a moment. Then she nodded.

Lydia made a guess. 'Daisy told you to do it?'

'She said it went under 'services'. I never ask for details when something goes under that label.'

'Fair enough,' Lydia said. It wasn't Jo's job to interfere or question. It was her job to keep the books and make them look pretty for HMRC or anybody else who came poking around.

Jo had straight highlighted hair and a thick fringe which almost touched her lush black eyelashes. She slow-blinked at Lydia, now, like an ageing Disney princess on the make. 'We're going to need an injection soon.'

'Cash?'

'There have been a lot of withdrawals and not enough deposits. Charlie used to-'

Lydia wanted to shut her ears to whatever Charlie used to do, but she knew that wasn't an option. 'Was he moving the money from another savings account? Something I can access?'

'Usually just cash. He was bringing it into the business.'

Lydia felt the admonishment. Charlie had brought money into the business. Lydia took money out. And she had shut down all of their most lucrative streams. It seemed weird that a crime family ran the same as any other company, but it seemed to be true. Without cash flow, they were heading for trouble. Lydia's mind caught on Jo's phrasing. 'Not always cash? Have there been transfers into the business account?'

Jo nodded, looking unhappy. 'Sixty grand came in. It seemed a bit odd, but it covered the services payment. The one to Stacie. And I have learned not to ask questions. Don't ask, don't tell.'

'Sensible policy,' Lydia said. 'But I'm asking, now. Where did the sixty grand come from? An electronic transfer had to have details of the payee. The bank name, at least.'

'Oh, I know which account it came from, that's why it was weird.' She ground out her cigarette. 'The money was transferred from Charlie's personal account.'

'Who has access to that account?'

Jo met her gaze. 'Charlie.'

Lydia held it together as she dismissed Jo, and made it up the stairs to the privacy of her flat before allowing the tears to fall. It was too much.

Jason rose from his cross-legged position on the sofa. 'What's wrong?'

Lydia swiped at her treacherous eyes. The tension that she had been feeling, the threats to the Family, the growing realisation that somebody was causing targeted trouble, and the worry over Fleet, it was all spilling out. She shook her head, unable to speak.

Jason hesitated. 'I could hug you. But I know I'm cold.'

'It's okay,' Lydia said, sniffing noisily. The tears had stopped as quickly as they had arrived, and she was already thinking more clearly. She began pacing. It had seemed scarcely possible that Charlie was orchestrating the threats to the Crows from his cell deep in the secret service building. That he had sent the note to Oscar, tipping him off that he had killed his father. That he had used Daisy to send instructions to Mikhail and to make a payment to Stacie. But this seemed to clinch it. If nobody else had access to Charlie's personal account, then he must have made the transfer. Which made it vastly more likely that he was behind the other actions, too. Was Sinclair giving him secure internet access? Surely not.

Jason was watching her warily. 'Shall I make you something to eat?'

'I just had a meeting with our accountant. Charlie made a transfer from his personal account to our business account.'

'Are you sure?'

'It's the final piece. I can't keep pretending that he isn't moving against the Family. Against me.'

Jason crossed his arms. 'Is that possible? From where he's...'

'He's been giving instructions to Daisy. She didn't admit it, but I'm pretty sure. It was a woman who gave the note to Oscar, and I bumped into Daisy at Mikhail's flat. She wouldn't tell me, but I think she must have been there to collect any stray evidence of Charlie's instructions.' A thought that had been growing suddenly solidified. 'I think I know how Mikhail died.'

'Charlie?'

'Mikhail always got his instructions written on pieces of paper, which he ate after reading. I think Charlie was able to imbue those words with Crow whammy, make them impossible to mess up or deviate from or ignore. I think Mikhail was carrying a slip of paper with instructions from Charlie as a kind of suicide pill. Something to take if he was arrested. The pay-out to Stacie occurred on the day after he had died, the day after he left that inflammatory message scrawled in his own blood.'

'You think he killed himself because he was told to? In return for cash?'

'A lot of cash, yes. Enough to make a difference to Stacie and his son, Leo.'

'I still don't understand...'

'What if the instructions could make Mikhail do anything? Even stop breathing?'

Understanding dawned in Jason's eyes and he swore quietly. 'Wait. Is any of this possible.' He waved a hand. 'I don't mean the magical suicide note, I mean Charlie managing all this from wherever he's being held.'

'He just needs a way to communicate. An internet connection.' Lydia could imagine Charlie sweet-talking a guard, promising them all kinds of riches in return for a little broadband.

'Unless he's out. Wait.' Jason shuddered, his whole figure shimmering at the edges. 'Could he be out?'

Well that was an awful thought. Lydia stopped pacing for a second as it hit. 'Escaped, you mean?'

'Or released.'

Lydia resumed pacing. Faster than before, as if she could outrun that terrible possibility. Charlie walking free. Ready and able to exact his revenge on the woman who had handed him to the spooks. 'He must hate me,' she said out loud. 'I've devoted a lot of energy to not thinking about him, about where he is or how he feels.'

'Good,' Jason said. 'Get back to that. He betrayed you. He doesn't deserve...'

She shook her head. 'But now I need to think about it. If he's active and able to reach out from... Wherever he is. I need to try to get inside his head, work out what he's going to do next.'

'He won't want to do anything to destroy the family,' Jason said. 'He was always loyal to the Crow business. Before everything else. I find it hard to believe he's behind the stuff with the Brixton Mob. Why would he stir trouble for the Crows?'

'To make me look weak,' Lydia said. 'But you're right, he'll be careful not to hurt the Family too much. Just enough to make the Crows turn on me, start looking for a new leader.'

Jason was vibrating, now, looking more ghost-like than usual. 'I can't believe this. I thought he was dead. I assumed he was...'

'I know,' Lydia said. Her mind was still racing. What else would Charlie do? If he wanted to hurt her? She swallowed hard. Might he go after Fleet?

IT WAS ONE THING THAT FLEET WAS LYING TO HER about his whereabouts, but now Lydia really needed to speak to him. She didn't think that Fleet's secrecy had anything to do with the situation with Charlie, but she couldn't be certain. And she wanted, more than ever, to lay eyes on him. To see for herself that he was safe and well.

Not to mention that she now had a working theory for Mikhail's death. Something which Fleet would want to know about as soon as possible. It wasn't, sadly, going to help with the Met inquiry into Mikhail's death, but it would allay Fleet's fears about it being the fault of his colleagues.

But since the previous day, Fleet hadn't responded to her phone message. The one where she told him she had a possible breakthrough on Mikhail's cause of death. Or any of the three she had left after that. He hadn't read her WhatsApp message or replied to her text. The modern world had given Fleet multiple ways not to reply. To mark the void of his absence with stubbornly grey ticks on an app.

Lydia went back to the GPS tracker on his car and confirmed that he was still in London. His car had been parked up by Hampstead Heath and was still in the same spot as the last time she checked. It suggested that it hadn't moved all night. Fleet was probably on foot. Or chilling at a friend's house for a well-earned break. Or a hundred other non-dangerous activities. None of which explained his lying, but also, thankfully, didn't put Fleet in mortal danger. Didn't have him lying somewhere bleeding to death. Or being held hostage in some sicko's basement.

Her phone was in her hand and she had scrolled to

Sinclair's number. Her finger hovered above the screen. Did she want to put herself in debt again?

Part of her brain didn't want to admit that things were that bad, that she was that worried, as that was terrifying to admit. The other part of her felt stupid for having wasted so much time already.

She pressed the home button and stared at the app icons. Fleet had lied to her. Fleet clearly didn't want her to know where he was or what he was doing. Fleet's car hadn't moved for over twenty hours. These were the facts.

She tapped his car's location into her phone and went to find Jason.

'I've got a lead for a case.' She didn't know why she wasn't telling Jason the truth, only that she couldn't face saying the words out loud.

'Do you want me to log it in the file?' Jason looked slightly confused. Lydia always kept her own records and had been known to be slightly shirty when he had offered to take over the job from her.

'I'm sending you the location. I just want you to be aware of where I've gone. If I'm not back this evening and haven't emailed by midnight, then can you call Aiden and send him after me?'

'Not the police?'

'No. Aiden.'

Jason looked like he wanted to argue but then seemed to think better of it.

Downstairs, Lydia blew through the kitchen door to find Angel.

With her dreads caught up in a hair net and a fine

sheen of sweat on her forehead, Angel was stirring a gigantic steel pot of simmering deliciousness. When she looked at Lydia, her eyes were glazed as if she was deep in thought.

Lydia told Angel where she was going, too. Just in case Aiden didn't believe Jason or decided to come looking for Lydia at The Fork.

Angel nodded and turned back to her food.

Sadness was rolling from her in waves. Lydia felt like she could reach out and touch it. She wanted to get going, to get to north London and Fleet's car, but she hesitated. 'You still having problems with Nat?'

Angel stopped stirring but continued to stare into the pot.

'I know who sent the letters and they're dead. You can tell Nat it's safe to come back to Camberwell.'

A pause. Angel dragged her gaze from the food and looked Lydia squarely in the eye. 'Was it because I told you?'

'I didn't kill them,' Lydia said. 'They were already dead when you told me. I swear on my life, on my Family, and on this coin.' She spun the coin in the air.

Angel nodded, looking relieved.

Fleet's car was parked on a side street near Hampstead Heath. There was a dusting of tree sap on the roof and bonnet. Cupping her hands around her face, Lydia peered into the vehicle. It was neat inside and, like any security conscious person, Fleet hadn't left anything of interest visible. There was a reusable water bottle in the central console, a map poking out from under the passenger seat and a wrapper from a protein bar on the floor.

Unsure of what to do, Lydia wandered around the corner and onto Spaniards Road, edging Hampstead Heath. At the first entrance to the heath, she walked in. Fleet was either in the nearby pub, The Spaniards Inn, or walking the Heath. Of course, he could be in any number of other places, but Lydia had to narrow it down for her own sanity. She would check these two locations first and then worry about the rest of London. She had a plan and if sheer bloody-mindedness was the key to success, then she couldn't fail.

Walking past manicured grass and ornamental trees, Kenwood House peeking over a gentle rise to her left, she tried to enjoy the relatively fresh air. The sky was a blue bowl, with only the barest wisps of cloud and the contrails of air traffic. She told herself it was a beautiful day for a walk in beautiful countryside. Of course, she wasn't a big fan of nature and her tattoos were writhing on her skin, mimicking the snakes of anxiety in her stomach.

The path opened to a gently sloping grassland and she began to get the idea of the scope of Hampstead Heath. In short, it was bigger than she had anticipated. She ought to have checked the pub first as combing this gigantic park was clearly not viable. Even if Fleet was sitting perfectly still on a bench, she could still fail to find him. She closed her eyes and breathed deeply, squeezing her coin for good measure. After a moment of this, Lydia accepted that she wasn't going to get some helpful sign from the universe and that she was going to have to wander the park like a lost soul.

An hour later and she was skirting the fifth pond she had stumbled across and wondering at what point she should give up. She had tried Fleet's mobile again, but it was going straight to voicemail.

Breaking through a stand of trees, another view of rolling parkland greeted her. There were people visible, but so few that – in London-terms – it felt deserted. There was something else tugging at her senses. A smell of roasted meat. Her mouth watered and she looked around, expecting to see a family with one of those disposable barbecue sets, but even walking toward the scent didn't reveal any such thing. She was tired and hallucinating food smells, which probably meant she should stop wandering Hampstead Heath like a lost duckling.

She headed to the pub. Google informed her that it had been sitting on the edge of the heath since the sixteenth century, originally built as a tollgate. Apparently Dick Turpin had drunk here and the narrow stretch of road had been a popular place for highway robberies, back in the days when it was another two hours' coach ride to London. Lydia did a quick walk through the premises and the pub garden before heading back inside. She ordered a double whisky and showed the man behind the bar a picture of Fleet. 'Has this guy been in recently?'

He barely glanced at her phone. 'I don't know. We get pretty busy.'

Lydia didn't need to produce her coin. She just thought about how much easier it would be if the barman would look at Fleet's image properly, and at once the man seemed very keen to be helpful. She had clearly perfected Charlie's air of authority.

He held his hand out and Lydia passed her phone across. He studied it intently for a few minutes and then looked up. 'I don't recognise him. I'm sorry.' And he looked it. Truly sorry. Then he brightened. 'Hang on.'

Before Lydia could react, the man had walked away with her phone. He disappeared through a doorway behind the bar. Lydia was just wondering whether she needed to vault over it and follow him, when he reappeared with a short blonde woman. She was wearing a tank top and had an impressive sleeve on her right arm and a completely ink-free left. She gave Lydia an appreciative look. 'What do you want to know?'

'Have you seen that man?'

'Your screen has shut off,' the man said, passing her phone over.

Lydia unlocked it and held it out to the woman. 'Has he been in recently?'

'Yeah,' she said. 'He came in yesterday. He had an IPA, but he only drank half.'

Lydia narrowed her eyes. 'You were playing close attention.'

The woman shrugged. 'He's very watchable.'

Well, she could hardly argue with that.

'Was he alone?'

'Yeah. He sat there,' she pointed to a table in the corner. 'Seemed like he was waiting for someone.'

'And did they arrive?'

The woman shrugged. 'Not that I saw. I didn't see your man leave, though, so I don't know.'

Outside the pub, Lydia hesitated. The staff had been surprisingly helpful, but there was nowhere left to go. She could call it into the police. Report Fleet as a missing person. But she was a Crow. Crows didn't run to the coppers for help. They kept things in the family.

CHAPTER TWENTY-NINE

A young woman with a baby on her hip opened the door to Lydia. The baby had solemn eyes which regarded Lydia with an uncomfortable amount of judgement. The mother wasn't much friendlier. 'Yes?'

'I'm Lydia Crow. I need to see Auntie.'

'Wait, please.' The door closed.

Lydia glanced up the open passage and saw a teenage boy in a baggy t-shirt returning from the local shop. He had a thin plastic bag bulging with groceries and when he opened his front door a thumping bass line became abruptly louder and then quieter again when it shut.

Auntie's door opened and the same young woman told her she could come in. 'Shoes off,' she said.

Lydia stepped out of her DMs and walked into the small living room. Auntie was sitting in her paisley armchair, and there were some brightly coloured wooden blocks on the carpet of the otherwise preternaturally neat room.

She explained to Auntie that Fleet was missing. His car was parked near Hampstead Heath and, presumably, had been there since the day before when Fleet had been seen in the Spaniards Inn. As she spoke, she felt a spurt of fear that she should have stayed put, watching it in case he returned. She opened the app on her phone and checked. His car hadn't moved.

Auntie listened without interrupting and then said: 'He lied to you about where he was going? Doesn't that suggest he doesn't want your company?'

'Yes. But he isn't answering his phone. I'm worried he's in trouble.'

'Perhaps he doesn't wish to speak to you? Had you quarrelled?'

'No,' Lydia said. Then, for the sake of being truthful, she added: 'Not recently.'

'Uh-huh,' Auntie said, her lips compressed.

'I just wondered if you knew of anyone he would visit or anything he might be doing in the Hampstead area? His car has been parked there for more than a day, now.'

The young woman, who still hadn't been introduced started to speak but shut up quickly at a sharp look from Auntie. 'The baby looks hungry.'

'I'm going,' the young woman said with ill-disguised irritation. 'You want tea?'

'No thank you,' Auntie said. 'Our guest won't be staying.'

As soon as the woman left the room, Auntie reached down beside her chair and pulled a sewing box onto her lap. Inside it was overflowing with ribbons and thread, buttons and other haberdashery items that Lydia couldn't name.

She pulled a pin from a cushion shaped like a tomato and stabbed her thumb without any hesitation whatsoever. 'Bring the matches,' Auntie said, tilting her chin at the window.

Lydia walked in the direction indicated and found a flowerpot with a large box of cook's matches and a briar bowl pipe tucked inside. She passed the box to Auntie, who was diligently squeezing drops of blood from her thumb.

'Shall I get one out for you?'

'Yes, please,' Auntie said, still squeezing.

Lydia held out the match and Auntie smeared her blood along it. Then, with no ceremony whatsoever she struck the match and held it up, watching the orange flame burn the wood and the blood.

For a moment, just before the flame touched Auntie's fingers at the base of the match and Lydia wondered if the woman was going to blow it out or let it burn her, the light changed in the room. A cloud must have drifted as the room was suddenly filled with bright sunlight.

Auntie nodded. 'He's alive.'

Lydia's heart leapt. Until that moment she hadn't realised that she had worried that he wasn't. 'Where is he?'

Auntie gave her a look of pure irritation. 'It's not that kind of spell.'

The word 'spell' hung in the air for a moment. Auntie's eyes seemed to be challenging Lydia to make something of it. 'Right,' Lydia said. 'Thank you for your help. I really appreciate it.'

Auntie nodded stiffly. 'Did you say his car was in Hampstead? Is it near the heath?'

'Yes, why? Do you know what he might be doing there?'

'I have nothing to tell you,' Auntie said. 'Except that people go to the heath for two main reasons. To lose themselves or to find themselves.'

Before Lydia could respond to that unhelpful commentary, Auntie added: 'You will let me know the moment you find him.'

Lydia agreed and left the flat. She replayed Auntie's last words, taking comfort from their definite nature. 'When' she found Fleet, not 'if'. At least Auntie had faith in her. Or it had been an order. Either way, Lydia felt better than she had all day.

FLEET'S CAR WAS STILL MOTIONLESS AND LYDIA needed to change her clothes and her car. When she found Fleet, she was going to need to be in a vehicle he wouldn't immediately recognise. Fleet had lied to her about his whereabouts and was now avoiding her calls, there was a good chance that he wasn't in a hurry to be found.

She had a quick shower, dressed in clean clothes and packed a go-bag for surveillance. She was keyed up and trying to be ready for every possible eventuality. She kept reminding herself that Maddie was dead and gone. And if Charlie was out, somehow, she would know about it. Sinclair had been finding out about the assets left in her care, which meant that he *was* still in her care. Thinking about the secret service brought another unwanted thought to the foreground.

Lydia did not want to contact Sinclair. She paced the floor of the office several times, trying to work out if there was a way around it. There wasn't.

The number she had been given was for a nail salon. She had to ask for a mani-pedi appointment at six the next day. Ten minutes of pacing later and the phone rang.

'Lovely to hear from you,' Sinclair said. 'And so soon.'

Lydia unclenched her jaw long enough to say, 'Just tell me if Fleet is doing something for you.'

'Why would I do that?'

Sinclair's cool tone floored Lydia for a moment. 'I thought you were cultivating me as a source?'

'Perhaps,' Sinclair said. 'But I think you misunderstand the role. A source gives information. You are demanding it.'

Lydia walked through the flat and stopped at the door to the roof terrace. There was a line of jackdaws just outside and a crow on the railing, looking into the street like a sentry. It was comforting. 'What about goodwill? Give and take?'

'Is that how it worked with Gale? I would ask him, but he's permanently indisposed.'

'Gale is dead,' Lydia said. 'You might want to think about that.'

A short silence. Then Sinclair's amused voice. 'Goodness. How chilling.'

Lydia waited. The jackdaws hopped about a bit, as if awaiting orders.

'DCI Fleet is not undertaking any action on my behalf or at my behest at this current time.'

'Thank you,' Lydia said. 'Your cooperation has been noted.'

CHAPTER THIRTY

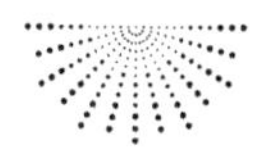

Aiden drove a sporty red Mazda which wasn't Lydia's first choice of surveillance vehicle, but Fleet would spot her grey Audi straight away and she didn't have time to mess around with a car hire place. The GPS on Fleet's car had started moving and she had got Aiden to bring his car around for her within ten minutes. The flashing dot was heading south from Hampstead Heath and she watched as it moved, wondering whether she should try to intercept Fleet en route or wait to see where he parked. There was no guarantee that it was Fleet driving the car, either, but she tried not to dwell on that possibility. It had to be Fleet. And it was easier to believe that now that Auntie had told her Fleet was alive. Easier to keep a lid on her worst fears.

Ten minutes of indecision was rewarded by the realisation that he was heading to Camberwell. She watched the dot until it stopped outside a very familiar address. Lydia let out a long breath, her head swimming from lack of oxygen. Then she packed her bag, told Jason where she was going, and left.

FLEET HAD BEEN INSIDE HIS FLAT FOR OVER FIVE hours. Long enough that Lydia had run the arguments for just going upstairs and knocking on his door, hashing this out in person, several times. Each time she came to the same conclusion, though. Fleet had been being secretive long before he lied to her about his whereabouts. The chances of him suddenly opening up were worryingly low. The chances of him clamming up and preventing her from tailing him, extremely high. At least this way she had a fighting chance of finding out what was going on.

She had parked at the far end of the building's resident carpark and was slumped down in Aiden's car. She had a crick in her neck and her lower back was complaining, but at least she didn't need the bathroom. Surveillance training meant that she had taken no liquid except for three small sips of water.

She was just wondering whether Fleet was in for the night, when the main door to his building opened and a familiar tall figure appeared. Lydia slumped down even lower, the tension humming through her muscles even as she tried to take slow breaths. She needn't have worried. Fleet was moving fast and he crossed to his car without so much as looking around. Lydia felt a stab of concern for him. He was a high-profile copper in Camberwell – he ought to take better care of his personal security. Of course, he usually did. Which just went to show how distracted he was.

He peeled out of the carpark and turned left. Lydia followed, keeping a couple of cars between and thanking London for its congested traffic. Unless Fleet put on flashing blues, she wasn't likely to lose him.

Lydia didn't know where she had expected Fleet to be going, but this wouldn't have even made the short list. He parked in a multi-storey on Pancras Street, close to the twin stations of Kings Cross and St Pancras. Lydia drove past the entrance and found some extortionately expensive on-street parking nearby. It was a thirty-minute limit, but she assumed Fleet would be heading to one of the stations. All she needed was time to see which train he was getting.

Instead, Fleet confounded her expectations again by walking in the opposite direction. He headed down Camley Street along the railway line, toward an industrial-looking area with old gas-holder structures and brick warehouses. He veered left and disappeared from sight. When Lydia reached the spot, she discovered there was a wrought-iron gateway leading to a hidden nature reserve, tucked next to the Regent's canal. London was full of these unexpected pockets of greenery, but Lydia was still surprised to find herself on a quiet canal path, surrounded by the sounds of nature, only moments after striding past the coffee shops and restaurants of the busy railway area.

The black water moved lazily in the dying light.

There was a bridge over the canal with steps leading up to it, framed against an orange-streaked sky. Fleet wasn't on the bridge, so she assumed he was on the path beside the waterway. She moved right, for no reason other than she had to go in one direction and it seemed as good as any. After a few steps, the path ahead remained empty and she thought she had lost Fleet. Then she felt a burst of warm sunshine hitting her back. She turned to find Fleet standing six feet away. 'You followed me.'

'You lied to me.' Lydia took a step toward him and then stopped, not wanting to send him in the opposite direction. 'I've been worried about you.'

Fleet inclined his head. He looked unhappy but resolute. Lydia knew that expression. She had seen it in the mirror enough times. Still, she had to try to reach him. 'What are you doing here? Who are you meeting?'

A convulsive action. Not quite a shrug or a shake of the head, but more an involuntary tremor. 'I can't.'

'Tell me.'

Fleet's expression closed further and he didn't reply.

The frustration and the fear bubbled over. Lydia hadn't decided to use her power, but she stopped even attempting to hold it back. Something was badly wrong and she had to protect Fleet.

Another tremor, but Fleet's lips remained tightly shut.

Her coin was in her hand. She knew it wasn't right to deliberately use her power on Fleet. She knew it was indefensible. But she could feel the tattoos writhing over her skin, the power running through her blood and bone. And, beneath that, a terrifying certainty that Fleet was in danger. She had to know what was going on, she had to be able to fix it. For his own safety. She squeezed her coin and pushed everything she could into her next command. 'Tell me.'

Fleet shook his head.

She pushed a little more, reaching out with her power to find his mind. It was there. Golden sunshine and the sound of waves on a beach. But that was it. There was no way for Lydia to take hold. She tried again and was met with a smooth surface, no strands to grab, no way in.

Lydia dropped her focus, a tight band of pain had wrapped around her head in response to the mental effort. She sagged a little in defeat, a combination of disappointment and relief washing over her as the enormity of what she had attempted hit home. She had tried to control Fleet. That was a line she would never have been able to step back from, a smashed trust that couldn't be remade. Knowing that she couldn't, even accidentally, control Fleet let something tense and hard break apart inside. She wanted to sink to the ground in relief. She wanted to throw herself into his arms. Thankfully, Fleet didn't seem to know she had tried. She hoped he never found out.

'You need to leave,' Fleet's voice sounded strained. 'He'll be here soon.'

'Who will be here? What is going on?' She still felt ashamed that she had attempted to use her power on Fleet, but that didn't stop the frustration breaking through. She wanted to force him – using non-magical means – to speak to her. She walked toward him, arms open and palms up. 'It's me. Fleet, it's me. It's us. You can tell me anything. You have to talk to me.'

For a moment, she thought he was going to reach for her. His eyes softened and he opened his mouth to speak. Then, his gaze shifted abruptly over her shoulder.

There was the sound of a motor and the scent of coal. Lydia turned to see a long low boat appearing around the gentle curve of the canal.

'You have to go,' Fleet said urgently. 'Go now.'

It was too late, even if Lydia had intended to heed Fleet's warning. The boat was close to the bank, and a man appeared from below deck. He stepped off the boat and onto the path as easily as if he was stepping off an escalator on the underground.

One second he was silhouetted against the sunlight, seemingly distant, and the next he was standing a few feet away from Lydia and Fleet on the canal path. There was something not quite right about the timing and the man's movement, but Lydia didn't have the spare mental capability to examine it. Her senses were filled with the threat and the knowledge that this was something new. His coat was the kind of dirty that looked like it would fall apart if it was washed. The dirt had become an integral part of the material's structure. His eyes were unnervingly bright in his stubble-shadowed face. He tipped his hat to Lydia, at complete ease.

She could feel Fleet just behind her. She glanced back to see that he wasn't moving. He seemed rooted to the spot, his eyes wide and his expression blank with fear. She had never seen anything like it.

The back of her neck prickled and she looked

quickly back at the stranger. He was average height and slightly built. His black hair was shot through with grey, his hat a peculiar old-fashioned style, and the eyes that were watching her, assessing, were uncannily light. Or there was light spilling from them. It was hard to tell.

When he spoke, his voice was soft and deep and she couldn't place his accent. 'You're far from home.'

Camberwell was barely five miles south from where they stood but she felt the meaning of his words and nodded. He was talking about way back in the Crows' history. Before they boarded boats in Scandinavia and headed to this rainy island. 'What about you? Is this place yours?'

He looked around, as if surprised to find himself in London. 'Not really. Maybe. For now.'

Well, that was clear. 'You're not a Fox,' she said, trying to sort the jumble of impressions. There was a tinge of animal, a sunshine gleam like Fleet and the creaking of wood in a high wind.

A flash of white teeth. Not a smile.

She felt Fleet move closer to her and she wanted to reach for his hand. She couldn't break focus from the stranger, though. She didn't dare look away. The impressions were still jumbled, refusing to fall into any sort of order she recognised. There was the call of a bird, piercing on her ears, even though the sound was only in her mind. She couldn't place it. 'I know you're not a Crow,' she said.

In contrast to the flow of images, sounds, smells, movement and feelings that were bombarding Lydia, the man was standing absolutely still. It was eerily like Jason when he forgot to fidget, but with an unmistakable life force. Coiled power waiting to spring. His voice seemed to echo with that power when he spoke. 'Why don't you tell me why you're here? You weren't invited.'

Behind her, Fleet cleared his throat. 'She followed me.'

The stranger didn't acknowledge that he had spoken, didn't break eye contact with Lydia. The soft dusk light was casting shadows across his face. 'Speak up, girl.'

'I'm just the welcoming committee.' Lydia smiled her shark smile. She felt Fleet take her hand, tugging as if he wanted to pull her back. She ignored the warning and stepped forward, spine straight and shoulders square. 'As long as you stay around Kings Cross we won't have a problem. I don't know how long you've been in London, but there are certain rules. Camberwell belongs to the Crows. It's not my problem if you head to the City to visit the Silvers or go north to Highgate, and there's plenty of room for you here. No need to bring trouble on your head.'

This time he did smile. Wide and delighted like a child on Christmas morning. Like clear water running in a stream. Like the sun coming out, flooding her with warm light. And she knew.

THE END

THANK YOU FOR READING!

I hope you enjoyed reading about Lydia Crow and her family as much as I enjoyed writing about them!

I am busy working on the next book in the Crow Investigations series. If you would like to be notified when it's published (as well as take part in giveaways and receive exclusive free content), you can sign up for my FREE readers' club online:

geni.us/Thanks

If you could spare the time, I would really appreciate a review on the retailer of your choice.

Reviews make a huge difference to the visibility of the book, which make it more likely that I will reach more readers and be able to keep on writing. Thank you!

ACKNOWLEDGMENTS

The Broken Cage is my thirteenth published novel (and the sixteenth I have written) and every single time I go through the throes of despair, the pit of self-doubt, the giddiness of a love affair and the frustration of fitting all the plot pieces together... As you might imagine, this makes me a *delight* to live with! I literally couldn't do this without the steadfast love and support from my wonderful husband. Thank you, darling!

And, as ever, thank you to my friends and family for cheering me on (and providing wine and sympathy when required).

A manuscript doesn't become a book without a lot of expert help, and I want to thank my excellent publishing team. In particular, Stuart Bache and Kerry Barrett.

Thank you to my advance readers, too: Beth Farrar, Karen Heenan, Jenni Gudgeon, Caroline Nicklin, Paula Searle, Judy Grivas, Ann Martin, Deborah Forrester, and David Wood.

Also, a shout-out to the members of my reader club. I

appreciate your support and correspondence more than I can say.

One of the many fantastic things about being a writer is that book people are the best people. I have met so many lovely friends through my writing and publishing career, and I thank my lucky stars for them. Thank you to Hannah Ellis and Clodagh Murphy for reading an early version of this book and for encouraging me to keep going.

Finally, special thanks to Holly and James for being loving, inspiring, supportive, and brilliant. And for introducing me to Stardew Valley.

ABOUT THE AUTHOR

Before writing books, Sarah Painter worked as a free-lance magazine journalist, blogger and editor, combining this 'career' with amateur child-wrangling (AKA motherhood).

Sarah lives in rural Scotland with her children and husband. She drinks too much tea and is the proud owner of a writing shed.

Head to the website below to sign-up to the Sarah Painter readers' club. It's absolutely free and you'll get book release news, giveaways and exclusive FREE stuff!

www.sarah-painter.com

LOVE URBAN FANTASY?

Discover Sarah Painter's standalone
Edinburgh-set urban fantasy
THE LOST GIRLS

A 'dark and twisty' supernatural thriller.
Around the world girls are being hunted...
Rose must solve the puzzle of her impossible life –
before it's too late.

Printed in Great Britain
by Amazon